MILES BAILEY GETS DOWN ON ONE KNEE

BOOK 3

JEN ATKINSON

Copyright © 2024 by Jen Atkinson

All rights reserved.

No part of this book may be reproduced in any form or by any electronic or mechanical means, including information storage and retrieval systems, without written permission from the author, except for the use of brief quotations in a book review.

Editor: Caitlin Miller

Cover design and illustration: Melody Jeffries

1. Romance—Fiction 2. Wholesome—Fiction 3. Romantic Comedy—Fiction 4. Stand Alone Series—Fiction

For Eryn
One of my very favorite people.

ALSO BY JEN ATKINSON

<u>Sweet RomComs</u>
Am I 30 Yet?
Romancing Blake

<u>The {INSTA} Series</u>
{INSTA} Boyfriend
{INSTA} Connection
{INSTA} Kiss
{INSTA} Family
{INSTA} Wedding FREEBIE

<u>Another Bailey Brother</u>
Levi Bailey has Butterflies
Owen Bailey Needs Advice
Miles Bailey Gets Down On One Knee

<u>Sweet Romance with Suspense</u>
Then Came You
Love, In Theory

<u>Sweet Romance</u>
Surviving Emma

The Amelia Chronicles
Knowing Amelia
Love & Mercy
Dear Kate
Because of Janie

Young Adult Romance
Paper Hearts
The Untouched Trilogy
Untouched
Unknown
Undone

Miles Bailey
GETS DOWN ON
ONE KNEE

JEN ATKINSON

3
ANOTHER
BAILEY
BROTHER
BOOK 3

1

MILES

I have never seen so many men lined up and drooling over one woman before.

"What are you watching?" I blink away from the screen to the three women glued to the reality TV show. My sister, Coco, my new sister-in-law, Annie, and my brother Levi's fiancé, Meredith. They all sit, watching, laughing, and not hearing a word I've said.

I'm not sure why the show even caught my eye. It's far from my thing. But I promised my niece, Alice, painting lessons for her birthday. That was a couple weeks ago. Lulabelle—her younger sister—turns one this month, and Alice has reminded me daily that I cannot give Lula a present when I haven't truly given her one yet.

"Lane Jonas is gonna get a husband," eight-year-old Alice says beside me.

"Lane who?"

"You know, from The Judys? They sing that song that Uncle Levi likes to hum. I think it's called "A Way Out," but he always says the wrong words, so now he just hums. Annie loves her and Uncle Levi isn't sure he likes having that in common with

Annie." Alice's eyes are glued to the screen where four men stand around one woman—they're all singing to her. Each belting more dramatically than the last. On national TV. *Yikes.* My stomach turns a little with the scene.

"I'm rooting for Broc," Alice says, plopping down onto a kitchen chair. She makes sure her view is directed toward the show, though she's looking at me now. She waves a paintbrush in front of my face as I can't seem to look away from the train wreck happening on the TV screen. "Are you listening to me?"

"Is this appropriate for you?" I wag a finger in the direction of the very PG-13 TV show in view just feet away.

"I just turned eight, Uncle Miles. I'm practically a grown-up now. I know all about kissing and paying bills."

I lift my brows. *"Right."*

"Did you bring the goods, man?"

I break away from the large flat screen on my sister's living room wall. This great room has us together and separated all at once. I pull two bags of king-sized M&Ms from my backpack. "This or… this?" I ask, pulling out a bottle of craft paint next.

"Yes!" Alice pumps her little fist and snatches the bags of candy from me.

"Only one bag up during our lesson. Got it?"

"Got it. I am a sophisticated lady, Uncle Miles. I know how to savor my M&Ms." Her blonde head pops up and she holds one finger in the air. "In fact, I have the perfect fancy bowl for these M&Ms. Wait here!" She scrambles out of her chair and hurries off down the hall toward her bedroom.

I cross over the carpet threshold and into the living room, my eyes super-glued to the TV. It's flashing the title:

CELEBRITY LIFE
CELEBRITY WIFE

"Is this what you do on Thursday nights?"

Meredith turns her head, seeing me for the first time, though I've been here for ten minutes. Her lips fold in on one another as if she's been caught doing something wrong.

"It is," Coco says, no shame in her tone. "If you're going to make fun of us, you can leave."

Annie reaches for another handful from the popcorn bowl sitting between her and Meredith. Her limb freezes in the bowl and she tilts her hand, looking at the wedding band that's been partnered with her engagement ring for only a few weeks now. She blinks away from the diamond that Owen will be paying off for the next five years. "There's a reason Owen, Jude, and Levi aren't here, Miles. We aren't afraid to kick you out too," she says.

I hold up my hands, suddenly afraid of the women in my life. "No judgment. Just a question."

"There's only two episodes left. Lane is down to four guys, but two have to go, tonight," Meredith says, pulling her feet up beneath her on the couch.

"Let me guess, you like Broc?" I say, repeating Alice's sentiment.

"No." Coco waves a hand in the air. "He's Alice's guy. And before you question my mothering, she's only allowed to watch the pinning."

"Pinning?" I have no idea what my sister is talking about. Or what my niece is viewing.

"Yeah. You know, like the rose from *The Bachelor*?" she says—but I don't know. I'll take her word for it. "Only on *Celebrity*, she pins the guys she wants to keep."

"The pin looks like a Walk of Fame star, like in Hollywood," Meredith tells me as if this makes me officially caught up.

The show starts up again and Coco holds out her hand, arm straight, remote pointing at the TV. She pauses the scene and peers back at me.

But I'm still pasted to the screen. The blonde on Jude and

Coco's eighty-inch TV is beautiful, stupidly stunning, in fact. So, sure she has a load of fame-hungry guys fighting for her attention in front of millions all for the sake of entertainment. But is she kind? Is she passionate? Does she care for others?

Huh. I watch a minute longer.

She looks kind.

Is that weird?

People can't really *look* kind, can they?

Her long ash-blonde hair is scooped to the side where a long braid trails over her shoulder and down her front, probably reaching her belly button. And I think there's a few strands of blue peeking out from the blonde. But I'm not really sure.

I'm staring, in a trance... maybe she's a witch and all these guys are under a spell because I can't seem to look away.

Coco hops up, standing by my side.

"Hey," she says, her tone hushed. "This is my one night out with the girls. Jude has Lula at Mom's place. Do you think you could distract Alice? I mean, nothing terribly risqué is happening over here, but—"

I blink my stinging eyes from the screen and give my full attention to Coco. "But she's eight. I get it. I'm here to paint with her. I will distract away."

My sister's cheeks go flush. "Because it's just a little entertainment with friends, and I don't want her thinking—"

"Coco. I got it. You aren't evil for watching a dating reality TV show. I can take her to my studio if you'd rather," I say, scratching behind my right ear.

Coco reaches up on tiptoes and kisses my cheek. "You don't have to do that. Your stuff is already here. I appreciate you spending some time with her."

I'm not doing her any favors, though. I'm happy to be helpful, but I love my nieces. I spend time with them whenever I can. We all do. Alice and Lula have four uncles, and we'd all fight for time with them. Even Coop, and he's a busy, semi-self-absorbed college student.

"Actually, a *marriage* show," Meredith says—though I hadn't realized Annie and Meredith were even paying attention to us.

Then again, maybe they weren't—because I don't follow. I glance at Coco. Can she decipher? "Ahh—what?"

"It's sort of a dating show—like you said," Annie explains, "but at the end, she'll marry the man of her choosing. That's why it's called *Celebrity Wife*. She's a celebrity, and soon she'll be a wife."

"Huh." I clear my throat. None of that sits well with me—I don't know why. It's not my sister, niece, or friend up there. So what do I care if some hot-shot rock star wants to marry a stranger?

I mentally shake my head. I *don't* care.

2

DELANEY

I hold to the armrests of my aisle seat on this plane that refuses to lift off. "My life will be normal in one week. My life will be normal in one week. My life will—"

"Hey, aren't you the lady from that show?" The bushy-bearded man next to me says. For a second, I pretend he's talking to the lady on his right—but I'm so not that lucky.

I clear my throat and stare ahead. He isn't recognizing me from The Judys, but from *Celebrity Wife. Joy.*

Filming has been over for months, but every last one of us, from the cast of guys to the make-up artist, had to keep our mouths shut until airing—or else. And I'm not paying CBS a dime—they have already turned my life upside down. They don't get a cent from my bank account.

I mean, my career is already in shambles, so why not add my love life to the ball of flaming cat poo we're calling Delaney's life?

Ash assured me that this was key to getting my fans to follow me on this new path… however, that was before I went and screwed everything up by *not* finding my prince charming. Let's just say I did not give the station their fairytale ending.

When Mr. Bushy Beard next to me won't stop staring, I find my voice. "I don't know what you mean." I barely give the man a glance. Normally, I don't mind sitting in coach. I like it even. But today... I should have paid someone in the very full first-class section a thousand dollars to swap with me.

"Yeah." He nods with each and every word out of his mouth, his beady eyes examining me top to bottom. "Blue hair. It's *you*."

I can't see his chin beneath the long bristles of crimped and curly facial hair. I keep searching for it—a really poor attempt to ignore what he's saying.

My hair is *not* blue, by the way. There are peek-a-boo streaks of powder blue through the blonde. It was a Judy thing four years ago. All four of us dyed our hair with just a peek of blue on the underneath during our "All Out" tour. We donated a quarter of our ticket sales that month to the Prevent Child Abuse Foundation, and we dyed our hair to match the cause.

I just happen to like the blue and keep it.

"You're in that *Celebrity Wife* show. You know, the one that Jaren Sparks hosts."

It's a miracle I've gone the entire morning without being recognized. I should be grateful.

I pull in a breath, tell my pounding heart to shut it, and lie through my teeth. "Oh, I've seen that. Isn't that happening in L.A.?"

"Yeah. That's it. You're *that* girl." He stabs a fat finger in my direction.

Why, oh why, did I not buy the *extra*-large bag of gummy bears? Instead, I went with the practical travel-sized bag. I am going to need the sustenance—I can tell!

Clearing my throat, I prepare for the performance of a lifetime—or at least, for this flight. I shake my head and grin as if he's funny, as if he's flattering me. You know, the ol' fake-it-until-you-make-it college try.

"If I'm her, shouldn't I be in L.A.? The last show airs next week." I clear my throat and roll with the fib. "At least, I think it does. I missed this week's episode."

"Oh, it was good," he says with another chinless nod.

The woman on his right side leans across his lap, her eyes peering up at mine from her awkward position. *Holy moly, tell me they know each other.* "Lane kicked off Mike and Austin. I personally don't like that Patrick fella at all. But he's still around." Her eyes go wide like she's doubting my good sense—and she should.

I sniff, clear my throat, and blink toward the aisle floor. "I don't like him either," I say through gritted teeth.

Patrick Stacey has made my life a living—

"Right," the woman says, interrupting my thoughts. "She's crazy." Then, resting her elbow on the man's thigh, she holds an awkward palm up to me. "I'm Rizzy. This is Manny."

I give her a fingertip shake and pray that Manny and Rizzy will find something interesting to say to *each other* soon.

"You sure look like her," Rizzy says. "You sure you ain't—"

My phone chimes with a text and I peer down, certain that Ash is sending me more scolding messages. "Excuse me."

"I don't think you're allowed to—" Rizzy starts.

"We aren't in the air yet," I tell her and give my device one hundred percent of my attention.

> **Mom**: I can't believe my oldest daughter is going to get married on national television without her mother there. How selfish can you be, Delaney Sage?

Just like that, Mom makes visiting with Rizzy and Manny feel like a relaxing day at the park.

Mom writes as if the whole thing isn't over and done with. Though—to be fair, maybe she doesn't realize that it is. She most definitely doesn't realize that I am still very, *very* single. I haven't shared anything of that awful show with her. Even though she'd be one of a few people CBS might have allowed. But then, why would I? She'd only make me feel two inches tall.

To be fair, I haven't told my dad either. But then, I'm not sure where he is at the moment... Vegas or Atlantic City? If he hasn't paid his phone bill, and there's a fifty-fifty chance he hasn't, then I wouldn't even be able to get a hold of him. So, why bother trying?

He may be more compassionate than Mom, but he's rarely accessible.

I shove my phone into my pocket and peer back up at my new *friends*.

Neither have wavered from studying my face. "Maybe she's her sister," Manny says to Rizzy, all while keeping those gray eyes focused on my face.

"I have one sister—Eryn Jones—and she's a freshman in college." All true.

"Well, she is your doppelganger, that's for sure." Rizzy straightens up, and with Manny's large frame between us, I can't see her at all.

Okay. I may make it through this flight, after all. If I—

"Can I get a picture with you anyhow?" Rizzy says, leaning over Manny's lap once more.

My brows cinch. "Uh. Why? What for?"

"I can still tell people you're Lane Jonas." Her eyes travel from my face to my hands clasped in my lap. "You're close enough. Though she's got that thing she does... with her eyebrows. You know?" Rizzy's brows are popping up and down, cinching in and out.

I do not do *that*. I mentally shake my head at the ridiculousness. Eyebrows? I do not do a thing with my eyebrows.

"*Jonas*," Manny says, interrupting my internal rant. He focuses his gaze forward at nothing, and I know what's coming. It always comes, and once again, I could murder Ash for insisting on Jonas as my stage name. "You think she's the sister to all those brothers that sing?"

"No." I moan at the same moment Rizzy says, "She must be."

Rizzy peers at me, expectant of my answer. "Did you google?" she says—as if Google is the Bible.

I swallow—I don't want to be outed. And I really don't want my picture taken. If I hadn't insisted on leaving California *today* —and alone—I'd be in my own apartment and later in my own little private quarters of first class. No bushy beards and no waggling eyebrows invading my space.

"Ah," I say, though it physically pains me. "I didn't. You might be right," I tell her. "And." I tap a finger to my chin. "That eyebrow thing. It's gonna give me away. No one will believe you that I'm her. And then, what will they think of you?"

I have no idea who "they" are. Let alone what "they'd" think. But I go with it. Because as much as I dislike being called the "Jonas sister" and that whole eyebrow nonsense is just that—nonsense—I need my privacy. I'm counting on it. Why else would I run away to a little Idaho town I haven't been to in a million years?

Rizzy's eyes pop open like a window blind unhinged with my question. "You're right… ah—I didn't catch your name." She holds out her palm again.

I swallow. Is Delaney too close to Lane? *Did* she google? Because if she did, surely she'd be gifted with my birth name.

My mouth drops open, but for three long seconds, no sound escapes. Rizzy blinks six times before I squeak out an answer. "Ah, *Dee*," I say, using the nickname my sister occasionally calls me.

Rizzy smacks her palm to Manny's thigh. "You're right, Dee. I'll just take a picture of you walking away. The back of you. That should be believable."

"You been to Coeur d'Alene before?" Manny says. He digs

into the front pocket of his overalls and pulls out a chicken leg. A crispy fried *chicken leg*!

My stomach turns as I watch him bring that leg, the skin falling from the bone, to his hair-covered lips.

I blink, but I can't stop watching. I'm pretty sure there is a piece of denim fuzz on the side of that leg and Manny is about to consume it.

"Oh, Dee," Rizzy sings—though I can't see her past the chicken leg. "Coeur d'Alene? You been?"

I'm so focused on the chicken fuzz that I don't even consider a lie. The truth just falls right out. "My family vacationed here once. Before my parents split up."

"D-I-V-O-R-C-E," Rizzy spells, and in my peripheral, I see her eyeballs slide from my face to Manny's.

A quiet whistle slips between Manny's tongue and teeth, wet with chicken leg grease.

"That's why Manny and I never did get married. You can't get divorced if you aren't married." She pats his leg with her balled-up fist.

I stir in my seat, then cram my eyes closed—and away from all things chicken and hairy. "That's so true." I flutter my eyes open and turn and peer out at the empty aisle just as the fasten seatbelt sign lights up. The airline workers stand at the front and go through the motions of showing us what to do in case of an emergency.

Rizzy and Manny listen, giving me space—at least for the moment. I breathe and think back to when I was young, when we came to this touristy little town and actually spent time together as a family. Mom acted human and Dad wasn't consumed with gambling. Eryn and I were just little—Eryn was so young she probably doesn't even remember the trip. We were together. We were a family. No one fought and no one judged. We played and laughed together.

That week was the most peaceful, sweet week of my growing-up life. I have one memory of a happy family and it takes place in Coeur d'Alene, Idaho.

So, who cares that I haven't been back in eighteen years—my life could use a little peaceful and sweet. I'm hoping Coeur d'Alene does the trick.

3

MILES

*L*ars stares at my newest piece hanging on the gallery wall. It's on display only. Owen and Annie by the lake on their wedding day. I used the bokeh effect to put emphasis on their figures. They look out at the lake, so their faces aren't seen in this watercolor.

"Why isn't this one for sale again?" Lars asks. "This one might actually sell."

"It belongs to my brother."

Lars sighs. "But if it's here, then you must be willing to recreate it for someone else?"

"With different subjects. Yes."

Another sigh. His brows raise in a look that screams insufferable. I'm pretty sure I'm not the insufferable one though—no matter what Lars Simon believes.

He just likes to have something to complain about when it comes to me. Usually, it's how little I've sold. I either have too many pieces in the gallery or not enough. I definitely don't sell enough. But today, it's that I'm displaying a piece that isn't for sale.

The thing about a gallery though, pieces are for show as

much as they are for sale. The majority of our visitors aren't looking to buy. They're looking to look.

But Lars doesn't want to hear that. He doesn't care about the visitors who aren't also shoppers.

If he weren't the only curator in town, I'd leave him. But he is, not to mention he's also the landlord of my loft and the small studio attached, as well as the owner of the building across the street. The very place I hope to call my teaching studio one day.

Whether I like it or not, I need Lars on my side.

My turn to sigh.

Lars crosses his arms. "If you want to sell more pieces, Miles, you have to be more open about letting some of these go."

"I let plenty go. But not this one. It's my brother's wedding gift." *Plenty?* It's not exactly true. My pieces aren't flying off the wall by any means. But I am willing to sell most of them, just not *this* one.

"Right." A breathy, impatient chortle vibrates from his chest. "Moving on. You wanted to see me…"

"Yes, I did." My eyes catch the one and only patron inside our little gallery at the moment. Maybe it's because I've never seen her before. I'm sure of it.

And yet, she's familiar.

She's staring at the one and only Manoli piece in this gallery. I'd like to tell her it's overpriced and nothing close to his best work. But I won't. Lars would wring my neck and never consider what I'm about to ask of him.

"You wanted to see me *because…*" Another impatient sigh falls from the man who has way too much control over my life.

This time, I can't blame him. I've been standing here contemplating how to tell our pretty blonde visitor what she should and should not buy rather than get down to business.

"Right." I clear my throat and blink my gaze away from the girl. "My studio."

Lars tugs on the vest of his three-piece suit and blows a

raspberry from his lips as he turns away from my painting. "This again?"

"Hear me out. The Inclusion Center brings in more than half my students, but none of them can make it up those stairs easily. And for some, like Walt, it's impossible. His wheelchair won't allow it."

Lars walks to the other side of the hall, past the girl, and stops in front of another one of my pieces. One that's been sitting there for a month without a single offer.

"You know, the longer it sits here, the less I like it." He stares at the songbirds emblazoned with bold colors and perched on a branch.

I've thought about giving it away a hundred times. But in the end—I always hope for the right owner to come in, to feel the joy in this piece, and to give it a home. More than a sale—that's what I want. I want my songbirds adopted by the right owner. The one who wants—*no*, needs—them.

He squints as if looking at the piece with different eyes. But mostly, he's changing the subject.

"I want the building across the street," I blurt. "I need it. You know that I need it." While I want someone to come and adopt my songbirds for all the right, sentimental, artistic reasons, I have to survive. And eighty percent of my income is brought in by my students—the elementary kids who come twice a week, the teens who come once a week, and the adults with disabilities group who come three to four times a week.

Turning on his heels, Lars faces me. His round spectacles slip to the ridge of his nose, and he bumps them up with the back of his hand. "You can't have it."

"You're using it for what? Storage? I'd be willing to go through it to find a new place for the things you have there. I'd pay additional rent for the space." I blow out an exhausted breath. "If I could use it for my teaching studio, my students would double." All true—but really, the building across the street would mean that Walt, Cinnamon, and half a dozen more would be able to join the regular class. That's all they want. They don't want the at-home one-on-one lessons I've provided. They want to join the class, to be like everyone else, to be with their friends. I don't blame them. "Double," I say again because Lars sees the world in dollar signs. I'm speaking his language.

"I don't see how any of that benefits me. No matter the amount of students you attract, you pay me the same rent."

I shake my head. "But I'd be paying you more—rent for my loft *and* the addition of the other building."

Lars wrinkles his nose. "You forget, Miles. I write the check for your cut of the pieces you sell. I know what you're making. You cannot pay me enough to use that building. This I know."

He's only half wrong. He knows my income based on what I sell but not with my teaching. Still, it's difficult to argue with him. My plan would require Lars to give me an incredible deal on rent—at least, in the beginning.

It's a deal he isn't willing to make.

~

"Hey, Walt." I peer down into the man's crystal-clear blue eyes and wave a brush in front of him, trying to grasp his attention. "You don't want to paint today?"

He sticks out his bottom lip and turns his entire torso away from me. "Not *here*."

"It's May. The sun is shining. I thought you'd like it out here."

Walt may be confined to his chair, and I heard one of the staff in this group home once say that Walt was a nine-year-old stuck inside a forty-two-year-old's body, but he is a force.

"No," he says, and I'm not sure that bottom lip could protrude any more than it currently is.

"It's better than the kitchen, right?" But it doesn't help that other members of Walt's house come to class in my second-floor studio. But not Walt. The building is too old, and there's no way we'd get his chair up that flight of stairs. Not to mention, my studio is a bit of a box.

Walt loves art and expressing himself through painting and drawing. So, I've been teaching him at the group home. But in the last few weeks, he's decided he doesn't want to be left out. He doesn't want to have anything other than what his friends have.

"What if we talked the guys into moving class into the garage for the summer? We could all work out here together. We could invite Cinnamon to come over too." I'm pretty sure Walt has a thing for Cinnamon. He talks about her enough.

But not even the lure of little Cinnamon is enough to cheer him today.

His head dips and his clear blue eyes drag over at me. Shaking his head, he stares right through me. I haven't enticed him, not even a little.

Sweat pools at the back of my neck. I rub it away but can do nothing for the tightening ache in my muscles. "I know, buddy. I'm working on a new place. I promise. But Lars—"

"Lars!" he spats, sitting up straight and shaking his head. Walt rolls his eyes. "Don't say his name. Don't say it! I do not like him, not one little bit."

I want to chuckle—I know just how he feels. I stuff the temptation deep down—it wouldn't help. "I get that," I tell him. "So, you can't count on Lars, but can you count on me?"

Walt tilts his head to the side, his lips protruding out again. He holds out a hand as if to shake mine. But when I set my hand in his, he claps his fingers around my thumb, holding on, dapping up, telling me he *does* trust me. He *does* count on me.

I don't know how, but I'll be securing a new studio. I have to.

4

MILES

*C*oco stands inside of her home, her eyes slits, glaring at me on her front porch. "You can only come in and stay if you're quiet and you don't poke fun."

"Poke fun?" I step inside, holding the bag of new paints I promised Alice. "I'm here for Alice."

She closes the door behind me, but I can feel her heat-driven laser eyes warming up my back. "She's at Mom's with Jude and the guys."

My brothers, brother-in-law, and nieces are all rendezvousing at Mom's and they didn't invite me?

"It's Thursday, Miles. You have a standing dinner invite," she says as if I've spoken my thought out loud—which I didn't. I'm sure of it.

"It's Thursday? *Already*. But it was *just* Thursday."

My sister smirks. "Yes, it was. One week ago." She takes the bag of painting supplies from my hands and walks it over to her kitchen counter. "How did your talk with Lars go?"

I clear my throat. "Not well." I made my request to Lars Simon days ago but had nothing good to share with my family. So I never mentioned it. "Lars won't budge."

"Maybe you could look for a different building."

"Maybe." But that single-story, multi-windowed, old structure has amazing lighting, great space, and it's the perfect location.

"One that doesn't involve Lars." Her eyes go wide and she crosses her arms over her Twizzler T-shirt.

Leaning against the counter, I breathe out a laugh. "I wouldn't complain about that."

Coco opens up her refrigerator and pulls out three cans of Mountain Dew—her favorite. Then, she grabs a fancy dish that looks like a miniature trough from the very top of her cupboard, the one Aunt Ally gave her for her wedding, and fills the thing with Twizzlers. Her obsessions run deep—the girl is fanatic about licorice and caffeinated beverages. "Maybe you should open your own gallery." Her brows lift and she pauses all busy work to peer at me, taking in my reaction.

I shake my head, though. "I'm not a curator. I'm an artist and a teacher. In fact, I might be a teacher who likes to dabble in art."

"Miles." She moans. "Don't sell yourself short." Coco's blue eyes cross to the living room, finding the watercolor of Alice I created years ago—long before she'd met her stepdaughter. Next to it is a brand new work of Lulabelle, her almost one-year-old. "You are gifted," she tells me.

I shuffle my feet, heat rising into my neck with the praise. I'm not here to beg for compliments. I know what I am.

"Listen," she says, a hand on my forearm, "I'm happy to have you stay, but like I said, you can't poke fun."

I shake my head. "Coco, I don't know why you think I'd make fun of you—"

"Meredith and Annie are coming over. It's the last airing of our show." She smiles despite the fact that she's watching something she has to tell others to not make fun of.

"The dating show?"

"Yeah. Lane Jonas will be a married woman by the end of tonight." She rubs her hands together, then drops them to her hips, looking at the spread she's gotten ready.

Still, I'm thinking about what she's said. Because I had to have heard that wrong. I was sure Meredith was exaggerating last week. My brows knit together—I can feel it, but I can't stop it. None of this makes sense, and my face knows it. "You're kidding, right? She gets married on the show? To some joker she barely knows?"

"Yeah. She's living the celebrity life, and by the end of the show she's a celebrity wife. Get it?"

The really lame title? Yeah, I get it. But I don't say any of that because she's asked me not to "poke fun."

No worries, sis. I don't need to stay to watch some girl—celebrity or not—marry someone who's practically a stranger. That's not my idea of entertainment.

There's a knock at Coco's front door, and on her way to answer, she holds out her hand, the remote in her grasp, and flicks the television on.

Her streaming provider has a dozen selections for her in view, but it must know what my sister watches on Thursday nights because *Celebrity Life Celebrity Wife* is already highlighted.

My cue to leave.

I hear Meredith and Annie greeting Coco when an ad for the show begins to play. A pretty blonde with a streak of blue peeking out from her long, silky hair catches my eye… just like last week.

Everything else in the room goes black. All I can see is *her*.

That girl. *That* face with the steel blue eyes and rosy cheeks and flawless skin.

I know that face.

That face came into the gallery last week. *She's* the girl.

I knew I recognized her, but I couldn't figure out from where.

I blink and try to recall a ring on her left hand. But I can't—one way or the other. I was too distracted by Lars. Too upset about Walt. Too sidetracked with the rejection of my building to look for a ring. I won't lie—Lane Jonas is an exceptionally pretty girl. And while I'm not currently looking for anyone, I did notice her. I couldn't help it.

"Miles," Annie says, "you're back. Did we convert you?"

Meredith giggles and sends me a happy wave.

"He's going. I think he's headed over to Mom's." Coco gathers up the Mountain Dews in the crook of her arm and holds the fancy dish of licorice with the other. She looks expectant my way, waiting for my confirmation.

But I know that girl—the one up on that screen. The one about to marry a guy she's known—what, six weeks? I *know* her. *Kind of*, anyway. I was in the same exact room as the girl lighting up the television. And somehow that fact won't allow me to leave.

"Um, actually—"

"You're staying?" Coco says, one brow bouncing up to her hairline.

"I thought I might." I clear my throat and tuck my arms in a cross. "If you don't mind."

She tilts her head, offering me a half smile. "Grab the popcorn."

I pick up the bowl of popcorn as well as a drink for myself. I set everything on the coffee table with the other snacks and take a seat next to Coco on the couch. She's already got the square glass table outfitted with cheese, crackers, and meats.

"You go all out, don't you?" I say, looking over the spread.

"It is the finale," Meredith says.

Annie rubs her hands together, eyes scanning from the table

to the commercial ending on the TV. "Yep, Lane's getting married, Miles. We have to celebrate."

"Speaking of married—" Coco leans over, snagging two Twizzlers from Aunt Ally's glass trough. "Mer, do you and Levi have a venue yet?"

"There's a house on the lake we're looking into renting."

Another ad on the screen ends and the intro to the show begins. I'm grateful when Annie hushes my sister and friend so that I don't have to.

The women watch and talk, but I keep quiet—*nothing suspicious over here, ladies, just really into your dating show.*

The two-hour episode is only fifteen minutes in when Lane —clearly not acting—leaves her scheduled interview and storms down the halls of the mansion she's staying in. She stops, glimpsing nervously back at the camera, and pounds on a bedroom door.

She looks on the verge of tears. They've put her through the wringer. They grilled her with questions about the two remaining men and her feelings for each. I'm exhausted just watching it all play out.

A woman with short black hair and tanned skin opens the door Lane pounds on, her eyes dragging over to the camera.

"Ash," Lane says. "We need to talk." She swallows and peers once more at the cameraman. Tears shimmer on her cheeks, and my heart rate picks up speed.

"She's regretting sending Mike away. I knew it," my sister says, pulling up her feet until she's sitting cross-legged on the couch.

I don't comment, though—I don't know who Mike is, and I'm too busy watching the girl who came into my gallery. It's her, no doubt about it.

"Sure, come in," the woman on the other side of the door says to Lane.

"That's her manager," Meredith whispers for my benefit.

I nod my understanding and turn my attention back to the screen.

"No cameras." Lane looks back. We see her sad eyes again. She shakes her head, telling them not to come in with her.

But someone off-screen objects. "That won't do," some faceless man tells her.

"It's going to have to do," she says—this time with force. She lifts the tail of her shirt, showing a skiff of skin, and pulling out a little black box tucked into the waistband of her jeans. She flips a switch—and suddenly we can't hear the rock star anymore.

"She turned off her mic," Annie says, on the edge of her chair.

The camera scans to the hall, where a blond man walks up to the door. "Lane went to see Ash?" he asks the faceless person, and they confirm.

"Patrick," Coco says, nose wrinkled. "She has no clue he's been lying to her." She groans. "I could never be a cameraman for a reality TV show. I'd spill all the beans of every jerk-a-saurus rex out there."

I blink from my sister back to the screen, where the *spineless*—according to Coco—Patrick slits open the door of the private quarters of Lane Jonas' friend.

Lane may have turned her mic off—but Patrick didn't. And with the door ajar, the long-distance microphone from the cameraman is picking up every private word.

Patrick winks for the camera, then directs his ear into the room, listening in on the women's conversation.

"Slime ball," Annie says.

"I do not like him," Meredith agrees. "Please tell me she does not end up with that one."

The figures are in the distance, but Lane's voice—no, her *cries*—come through. "I can't do this, Ash." She is a small image inside the room. Her face isn't as clear as before, but her words are heard as well as captioned for the audience. We get it all.

"You agreed to this, Lane. Do you have any idea how much this show has done for your public image? If you bow out now—"

The camera scans back to Patrick, eavesdropping on the conversation. His brows knit and angry wrinkles cover his forehead. He mouths the words, "Bow out?" for the camera.

"Just pick one," Ash tells her.

"How? I don't love either of them."

A shrill gasp sounds from all three of the very real, live, tangible women sitting in my sister's living room, making me jump in place.

Meredith stares Coco down. "So, that's why she's never said it. They said she was waiting, but—"

"So, you stay married for a few months, and then you both go your separate ways," Ash says.

"But they've both told me that they love me. I—I can't do that to someone. I can't hurt them like that. You kept saying it would come—but it never did. I don't love these men, Ash. This isn't fair to them."

"Either way, tell them now or tell them later, someone is getting hurt, Lane. Can't we help your image first?"

"But isn't it better to be hurt *before* a wedding ceremony?"

Lane is still crying when the camera zooms back to Patrick. The man's jaw is tight, and his eyes slits. He doesn't look hurt; he looks pissed.

The next half an hour my skin crawls as I watch this piece of work find Lane's option number two—some guy named Broc—and tell him exactly what he witnessed, with his own little flair on the story. Neither man is happy with the news, but it's Patrick who creates, lays out, and convinces Broc of a plan to *get her back*.

"Get her back?" I say, repeating the doofus's words. "Because she doesn't love him? Because she's choosing to be honest with them?"

Coco turns to look at me, one of her brows hikes up on her head.

"You're so in tune with your sensitive side, Miles," Meredith says, her smile small and kind.

I'm not sure what to say to that. I think I do see and feel things differently at times—it's the artist in me. But then there's only one way to see this guy, and it isn't good.

He's devised a mean, spiteful plan to make a fool of her—on national TV.

And that's exactly what he does.

It's painful to watch and yet I spend the next hour rooted in my seat, flinching as the two men lie and deceive her about the future, about their intentions, knowing that she's being torn up inside with the truth. And every time she opens her mouth to tell one of them that she's not ready for a proposal, they kiss her, or they hurry off, or they mention an ill parent or a dead dog—something painful and sad that makes her shut right up. It's clear she doesn't want to deliver more blows, more pain, and it's also clear they know that. They pick their moments carefully. They calculate all of their words to orchestrate hers.

We're all quiet and watching when she exits her room for the last time, ready to approach each man, one at a time. One last pinning. Normally, I guess, this is the point where she'd tell one goodbye and the other that a wedding party awaited them.

Only this season, no wedding party waits for an expectant bride and groom. There will not be any such ceremony.

Who thought this stuff up?

"Are you ready?" Ash asks her, a small shake of her head but a supporting hand on Lane's back.

"I'm ready. Time to say goodbye. I'm not who they need. They both deserve someone all in." She looks at Ash again. "That isn't me."

I swallow, knowing that Patrick will have something up his sleeve. He has for the last fifty-three minutes of this show.

Lane walks on the sand of the beach. She's told she's headed toward Patrick. But when she arrives, Patrick *and* Broc stand waiting for her, hands in pockets, eyes on the girl, scowls on each of their faces.

5

DELANEY

I sit in the hot tub of my Airbnb—no television in sight. Though my phone won't stop its buzzing. I should have left it inside the house. I am so tempted to drown it in this tub and buy a new one tomorrow. Instead, I glance down at the names lighting up my smart screen.

Mom.

Mom.

Mom.

And Eryn.

But I can't answer. I know what's happening right now. Yes, they're watching it. But I lived it.

I walked down that beach, trying to be a good human, doing what felt right inside. I went to say my goodbyes, to wish them both good luck. To tell them they deserved to be loved—a kind of love that I couldn't give them. I wanted to do what was right, not easy.

Instead, Patrick and Broc stood united against me. They each told me how they never loved me, how they could never be with someone as selfish and out of touch as me. Instead of allowing me to say goodbye and God bless, they each rejected me on a very personal level—rejection with a capital R.

Such an intimate attack on my character and integrity hurt. But I didn't love them either. I didn't want a life with either of them. I think I could have lived with the jabs and rejection with peace had it not been for the plotting, the scheming, the lies. I tried to tell them both sooner—neither allowed it. I wasn't trying to humiliate them or ruin their lives. I was just trying to be honest with myself and with them.

I am certain that after tonight, Patrick will have killed his own image. The world—at least, anyone decent—will find him as repulsive as I do. However, he took me down with him.

My image is scarred—and possibly for life. If my job and passion didn't put me in the spotlight, it might blow over. But the world is watching, and this... I have no idea how I'll recover.

Unfortunately, in the world of fame, loving yourself and wanting yourself isn't enough to make the world want you too.

I sit in the torrid water and steamy air for another half an hour before I'm brave enough to listen to my voicemails.

"Delaney," my sister says, her tone thick with worry. "Are you there? Are you okay? Why didn't you say anything? Call me back, sis."

I sigh. I didn't say anything because I couldn't face another human, not even my sister. Not with this.

And then my mother's voice sounds through the speaker of my phone. "You couldn't have just married one of them, Delaney Sage?"

And another— "Do you know what you've done to our family image? Does your selfishness have no limits? That boy may have been right about you. You should have given him a chance."

A third message begins, but I dunk my head beneath the hot water and shut out all of Claire Jones' words. I hold my breath as long as I can, as long as humanly possible. And when I come up for air, Mom's voice has left the building. Her lecture is over and I can breathe.

~

*C*rap. And double crap.
    Thank you sooo much, Rizzy—my airport friend.
You just *had* to take that far-away photo of me. You just *had* to share it on social media. You just *had* to tag your location.

The Judys exploded during our first two years as artists. We toured, we hired stylists and bodyguards. We stayed on top of the charts for four years. But the last two years have been—well, slower. Steady, but fixed. Our original fans still like our original stuff. But the new stuff, in my opinion, has no heart. It's the old stuff worked over and half our fans aren't buying it. Why would they? I'm not buying it.

Still, sales are steady—but no longer increasing.

With the slower pace, we stopped needing certain things—like those helpful men called *bodyguards*.

Until today.

It's the day after my fabulous *Celebrity Wife* finale and Rizzy has led the media right to me. Somehow right to my Airbnb welcome mat.

Once again, new friend—thanks for that.

I feel like a mouse trapped in a box with a dozen cats surrounding me. Really, there's a guy with a camera on my front porch, and I swear I saw one in the backyard, though I booked a house with a six-foot fence. I'm not surrounded by a hoard. But I won't stay in this trap. I'm growing claustrophobic by the second.

I need out.

Stepping out of the shower, I throw on my ripped jeans, a short-sleeved, mint-green tunic top, and my cross-strap wedge sandals. I don't bother drying my long hair; instead, I gather it to the side and weave the thick mane into an ash-blonde braid. I throw on a baseball cap and find my shades before making my escape.

I watch secretly, waiting for the vulture out front to cross to the sideyard, and then I slip out the door, closing it as if there were a newborn infant sleeping on the other side. I knew I should have gotten a house with a garage. I had to choose—garage or hot tub—and I chose the tub.

I almost make it to my rental before vulture number one spots me. Thankfully, it's just the two vultures on the prowl today. A hoard would make it hard to escape at all.

The windows of this car are dark, but not dark enough. I lock the doors, but he's still trying the handle, and that makes me jumpy. With my pulse thrumming a thousand miles a minute, I peek in the rear, like someone might be waiting for me in the backseat. I wouldn't put it past the media.

"Lane!" I hear him yell through the safety of the vehicle. "Just a few questions!"

Again, the lack of a crowd is encouraging. The slime at my window has his camera out and flashing, but at least there's no one behind me. I can back out.

I do, just as vulture number two finds his way to the front of the house. The first man waves a hand at him—they must be together.

Good, because while he's getting his partner to hurry to the car, I will be gone. I hit the gas, and take off like a bullet in this quiet residential area.

I make my way around the lake twice when my stomach starts to growl. There was that sandwich place right next to the gallery I went to the other day, and it had a back parking lot. My car wouldn't be visible from the main road for everyone to spy.

After another lap around the lake, I decide that no one around me looks suspicious, and no one is following me. We are in Idaho, after all. I drive to the sandwich shop and google before I get out of the car to see if they have an online ordering system. They don't. So, I sit another minute before donning my darkest pair of sunglasses and stuffing my giveaway hair up into my ball cap. It isn't an easy task with my thick hair, but I get most of it stuffed inside of the L.A. Dodgers cap. I throw on a jacket, though it's seventy degrees out. I'm feeling pretty smothered between the cap and coat on this sunny May day.

I head into the shop, but it's packed. Is this the only place to eat in this town? Instinct has me turning right back around. Chances are at least one person in that room watched *Celebrity Wife* last night. And I don't want to be anywhere near them.

Ugh. Is that dumb show going to haunt me for the rest of eternity?

So much for Ash's brilliant plan. Still, I can't blame her. I'm not looking for love. I know that. I knew that going in. I went in without the right intentions, so of course it came back and bit me in the butt.

There's a man with a camera across the street. Not a phone or a Polaroid, but a big-man camera. I can't tell if he's the man who hid in my backyard, but it's enough to send me to the closest, quietest place available.

6

MILES

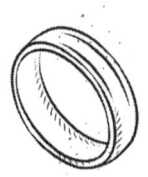

"It looks angry," Walt says. He stares at the modern painting of a local artist.

"You think?" I look at the rapid, hard brush strokes and rest my arm around Walt's shoulders. He isn't wrong.

"Yes," he says, his wild brows furrowed.

"I think you're right. See this stroke?" I say, pointing to the piece.

"It's dark. And mean." Walt ignores my instruction. "I do not like it."

"Would you like to move on?"

"Yes. Songbirds."

My piece. I started painting songbirds when Coco came home. Our sister had been adopted out as a baby—as brothers, none of us even knew she existed until she was suddenly back. But once we discovered our sister, we all dealt with it differently. We love her and feel thankful to have her home—but we also feel loss for the time we lost.

Still, the joy outweighs the pain. And I express that with songbirds. In fact, I became a little obsessed. I put out three more pieces. One found a home with Coco, of course, and the other two eventually sold. This is the piece that Lars hasn't sold, to his chagrin.

I push Walt along slow and steady, letting him take in the other work here. There are some really beautiful pieces—works that shouldn't just be passed by but enjoyed.

The door to the gallery opens and I glance over as if I work here. I don't—but most of the people who come in wouldn't believe that. I do live right upstairs.

The top of a strangely full and deformed baseball cap comes into view. The owner's eyes are covered with dark glasses, and as far as I can tell, focused on the ground rather than looking around the gallery. The curved figure, slender jawline, and tight jeans tell me this person is female.

Turning back to Walt, I steer his chair over to the bench I happened to situate right in front of my songbirds—this way we can sit together. Lars hasn't noticed. If he had, he would have moved it by now simply to irritate me.

"I like the colors," Walt says. His bottom lip protrudes out, but the corners raise up in a grin. He raises his stiff arm. His thin fingers clamp together in a claw and point to the painting.

"You know, you could take it home, Walt." I rest an ankle on my knee and peer at my friend. I've offered him the piece more than once.

"No. Like it here."

"I know," I say—and I can't help but grin. Walt loves it here and Lars hates it. It's almost poetic.

"Someone else wants to buy it," he says.

"Is that so?"

"That is so," he tells me, his I-told-you-so tone in full mode.

I laugh and, in my peripheral, notice the girl with the cap walking several feet away, staring at the angry painting Walt and I just left.

"That one is no good," Walt tells her, though I'm not sure she knows he's talking to her.

"Whoa. Remember, art is subjective. Everyone gets to like what they like."

He nods and gives me a small teenager-like eye roll. "No such thing as bad," he says, repeating my words. He huffs out a breath. "Mine is always good."

"Well, that's true." I pat his shoulder. There isn't much Walt loves more than his own watercolors and paintings.

His eyes cross to the window, landing on our wishful studio across the street.

"I know, bud. One day."

But I'm easily distracted as the girl pulls the cap from her head and ash-blonde hair comes spilling out. She shakes her head and splashes of blue catch my eye. *The girl.*

It takes me a second to remember that it's *Lane Jonas*, not just the girl I saw the other day. I only ever listened to The Judys first album, nothing more—but I did watch as she got the runaround by a *jackweed* named Patrick. I blink, clear my throat, and force myself to look away. She isn't here so that I can make her uncomfortable. She's here for quiet, for peace, and maybe… it's possible… she even likes art.

The thought makes me smile—but I still look away.

"Hey, Miles," says a friendly voice.

I turn to see Dolores, Walt's sister, at the door.

Walt groans as I turn his chair and he sees her too. I chuckle under my breath and wheel him over, ignoring the eyes of Lane Jonas.

"So unhappy to see me?" Dolores says. "*Rude.*"

"We just got started." Walt groans.

"An hour ago! Besides, you have lessons tomorrow. You'll see Miles so soon you'll be sick of him."

"True," I say, handing off his chair to Walt's younger sister and guardian.

Another groan leaves my friend's mouth.

"Tomorrow. Okay, bud?"

"Say bye to Miles," Dolores tells him.

"Bye Miles." Walt moans, and I am certain the workers from his group home are wrong—Walt can't have the intellect of a nine-year-old because he acts just like a teenager.

Dolores starts for the door. I hop over and open it up for the pair. A man with a black jacket and dark hat has his phone out and directed at the gallery. He's outside, but I have no problem telling him to *get lost*—the people in this gallery work too hard to have their work ripped off.

"Hey," I say as he steps out of the way of Walt and Dolores. "No photography or video of the gallery. No exceptions."

"Right," he says, shoving the device into his pocket.

I watch as Dolores walks Walt down to the handicapped parking space. Walt's mouth is moving while his stiff fingers lift to point to the building across the street.

I'm not sure what else I can do. Lars isn't budging. I don't have enough credit to take out a loan on this or any other building. I'm thinking and zoning out when I notice the man in the dark jacket hasn't moved on. He still stares at the gallery from the outside in.

I'm not inviting him and his camera phone inside, that's for certain.

I'm ten steps into the gallery when I peer back at him. "I'm calling Nina," I mutter to myself. My police friend will be happy to drive by. Maybe she'll even yell at the guy. It'll make her day.

I move forward, ready to pull my phone out of my pocket, but blonde, tiny, and curved is parked right in front of me.

Lane.

In motion, I'm unable to stop and we collide. Her hands hit my chest, and the lip balm she's holding tumbles out of her fingers and onto the ground.

"Shoot. Sorry," I say, bending on one knee to retrieve the thing. I reach up to hand her the pink gloss. Lane stares down at me, tears in her eyes and a small grin on her pretty pink lips.

My hand slips into hers. Is she crying? I saw her cry on that dumb show and it broke me a little. She'd tried to be honest, to be decent, to show respect to those men. They not only derailed her but did the exact opposite: making sure she was disrespected.

"Are you okay?" I whisper.

She nods and one tear falls onto her rosy cheek.

A flash from outside has me remembering my purpose. But when I stand, there are more tears on Lane's cheeks, and I can't quite leave her side. So, I pull out my phone right where I stand, peering down at the woman.

"Nina," I say, "there's some punk outside the gallery taking photos. Can you drive by, maybe scare him off?"

"I'm a block away and I've had zero action today. I'm on my way." She sounds giddy with the opportunity.

I smirk out a laugh with my friend's response. "Thanks," I say and end the call.

My eyes find the steel blue of Lane Jonas'. Her brows knit and another tear falls. "Thank you," she says, though I'm not sure why.

I lean in without thought or apprehension. I cup her cheek and, in a very un-Miles-like fashion, I press a kiss to this sad stranger's forehead.

There's another flash from a camera just before spinning red-and-blue lights shine out the gallery windows. *Good.* Nina will scare him away. It's her specialty.

"Do you need a drink?" I ask, sticking with my not-so-normal behavior.

Lane blinks, her blue eyes shining like glass. "I'd love one."

7

DELANEY

I'm not sure what's happening. I may have lost my mind. It fell out of my head when I agreed to do *Celebrity Wife* and it's never been found.

All I know is how I feel—and my gut tells me this man is *real*. He is safe. And I'd really love some alcohol about now.

I follow behind him, my eyes zoning in on the major muscles of his back, the ones his T-shirt seems to hug.

What am I doing? My mother would kill me right now—he's a stranger. *How stupid can you be, Delaney Sage?*

Even Ash would shake her head at me—this is reckless. *Be smart. There are crazies out there and you have to be smarter than they are.*

Eryn would yelp in shock at my behavior. *Where's your pepper spray?* It's in my purse, little sister. Stop your worries.

And while I don't think Grandma Judy would exactly push me into a car with a stranger offering me liquor—something that will surely mess with my already questionable decision-making ability—she always taught me to listen to my gut. When I left The Judys, it was my gut talking. And while things haven't been easy since I left, it was the right decision.

My gut screamed at me, telling me *not* to do *Celebrity Wife*, and yet I listened to Ash instead.

Mr. Tall, Dark, and Curly doesn't take me to his vehicle. Though I thought we were in search of a bar. I follow him to a back stairwell. The space has no outside door and no windows. A great place to be murdered. And yet, for the first time today, I feel like I can breathe.

He pauses and turns, those muscles in his back flexing with the movement. Standing on the first stair, he faces me, making himself a full foot taller than my five foot six. He's already tall, but now he's looking down at me. "This staircase leads to my home. I don't want to give you any misinformation. I'm not an assassin and I don't plan to seduce you. But up this stairway *is* my personal living quarters."

My lips quirk up in a grin. "I'm pretty sure an assassin wouldn't claim to be an assassin."

He ignores my lame joke, though a hint of a grin plays at his lips. "This is my place and this is where the drinks are—if you still want one. If not, I can show you out. No problem."

I nod. Swallow. And listen. My insides tell me this is exactly where I want to be. "Let's go," I say, pointing up the staircase.

"Okay, then." He gives one curt nod, then swivels his gaze to the stairs once more. With his hand on the rail, he glances back. "I'm Miles, by the way."

"Miles," I say. Even his name is comforting. No Miles ever murdered a rock star in a stairwell. I am certain of it.

He doesn't ask for my name, and I don't give it. I'm not sure he knows who I am. I mean, whisking me away from the photographers makes me think he should. But then he doesn't act like any stranger who's known my identity ever has before. My gut is giving me zero clues on this one. So, I keep my trap shut. I'll just get to be the mysterious, nameless girl who had a drink with him once.

He's waiting, but rather than offer my name back, I say, "I'm ready for that drink, Miles."

He nods once more, quiet and strong, then walks up the flight of narrow stairs.

I'm expecting something dark and cold at the top of this walk. But Miles opens the small, rounded door, and light spills out of the space. He ducks himself inside and I follow after, suddenly anxious for what I'll see. Slanted ceilings make the small quarters of this room feel even smaller. But the big windows built into the right half of the skewed ceiling bring in the sunshine and light up the space beautifully. There's a worktable, a couple stools, and several easels about the room. The wall at my left is covered with a myriad of colored paper—construction paper, I think. Each hue blends into the next, making a rainbow of color in a nonsensical way. There are canvases with half-finished paintings on two of the easels. I can't stop looking—there's too much to see—but Miles just walks past it all.

"My place is through here." He points to another hobbit door at the back of the small room. I almost missed it with all the light and color and work to be seen.

"This isn't—"

"This is my art studio. But I live in here." He's still directing me to the closed door within the small studio.

"You live in the gallery?"

"Above it," he says. He stops at the door, his eyes finding mine. "You still okay? I can always take you back down."

"Let's go," I say while the women in my life scold me inside of my head. They aren't wrong—going to a strange man's apartment *alone* at any time of day isn't something I'd normally recommend. But somehow, I still feel good about going.

Besides, it isn't like I know nothing about the man. I watched Miles last week and again today. I heard him speak to his friend—the man in the wheelchair—and the other man, who I'm certain is *not* a friend. I even know a little about him. He wants that building across the street for something, and the rude man he spoke to refused.

Okay… not a lot to go on. But I do know something—and I know my gut. *Don't be wrong, okay gut?*

Somehow, Miles' home is even smaller than his studio. There isn't even enough room in this place for a full-sized refrigerator. There's a couch for two and a small television. And one more hobbit door off to the right.

"I'd give you a tour, but…" He shrugs.

"I think I've seen it all. Well, except your bedroom." I point to the door.

"That's the bathroom." His brows lift. "We are standing in my kitchen, living room, and bedroom."

"No bed?" I peer around as if I could have missed one in this small space.

"The couch turns into a bed."

"Ah." I laugh and finger some of my messy hair behind one ear. My hat is stuffed inside of my crossover bag and part of me is tempted to put it back on. I'm probably a mess. But the thing was giving me a headache.

Besides, Miles doesn't care, and no photographers know where we are.

And yet, I'd love to freshen up. "Could I use your bathroom?"

"Sure. I'll grab your drink. Water or Coke?"

I narrow my gaze. "Nothing stronger, huh?"

His lip twitches with the start of a grin. I wait just a second for it to bloom, wanting to see his full grin. But he doesn't give it.

He blinks down at the ground, scratches the back of his curly-haired head, then peers back at me. "Not at the moment." Miles is handsome. He's kind. And in the few minutes that I've actually known him personally, he's genuine.

I knew my mother was wrong.

Good job, gut. I like him already.

8

MILES

*L*ane is in my bathroom long enough for me to pour two Cokes over ice. She's donned her black cap again—only this time her hair spills over her shoulders and down her back like a waterfall. The girl isn't lacking in the hair department. She's got a lot of it. Like she's Elsa with blue streaks... I may have watched that movie with Alice, once, twice, or eleven times.

I open one of my few cupboards and pull out a bag of M&Ms, the stash I keep on hand for Alice. It just feels right. Tears equals chocolate, right? Although, I think she's stopped crying. She's been through a lot, something big and difficult, and those emotions were triggered again—that's clear. Or maybe I have no idea what I'm talking about. I'm really just assuming every ounce of this.

I walk our drinks over to her, hand her one, and sit on my couch. I bought the thing after the sale of my first painting. It felt like a very grown-up way to celebrate.

She sits with me, and I pass her the bag of M&Ms.

"I brought sustenance."

"Oh!" She nibbles on her bottom lip, and her eyes flutter up to mine. "Any gummy bears?"

"Ahh—no. Sorry." I clear my throat, hiding a chuckle.

"I'm sorry," she says, her eyes cramming closed for a brief second. "You aren't a convenience store. This is wonderful." She tears open the package with her teeth—her other hand holding to her soda. She tips the package up and shakes a couple into her mouth. "Do you often bring strange girls up to your apartment and feed them chocolate?"

"Only the sad ones," I say as a joke. But it isn't funny. It's more than I should have said, more than I'd normally say. But something about this girl makes me want to speak. Still, her face falls a little with my observation.

"I'm that transparent, huh?"

"No." I clear my throat and sip from my drink. "Maybe. A little."

"No coffee table, huh?" She holds up her glass, unsure where to put it.

"Sorry." I wobble my head *no*. "But no dog either. So you can put your glass on the floor."

She does, then shakes a couple more M&Ms into her hand. "Want one? You look a little sad yourself."

"I do?"

Lane swallows. "I heard you talking about the building across the street. You want it for..." She glances at the door to my miniature workspace. "A studio?" Her nose wrinkles. "That guy—he seemed pretty adamant about his *no*."

My forehead furrows as I think about what she's said. She heard all that? Was I talking to Lars so loudly? "For a teaching studio, actually."

Lane's eyes narrow on my chin—my scar from more than a dozen years ago.

I tap the pale, flat moon with my pointer. "I fell ice skating when I was ten."

Her eyes study, listening.

"My brother, Levi, was so mad."

Her brows cinch, confused, but still, she sits quietly as I say more to her than I normally do to anyone.

"He was more mad at himself than anyone. As if my falling was his fault." I shake my head. "Mom patched us both up though. I got a trip to the hospital and three stitches, and Levi got the longest mom hug known to man." I'm not sure why I'm telling her this. She hasn't said anything. And normally I'm content with quiet. Why do I need to fill the silence?

"That's nice." She says it earnestly but also as if my story is a UFO—something totally foreign to her eyes.

I'm ready to ask if she never fell as a kid. Maybe she was wrapped in bubble tape like Meredith. Which is a ridiculous thought because out of the two people sitting in this loft, she has lived a much more exciting life than I have.

"You said you wanted a *teaching* studio. What does that mean?"

"I paint, but I teach art too. The majority of my students are people with disabilities. Most of them can't make it up the steep stairs to this studio." I motion toward the door to my workspace. "Sometimes, I go to their residence to teach, sometimes their life-skills center, but it isn't the same for them. They like going to class like everyone else."

Lane's teeth nibble on her full bottom lip. She draws my eyes there like a moth to a flame—or like Levi to a ham kolache.

"That's really nice, Miles." Her eyes latch onto mine and hold me there. "You're a nice guy."

I study her. Is this how she ended up on a reality TV show dating strangers? Did she trust too easily? "You don't really know me."

"That's true. But I still say you're a nice guy."

Lucky for her, I am.

9

MILES

"*I* should go," Lane says after downing the last two sips of her cola.

And while I'm not Levi, I'm not the overprotective type, I'm not *un*protective either. Something inside of me won't let her leave yet. Just in case. "Here's my number." I grab a sketch I started last week sitting on my kitchen counter and rip off the corner—I'm redoing it anyway. I sit back beside her and scribble down my number, holding it out to her. "Just in case you need anything."

She tilts her head. "And now you want my number? Right? Just in case you *need* anything?" Her brows lift.

I guess I can't blame her for being skeptical in her line of work. But I don't want it. I won't need it. I'll be fine. I shake my head. "I don't need your number. I just want to help—if you need it." I lift one shoulder. "Call me from a payphone if you want. This isn't a scam to get your number."

"Nice guy," she says, meshing her lips together. "You know payphones don't exist anymore, right?"

I breathe out a chuckle. "Fine. Call me from the sandwich shop next door. Or don't call at all. It's up to you. It seems like you're alone. Like maybe you could use a friend. And if you need—"

"Got it." She swallows and takes the slip from my hand. Her fingers brush mine, and maybe it's been a while since I've really looked at a woman because my hand lights up like the Fourth of July. Her steel blue eyes lock onto mine and refuse to let me go. "If I need a friend, I'll call."

I'm just trying to help—and yet I'm sweating more giving this girl my number than when I helped build Walt's wheelchair ramp at the new group home. She's a workout, no doubt about it.

Lane stands up from my couch and runs her hands down the thighs of her denim pants. I follow her up, certain the air will be cooler up here.

"Thanks for the drink," she says, holding out her downed glass of Coke.

She gives me a small side eye before pulling off her hat, then stuffing her long, thick hair up into it and forcing the thing back onto her head. I walk her through the studio and to the top of the stairs.

She slips her dark glasses onto her face and peers up at me, though her eyes are hidden. "Bye, Miles. Thanks for being a decent man."

I pinch my lips together. "Bye, Lane."

She trots down three of the stairs before pausing, turning back, and sliding her glasses to the tip of her nose to see me better. "You knew?"

I stuff my hands into my pockets and gulp down the knot in my throat. I know exactly what she's asking. "Yeah."

Her brows pinch together, but she doesn't say anything else. She pushes her glasses back in place and skips down to the gallery door.

～

The air smells as if we've entered an Italian bistro. Mom stands at her stove, stirring a white sauce in her oversized pot. I'm not complaining. I love it when my mother cooks.

"Miles, will you get the bread out of the oven, honey?"

"Sure." I may be thoroughly distracted, but I can pretend I'm not. I reach around her, hot pads in hand, and pull Mom's homemade bread from the oven. I set the loaf pan on the counter and turn back to my phone. Yep, I'm reading the latest Google has to offer me on Lane Jonas.

"Miles! The counter!"

I reach for the pan—that's currently leaving a mark on my mother's Formica countertop—without a hot pad. It only takes a second for my fingers to fry. I drop the loaf pan into the empty sink, bread side down. *Crap.*

"Miles." Mom moans. "Honey. Are you okay? You are distracted today. What's up?" Setting her spoon to the side, Mom snags the pot holders I didn't bother with and pulls her bread upright.

What's up? Oh, I don't know, I just entertained a rock star in my loft for half an hour. We had Coke and M&Ms and talked about how I'm stupidly decent and suck at skating. That's all.

With one hand on her hip, she studies the mess I've made. "It's just a little wet. It'll be fine. Hand me that knife and I'll trim the top off."

"I'm sorry, Mom."

"Is everything okay?" She takes the knife from my hand and saws off a skiff of her golden-brown bread.

"Yeah. Same ol' stuff." I run a hand through my hair, looking at her bread that now has a flat top. "I must be tired." I pull in a breath, keeping my lips shut on the Lane subject. *Yep, nothing to tell here.*

"It's Lars, isn't it? He won't budge. I knew it. That man is rotten."

"He isn't rotten. He's just... selfish."

"That sounds rotten to me." Mom huffs, sliding one arm around my back. "You're doing good things, son. Just keep doing them."

"He is doing good things. He'd be doing even better things if he'd ever take my advice!" My sister shuffles in with baby Lula in one arm, a diaper bag over her shoulder, and a big bowl of something in her other arm. "I mean, I'm older and therefore wiser and—"

"Not that old," Jude says from behind my sister. My sister's husband ducks through the doorway with his daughter Alice on his back and two bags of green salad in each hand.

"Still *wiser*," Coco insists.

"Of course," Jude says, setting the bags of greens on the counter and kissing her cheek.

"And I had the perfect girl for him!" Coco tells Mom, then hands the bowl in her grasp off to Jude.

As if they were waiting for their cue, more of my family files into the kitchen. Levi, Meredith, and just behind them, Owen with my new sister, Annie.

"*Nope*. You shouldn't be allowed to fix up anyone else in this family," Levi mutters.

"Ah," says Owen, "I'm gonna have to second that."

"Owen." Coco gasps, clearly offended. "I helped you get Annie!"

"Yeah, but after you set her up with Levi and helped her find me a bunch of pretty terrible blind dates."

"Will you never get over that?" Annie asks. She'd been more of the coordinator on all those setups than even Coco.

Owen wraps an arm over his new wife's shoulder. "I am over it. I'm just pointing out that Coco doesn't have the greatest track record."

"Well, that's not very nice. My track record is just fine. I knew Annie was right for you, and I knew Meredith was right for Levi." She nuzzles Lula's cheek, but my almost one-year-old niece wiggles until her mother sets her on the ground.

"Any more steps?" Mom asks, glancing from the baby to my sister.

"Not yet. But Mom is coming for her birthday, and I'm hoping she can wait for Grandma Heidi."

Grandma Heidi—Coco's other mom. Because my sister was adopted as a baby, we've only reconnected with her these past three years. Heidi is her adopted mom. It's not nearly as confusing as it sounds—only *sometimes*, when she talks about her *other* mother. It's easy to forget that Coco didn't grow up with us because it feels as if she's always been ours.

"That would be perfect," Mom says, picking up Lula and giving her a snuggle before setting the wiggly girl back on the floor. My mother is one of those angelic souls who holds no jealous feelings or animosity. She's full of love and light and thanks. And that's all she has for the woman who raised my sister.

"I think Miles should allow Coco to set him up," Annie says, looping her arm through Owen's.

Levi scoffs. "You do?"

"Yes, and I am the family advice columnist."

"No need to remind us," Levi says. Though he likes to tease her, he and Annie are friends—*now*.

"It's like a Bailey family tradition. A rite of passage. You wanna be a Bailey? You've got to let Coco work her magic." Annie grins, clearly trying not to chuckle. "Really, it's only fair of Miles to let his sister do a little matchmaking."

Meredith looks up from her crouched spot next to baby Lula, who is trying to crawl over her and into the living room. "I agree. That sounds like a fun tradition."

Blinking, I scoop up my little niece. "Not fun." I narrow my

MILES BAILEY GETS DOWN ON ONE KNEE

gaze at Coco, who beams as if she's won the race. *Coco for matchmaking president.* Nope, I'm not voting for her. "Not happening," I say.

"Come on, Miles." Coco moans. "Coop is the only Bailey man who ever attempts to find himself a date. If I don't help you, who will? You're all hopeless."

"Hopeless?" Levi says with a short growl. "Engaged." He points to himself.

Owen raises one hand. "Married," he says with a pleased nod.

"Granddaughter!" Alice belts from her father's back. She slips down to the ground. "Shirley Aldred says that her dad is her grandma's favorite because he is the only one to give her any grandchildren. And that makes perfectly good sense to me."

"Right!" Coco holds out a palm, high-fiving her stepdaughter. "So, we're the favorites!"

"I do not have favorites," Mom says, that rare, exasperated tone rearing its head. "Except... my grandchildren are my favorite." She holds a hand out to Alice and they disappear down the hall and into the dining room.

"We weren't arguing about favorites," Annie says. "Did you all forget? Coco was pointing out that the Bailey men are fairly hopeless when it comes to women." She lifts one shoulder. "And she isn't wrong. It needs to be stated."

"Hey." Owen's brows pinches. *"Married."*

"Yes, but it took you fourteen years to ask me out."

Meredith nods. "And"—she looks accusatory at Levi—"you denied your feelings for weeks. Coco might be right."

"I'm always right," my sister says, her eyes on me. "So, Miles—"

"Sorry. Not this time."

10

DELANEY

I can't sleep. That's never a good sign. I can always sleep. My mind keeps returning to Miles the artist who didn't ask for my number or a photo or even to have me sign anything. It's not the norm. So not the norm that I was sure he had no idea who I was.

I knock my head against the wooden headboard of this king-sized bed and nibble on my thumbnail.

My eyes refuse to close. I snatch my cell from the end table and bring the thing to life to see a text from my sister. When I open it up, there's a screenshot of a tabloid. A photo of me and a kneeling, curly-haired, deliciously decent Miles. She's written one word and a million question marks.

Eryn: Who???????

Flailing my arms, I sit up. "Crap." I open my celebrity news app and— "Double crap!"

Multiple photos light up the screen—several of me, from my time with the Judys to walking into my Airbnb the other night. And then there's the big one, the framed photo. While it's not flawless since taken through the gallery window, I still know who that is. Miles kneels in front of me, and it looks as though we're holding hands. I scroll down to more photos from yesterday. None of the gallery pictures are crystal clear—but they all clearly imply that something is up. They've zoomed in on Miles' face, our hands together, and the knee he's kneeling on, all a little distorted and all hinting at things that didn't happen. The captions don't help.

Who is this nobody proposing to Lane?

Did Lane Jonas finally say yes?

No wonder Lane didn't want Patrick. She was already in love.

I glance down at one more, pull in a gasp, and roll over in this borrowed bed—only I turn left when I should turn right, falling out of bed like a cat who has used up her nine lives. My back hits the ground, forcing all the air from my lungs. My hands still clutch my cell and my eyes are still glued to the text on the screen.

Wedding bells in Jonas' future.

I'm not sure if it's the headlines or if hitting the ground so hard knocked all the sense out of me, but all at once, I have a plan.

A good one. One for me and maybe even one for Miles.

That is, if I can get him to go along with me. He's so darn decent and sensible, he may never agree.

∼

I wait until five in the morning, and then I text my morally strong, artistic hero. I'm counting on the fact that Miles didn't seem glued to his phone or act like a starstruck puppy being on my side.

With all of those vibes mojoing inside of me, rooting me on, I write to Miles.

>**Me:** This is Lane.
>**Me**: Can you meet me in the gallery first thing this morning? I have a favor to ask.

I clamp down on my bottom lip. *A favor?* Yeah, that's all this is… one teensy, weensy, little—*enormous*—favor.

I'm hoping he'll see the message before he starts his day—before the crap hits the fan and my little twisted plan never sees the light of day.

I jump up, ready to shower, ready to be ready for when Miles does text me back. Because good intuition tells me he isn't the kind of man to ignore a girl. That, and he literally told me to call if I needed anything. Toss out the fact that I'm famous. He didn't seem to care.

I'm in the bathroom, half stripped when my phone pings at only 5:30am. The man is awake—already?

Either that, or my mother has seen the photos and she's texting—again…

Nope—it's Miles.

Bless him.

>**Miles**: What time?

I turn the shower water on, letting the hot water steam up my rented master bath's windows and mirrors, creating my own personal sauna.

Me: How soon can you be ready?
Miles: I am ready. Sort of.
Me: Does that mean you've showered?
Miles: Well… no. That means I'm up, I've worked out, and I've spent twenty minutes on a piece that's going nowhere.

Huh. Early riser. I don't know why it makes me smile. I sleep in as long as the tour or Ash will allow. Still, I like this about Miles. It says more about his character. For some dumb reason, the fact that Miles Somebody wakes up early to work out and paint makes me trust him all the more.

Me: When does your boss open up?
Miles: Lars comes in a little before eight, but I can always open up for you.

Eight. Perfect. I need Lars there.

Me: Eight works. That way you'll have time to shower all the man stink off of yourself.
Miles: And you'll have time to eat a nutritious meal of gummy bears for breakfast.

I giggle and rub away the moisture beading on my neck from my homemade sauna. Already Miles-the-decent-adorable-artist gets me.

This is going to work out. I have a feeling.

11

MILES

I cross over from the stairs that lead to my loft into the gallery. We don't get any patrons until after ten, though Lars opens the doors at eight. It's only 7:49am. I worked until after seven and then hurried to shower and get ready. I didn't even bother putting in my contacts. I don't want Lane to have to wait on me.

I'm not normally overly curious. I see things as they are. I hear what people say. I can usually read and understand them well.

But that text—I don't have any idea what kind of favor Lane Jonas needs from me. Still, I offered with sincerity. I'm happy to help.

Lars' office door is shut, but light spills out from the bottom of the entrance. He's in there. I know better than to bother him this early. If he opens it up, I'll explain that I'm meeting Lane here. If he doesn't, he's none the wiser.

My phone pings with a text, and I peer down at the smart screen. It's from Coco, but the banner has only told me that she's sent a photo—no text. I am centimeters away from opening up the messaging app when Lars' office door swings open.

But Lars doesn't walk out.

Nope. Lean legs, ash-blonde hair with a hint of blue peeking through its braided strands is somehow leaving the curator's quarters. And while I don't know Lane all that well, while she isn't my sister or friend or anyone I should truly be worried about, my stomach churns with the sight.

Nope, I don't like that.

Not one bit.

She swivels, her profile facing me. I can only see part of her face, but there's a hint of a smile there. While Lars, head-on, is giddy with the largest, eeriest grin I've ever seen on the man's face. She holds out a hand, and he accepts, shaking while assaulting her with that grin.

It's not a greeting or a goodbye but the sealing of a deal.

What is happening?

I walk toward the two. Lars' gaze flicks from Lane to me and his smile vanishes.

"What are you—" He snarls.

But Lane finishes for him. "Miles. Thanks for meeting me so early," she says, slipping her arm through mine.

Lars clears his throat, swallowing down the remark he had built up for me. "I'll be in touch, Ms. Jonas."

"*I'll* contact *you*," she says, making it clear that he doesn't need any contact information from her. *Good*—at least she's a good judge of character. With her arm still snug through mine, she walks me away from Lars' office.

I wonder which painting she's purchased. I wonder what her taste is. I also wonder how much Lars jacked up the price when he found out who she was and what she wanted. I wish she'd asked me to be with her when she made the offer. I'm not afraid to remind Lars of worth and fairness.

We pass the janitor's closet, then the local artist's corner, and

Lars is officially eating dust. My pocket pings with another text. And then another.

"Sorry," I say, knitting my brows and peering down at her. "My phone is blowing up all of the sudden."

Three texts in five minutes to anyone else may not be crazy, but it is for my cell. I slip my hand into my pocket as another text chime rings.

"Weird." I pull out my cell. This time the banner tells me it's a photo from my mother.

"No, Miles!" Lane shrieks—and it sounds like madness in the quiet space of the gallery. I jolt my attention up from my screen just in time to see her hands snatching away my cell. She slips the device down the neck of her pink, tucked-in T-shirt.

My brows lift, confused. "Ahh—"

"I'm sorry, but I have to talk to you first."

My eyes drop to her abdomen, where a rectangular outline shows me exactly where my phone sits against her skin.

"O—kay, but my—"

Reaching out, Lane takes hold of the front of my T-shirt and yanks, pulling me into the small janitorial closet behind us. She slams the door closed, leaving us in the dark. Soft fingers trail past both my wrists and over my forearms. She holds me there, and while I can't see her face, I hear the rapidness of her breath and maybe even the beating of her heart.

"Lane?"

"I have to ask you something."

"In a closet?" I attempt to move my arm from her to search for the hanging string connected to the lone light bulb in this storeroom, but she doesn't let me.

Her fingers grip tighter, holding me in place. And I'm starting to wonder—sure, she's a good judge of character, but maybe *I'm* terrible at reading people. Because I swore this girl was sane.

"I'm just going to turn the light on," I tell her.

"Oh. Um. Okay." Her grip loosens enough that I can tear one arm away from her Dwayne-The-Rock-Johnson hold on me.

I search in the dark air above me, feeling for the dangling string—there it is. I tug and Lane Jonas lights up like an angel—an angel with a fluorescent halo surrounded by Windex and toilet bowl cleaner. The light bounces off of the rainbow charm around her neck, forcing my eyes there.

I clear my throat and toss away any thoughts of angels and throats. "All right, ask away."

She lifts her blue eyes up to me, swallows, and opens her pouty lips—err, not pouty, really, just regular ol' lips. She opens her lips—err, even better, she opens her mouth and says, "I want you to marry me."

12

MILES

I would choke, only there's nothing in my mouth. Not even a drop of spittle to block my airway.

Maybe I didn't hear her right.

Maybe she *is* crazy.

Maybe I'm dreaming.

Maybe—

"Just for a little while," she says.

Crazy it is!

I am one confused man. I mean, sure, I am a *man* and we confuse easily, but I think this would confuse even the brightest of male specimens. I scratch behind one ear. "Weren't you just on a dating show? One where you could have gotten married in the end?" And while I thought marriage after a few weeks was insane, we've known each other for a day.

She licks her lips and my eyes draw there, lingering far too long. "Yes. But those men claimed to love me. And—"

"And, sure, why would you want your husband to love you?"

"They had *feelings*—feelings I didn't reciprocate. I didn't love them back, Miles."

I swallow. She didn't. I remember. And she attempted to be

really honest and decent about the whole thing. Which doesn't make me understand this situation any better.

She huffs out a breath and drops my one arm left in her grasp. "Listen, I'm making some changes in my career—at least, I'm trying to. It's ruffling feathers. My PR manager was certain that show would boost my image." Her eyes close and the light above us illuminates the sparkles in her eye shadow.

Like a trance, I stare at her closed lids until steel blue eyes look back at me once more.

"The thing is, I think Ash may have been right. My image needs some... *love*. But I ruined everything when I didn't fall for any of those men, when I couldn't go along with it all. I just couldn't bring myself to falsely marry someone with them thinking that I actually loved them. That's above and beyond wrong. You know?"

I nod, still unsure what's happening here.

"But you don't love me, Miles."

I swallow. I don't? I mean, of course, I don't. I don't even know her. "I don't," I say—and I mean it. No matter how pretty her lips may be or how saintly this light makes her appear, to love someone after one meeting would be crazy.

And I am not crazy.

Then again, I am in a closet, listening to a plan that makes no sense at all. Maybe sanity and I are only partial friends. I blow out a breath and clench my jaw. No matter the desperate look in her eyes, I determine that I am mostly sane. "I can't marry you, Lane."

"Delaney." She lifts her chin, her long, dark lashes fluttering up at me.

"Excuse me?"

"If we're going to be married, you should know my real name. Delaney Jones."

Perhaps she's hard of hearing too. "I can't marry you."

"Miles. You are a decent human. I promise to help you if you will help me. The only way this gets screwed up is if you fall in love with me. And you're not going to do that. Right? So, we're good." Her chest fills just before she sighs out an exhale.

"Are you—" I shake my head. "Did you take something? I mean, you aren't on something, right? Because—"

"You think I'm on drugs?" Her shoulders shoot back, her chest puffs, and she gives me an epic glare.

"Well, you aren't making sense, and you assume that I'll just go along with this crazy charade."

"Miles. I have been stuck. I have been unhappy as a Judy for the last two years. My heart is in folk. But I can't just cross over, not with my image in the mud the way it is. I would flop before I ever got my start. Help me build my image and I'll help you get your art studio. The building across the street," she says. "The one for your students."

I pause, resistance on the tip of my tongue, but... My art studio? My teaching studio? The one Lars refuses to give up? How could she possibly help me with that?

As if Lane Jonas—no, Delaney Jones—has read my mind, she says, "I just bought the building from Lars." She licks her lips, her eyes on me.

I can't speak. I can't breathe. My jaw goes slack, but I can't lift it. She bought the studio? My studio? As in, it's a done deal?

Delaney reaches up, one hand on either side of my face. Her fingers brush my jaw, and both her thumbs tap my chin upward, closing my gaping mouth.

"So, what do you think?" she asks.

"You bought my building?" I finally get out.

"I did. I've been on the phone with my lawyers all morning." Her blue eyes sparkle as she stares right through me. "As a wedding gift for my soon-to-be husband."

13

DELANEY

I can see the wheels turning. Miles can't turn me down flat—not with the studio as a bargaining piece. Some super villain side of me is banking on the love he so clearly has for his students. But really, this is what makes Miles perfect. Because I wouldn't only be serving myself but him too.

I don't love Miles. And Miles doesn't love me. No hearts will be broken when this farce of a marriage is over and done. Besides that, I *like* Miles. He's a decent human and a standup guy. He isn't selfish. He wants to do something good for others and I can help him get there.

Here's the thing—even if the man says no, even if he refuses to help me—the building is his.

See, I'm not really a super villain.

But I don't think he'll say no. I think I'll help him and he'll help me. In the end, we will both find ourselves exactly where we want to be in our careers and in our service to mankind. Sometimes you take what you want. Sometimes you earn it. And other times you have to convince the people to see what you're offering in creative ways.

That's all I'm doing.

"Why—why—marriage?" Miles stammers. The lamp in this room is giving the man a funny glow. I think it's foretelling. Miles is an angel sent here to help me. And why wouldn't I want to help an angel?

I breathe in and buoy my confidence because this is where I get triggered too. "Because. Ash says when I abruptly left The Judys and *Celebrity Wife,* I gave myself a reputation." I clench my jaw. "I didn't mean to. I don't deserve a terrible rep. I want to try something new. I'm following my heart. My heart was never in that TV show. Again—Ash's idea."

"Sounds like you should fire that guy."

"*Girl.* And I've considered it." I drop my gaze to the front of Miles' shirt. "Only she's trying to help me. She knows what I want. She's trying to get me there. My heart is no longer in rock or The Judys. I needed change—for my peace of mind. I don't know if that makes sense to you." I nibble on my bottom lip and stare straight ahead into the chest of Miles Somebody.

"It does, actually."

"I could jump into folk," I say. "I could fail." I bring my eyes up to his. I need him to understand this. "It's not about failure. But singing—well, it's for me what teaching is for you. If you have no one to teach, then what's the point? I want to sing. But I need someone to listen." I lift my shoulders in a small shrug.

"And because of that—which all makes sense, by the way—we need to get married?"

"Yes! You got it." I beam, hoping my face screams major (fake) wife material.

"I still don't—"

"Miles, I will be the best fake wife you ever had." I snag a hold of the front of his T-shirt, tugging him two inches closer to me. "I promise. You want me at the Miles' family reunion, I'll be there. You want a home-cooked meal—" I wrinkle my nose. "Well, I can't cook, but I know people who can."

He smirks. "Why *marriage,* Delaney?"

He calls me by my given name, and it catches me off guard—even though I gave him the name. The only time I hear it is when I talk to my mom or Eryn. Heck, half the time even Eryn calls me Lane or Dee. Lane was always a nickname, even before The Judys topped the charts.

"I need some positive press. Something to write home about."

"Why not an engagement—"

"No. It has to be a marriage."

I can see his teeth grind. "Holy matrimony?"

"Yep."

"You know, this kind of arrangement takes the *holy* right out of it."

"It doesn't." I press my hands together as if in prayer. They bump between my chest and his. "I promise, it'll be holy with a capital H."

His chest rumbles with a laugh. "You've already bought the building?"

"It's mine." I blink up at him. "It's *yours*, Miles—" I blow out a breath. "What is your last name? That might be important for me to know."

"Bailey. Miles Bailey. And it's one of a million things you might want to know about your future husband."

I grin. I can't help it. I like him and his name. And I think I'm wearing him down. "Miles Bailey."

"So, we get married, and then what? We keep up the sham as long as I want to teach and you want to sing?"

I shake my head. I thought about all of this last night. "Give me a year. I am certain I can build up my image in a year. Then, we can go our separate ways—you with your building, me with my new fan base."

Miles coughs, running his fingers through his curly head of hair. "A year? That's—that's a long time, Delaney. And I don't see how I—a nobody—will be helpful to your career."

63

"It's the image—Lane Jonas, *in love, happy, settled, wife*—that's helpful."

He shakes his head.

I twist my lips to the side, thinking. There are things I didn't consider as I jumped into this plan. While I've thought of so much. I didn't think about Miles having any attachments. "Do you have a fiancé?"

He scoffs. "No."

"A girlfriend?" I swallow, and that one drop of spittle plummets into my stomach like a boulder. A girlfriend would definitely put a snag in my plans.

"No. No girlfriend. But a house full of Baileys. I can't lie to my family."

No girlfriend. No problems. I hold a hand to my stomach. "Miles, you'd have to lie to your family. If you agree to this, no one can know it's fake."

His brows furrow. "You don't think my in-tune mother and extremely observant sister won't know that something is up?"

"They can't! The paparazzi can fish a false story out of a bucket of trout. Your family has to believe it too." I press my lips together. "As does mine."

Another hand through his hair. This time, the right side stays up on end.

"I just don't see how the people I see every day will believe this."

"Listen, that dumb show that turned my life upside down finished filming months ago. Say we met online. Say I wasn't allowed to tell anyone the outcome of the show, and so we kept our relationship a secret." I tug on the front of his shirt, pulling him closer until his chest bumps mine. I peer up at him. As far as fake husbands go, I'm pretty sure I picked a winner. Still, he stares down at me, his brows knit. Behind his rectangular glasses, his hazel eyes bore into me with doubt after doubt. "Miles," I say, taking the hand that's balled up a fistful of his shirt and flattening it out onto his chest. "Unless you have another plan, I am offering you everything you've been wanting on a silver platter."

"Not on a silver platter," he says. "A golden band."

I smirk. "Technicality. Listen, you won't have to deal with me much. I work in California—"

"You can't work from anywhere?" One of his brows lifts.

I lick my lips. "Well, The Judys were based in Cali."

"But you aren't with The Judys anymore, correct?"

"Yes, I'm just saying. I can have reasons to be gone. You won't even have to see or deal with me."

He studies me a second in this dim closet before saying, "That doesn't exactly sound like newlywed bliss."

He's right. If this is going to work, that won't do.

I swallow. "Are you saying you'll do it?"

Miles' heart thumps beneath my hand. I feel it. That rapid heart says he's considering it. Another tha-thump, and then: "Yeah. I'll do it."

Just like that, I've got myself a husband. I hop on both feet, looping my arms up and around Miles' neck, hugging him close —just as the closet door opens up. With my arms snug around Miles, I peer out at the bright light shining in—to more flashing lights. Lars stands at the front, but there are a handful of photographers just behind him. With the closet opened and my arms tangled around Miles, their flashes go off like fireworks on the Fourth of July.

"Miles?" Lars spits, his lip curled in loathing.

Miles has one arm around my back, and with the bout of flashes, he holds me a smidgen tighter. He holds up one hand, blocking the lights from his eyes, before reaching for the door and closing it back up.

14

MILES

"You know," Delaney says, "they aren't going away. In fact, with the proof that we're in here, only more will come." Her arms are still draped around my neck, her breath sweet and warm on my neck.

"Yes, but not even Lars will like photography in the gallery. And I've got a police friend in my pocket." With my hands, I gently pick up Delaney's wrists and lower her arms to her side.

She swallows and pink floods her cheeks. "Sorry," she whispers.

"Actually." I drop my gaze to her stomach. "My cell is still—" My eyes lock on the small bulge at her tummy.

"Oh." She gives me a false grin. "Right." She untucks her pink top and catches my phone as it slips past the snap on her jeans. She holds it out to me.

The cell is warm and clammy after spending the last twenty minutes next to Delaney's stomach.

I dial Nina and hold my phone—that might even strangely smell of Delaney, sweet and floral—next to my ear. "You might need a little help," I tell her after explaining the situation.

I shove my cell into my pocket, and Delaney pushes her long

blonde braid off her shoulder to hang down her back. "All right. Ready?"

"Ready?" I say, not computing.

"Are you with me one hundred percent, Miles Bailey?"

Engaged. Married. It's not as if this deal is going to mess up my social life. So, why not marriage to get my building? I run my hand over my chin and blow out an exasperated breath. I might be going crazy. "One hundred percent."

Delaney nods and loops one arm through mine. With her other, she leans forward and opens up the closet door.

A myriad of flashes blind us and I hold out one hand, trying to block the blinding lights.

"Are you done?" Delaney asks.

"Who is he, Lane?"

"How long have you been seeing this man?"

"Is this why Patrick dumped you before you could dump him? Were you cheating behind the scenes?"

"No," I say before Delaney can get anything out. "No cheating." My mother would kill me.

Her hand on my forearm squeezes, while her other sets to her hip. "You all saw the show. I was not in love with any of those men—and I tried to tell them as much. They wouldn't let me. Miles wasn't in the picture then. The show may have aired recently, but it ended months ago." She gives a small definitive nod, letting them know this is the end of the cheating talk.

"Lane, are you saying you're in love with this man?" the man I called Nina on yesterday asks. So many things fall into place with that recognition.

"I would hope so. He is my husband."

Her words only get us another round of flashing cameras.

"So, why hide in the closet?" says another.

"Miles is new to this." She nods toward the men and their cameras. "Besides, I wasn't ready to share him with you or anyone else." She peers up at me with her words. Her eyes remind me that my job is to make this believable. No one can doubt.

Right?

Her chin lifts, her eyes scanning from mine to my lips. Lane Jonas is giving me permission to kiss her. I see it in her eyes.

"Miles?" says one of the men. "Miles what?" He's holding out his phone, ready to record whatever it is we recite. And I'm guessing, ready to look up every ounce of dirt he can find on me.

Great.

There isn't any dirt. At least nothing criminal. Unless giving Owen a wedgie when I was ten is against the law. But that doesn't mean the thought of someone creeping through my personal life isn't disturbing.

I turn back to Delaney, who continues to watch me, still giving me permission. I slip my arm around her back and pull her closer to my side. "Miles *Jonas*," I say before leaning in. Delaney blinks, her eyes fluttering closed. But I touch my lips to her forehead, pressing a lingering kiss there. The woman smells like she bathed in a tub of roses: sweet, floral, and completely inviting. Her skin is soft and smooth. And I swear it wants me to touch it.

I'm trying to remember what it is she asked me to do. *Not fall in love with her*, right? Because that's the only way our plan fails.

15

DELANEY

It isn't even noon and I've got my lawyers and Ash working hard. Ash has procured the license and the officiator. They are ready and at my beck and call. She's a very handy woman. She's also holding a press conference in Cali without me, announcing my recent nuptials.

Very recent.

In fact, we may be saying "I do" while she's telling the world that it's a done deal. *Lane Jonas is making changes in her life—and those changes look good. So, keep looking world. She isn't a has-been. Nope, she is just getting started.*

"You don't want to change?" Miles asks me. "Or should I?" He tugs at the front of his T-shirt.

"I'm not really worried about our clothes right now. We just need to make it official. I can have Ash set up a photo shoot later."

"Photo shoot?" He swallows, his Adam's apple bobbing like a strong man game at the town fair.

We stand in Miles' one-room loft waiting for the people Ash is sending over. One witness and one officiator with all the official paperwork. My heart thumps in my chest, though I know none of this is real. There are no real feelings involved. The paperwork is legitimate but that's it, which is why this plan is so perfect.

Could I have married Patrick? Sure. But at one point on the show, he insisted that he loved me, that he'd do anything for me. So, that commitment came with loss and heartbreak. This comes with a gift for Miles, something he's always wanted, and no broken hearts. The thought helps me breathe easier.

However, my husband-to-be looks a little pale.

There's a tap on Miles' door, and I open it up to a man and woman I've never seen before. "Alec? Bonnie?"

They nod.

Miles leans closer to my side, whispering, "So, they can know, but my mom has to stay in the dark?"

This guy really likes his mom—I cannot relate. I don't dislike my mom, but we've never seen eye to eye.

"They don't know. They only know what their jobs are," I mutter back.

And that's the only introduction we get. These two are confidants of Ash's. And Bonnie, as of fifteen minutes ago, via the Internet, is legally ready to officiate her first wedding ceremony. Alec is here to witness.

We sign paperwork without bothering to read any of it and we're ready to vow one year of our lives to the other.

The ceremony takes a measly three and a half minutes. Miles and I stand face to face, not even touching. We both offer "I do's", nothing more, and, without a kiss-the-bride, Bonnie gives us a nod.

"Legal and binding. You are wed."

I breathe in, my shoulders rising, looking up at my new husband. It's done. "You may kiss the bride," my nervous instincts say—out loud. I don't mean to. Still, the words are out and I can't take them back. It doesn't feel official without *those*

MILES BAILEY GETS DOWN ON ONE KNEE

words. I wait to see what he'll do. Miles has the sort of full lips that look kissable—just as an observation.

Miles cups both my cheeks, his eyes on mine, and the pulse in my wrists picks up speed. Okay—here we go.

Husband.

Let's do this. You know, for our audience.

I can allow a kiss. Again—for our audience.

He's giving me a year of his life. I can give him a kiss.

I watch as Miles moves closer. But his hands on my face tip down, not up. He presses—yet another—soft kiss to my forehead. His hands warm my cheeks, and though Miles *doesn't* kiss my lips, blood still rushes to my face with his touch.

Somehow this man's forehead kisses leave me spinning more than any kiss from a contestant on a TV show ever did.

It must be the strangeness and the newness of this situation. Not him. It couldn't be him. Because I hardly know the man. His morals are the only reason he stands across from me now.

Before Miles can take his lips from my head, Alec is talking. "Okay, Ash has a small press conference set up for you at—"

"We cannot tell the press," Miles says. "Not until we've told my mother."

Yikes. *His mother.* I'm already a little terrified of the woman. All mothers give me hives—well, all mothers other than my grandma.

I can do media. I can do press conferences. I can do a lot of hard things. Meeting mothers is not counted among them.

I've had a handful of boyfriends over the years—I don't know any of their moms.

Alec looks to me.

I nod. How can I deny Miles this? He's giving me *marriage* and a commitment of some sort. "We're talking to Miles' family first, then we'll talk to the press. Tell Ash to hold off until—" I pause, looking at my Miles.

"Tomorrow," he says. "We can tell her tonight."

I nod. "Tomorrow it is. Just have Ash text me."

"Will do." Alec gathers his things and starts for the door.

"Congrats," Bonnie says, holding out the signed marriage license and prenup entitling Miles to the studio building and nothing else. They slip out of Miles' loft without a sound, and I am left alone with my *husband*.

"We need to get a few things straight," he tells me. "Or this isn't going to work. I don't think I would have met you online. It's just not me. My family won't believe that. Maybe you visited Coeur d'Alene before."

"Sure," I say, plunking myself onto his couch. I peer about the room. "I was here before, years ago, so that's plausible." I bounce a little on the thin couch cushion. "Where do you sleep, Miles?"

"Couch bed."

That's right. He mentioned that. That does not sound comfortable.

"So, a visit?" He sits next to me, getting right back to business.

"Yeah. I mean, my family came to Coeur d'Alene before my parents split up."

"Your parents are divorced?" His brows furrow. "Mine too. There's so much we don't know about each other."

I breathe in, then out, pursing my lips. "It's true. And we aren't going to learn it all in an hour. So—maybe we had a rapid romance. Something neither of us expected. We threw caution to the wind and jumped in."

"That doesn't really sound like me. Besides, we should know at least *something* about the other." His brows raise as those hazel eyes—more green than blue stare into mine.

"We should." I pull up my legs and cross them, sitting on this couch sideways so that my body faces his. "Well, I know that you got *this* ice skating," I say, tapping the scar on his chin, maybe a little too proud of myself. "And your brother... Lance—"

"Levi—" He smirks. "My brother *Levi* never forgave himself for letting me fall."

"That's right, a brother. You have a brother. I have a sister, Eryn."

"I have three brothers and one sister."

"Holy." I puff out a breath. Such a big family. My parents did not like one another enough to produce such a large family.

"Yeah. You should know their names. I would have talked about them. My family is very important to me. My nieces especially, Alice and Lula. They're Coco's girls, one stepdaughter and one biological. But they're both hers."

"Oh, boy." There's a lot more here than we have time for. "Okay, give it to me." I memorize lyrics for a living. I can remember Miles' family.

"In age order: Levi, Coco—"

"Coco?" I smirk.

"Yeah, Coco is a nickname. Mom named us all after something she loved, and Coco's given name is Cora, after the color coral."

I tilt my head and watch him. "And you were named after?"

He pulls in a slow breath, his broad chest expanding. "A soap opera star. Some character from *Lovers Love—*"

"*Lovers Love Twice*! I used to watch that show with my grandma." I bounce in my seat. "You're named for Miles Howard, the debonair surfer who stole Charlotte's heart after her husband died and she thought she'd never love again." I throw a hand across my forehead for dramatics.

Miles cracks the smallest of grins. "How do you know that?"

"My grandma had all the seasons taped. I used to watch them with her on her old VHS player." I laugh. "This is awesome. Grandma is going to love you, Miles Bailey." My eyes widen. What if… "Ooo! Tell me your middle name is Howard. Tell me. Please, Miles. If your middle name is Howard, then that hideous green doily she has hanging on her wall is mine!! Eryn can suck it!"

He chuckles at my outburst. "Why would you want a hideous doily?"

"Because it's Grandma's, and she's had it hanging on her wall for half a century. Eryn and I have both asked for it for the last decade. So, tell me your middle name is Howard, Miles." I cross my fingers on both hands and hold them up, waiting for his answer.

"Sorry. I'm named after my dad. Miles Gavin Bailey."

"Are you close with him? You haven't mentioned him." Granted, this is the first real in-depth conversation we've had.

"Ah, not really. We were, kind of, when I was young. But after my parents' divorce, Dad started traveling, and now it's a rare occasion for us to see him. He checks in every couple of months."

"Doesn't that piss you off?" I stare at him, waiting for his response. But there is no malice in this man's voice. It's an unfair question. I'm not angry with my dad for being more committed to his gambling addiction than his daughters. It is what it is. I'm just grateful when I do see him because I know I won't be judged.

"How would that help anything?"

"Okay, so Miles isn't an angry soul." I can't take my eyes off his. He doesn't care that he's sitting here with someone famous, or that we were just married, or that his dad is an apparent loser. Okay, harsh, but who wouldn't want to spend time with Miles?

"Are you an angry soul?"

I twist my lips. "Not angry. But in weak moments, a little bitter and extremely cautious of who I offer my time to."

"Says the girl who just legally bound herself to a stranger."

I lift my brows once. "I have a good feeling about you. And if my grandmother's lessons, my mother's judgment, and *Celebrity Wife* have taught me anything, it's to go with my gut."

"Your mother's judgment?"

I press my lips together and squeeze one eye closed. "Yeah. We don't exactly get along, and she doesn't approve of ninety-nine percent of my life choices."

"Ninety-nine, huh?" he says, his words laced with doubt.

"When she thought I was getting married on national TV without inviting her, she left a message asking how I could do this to *her*. When I ended up not marrying anyone, she left another message asking why I couldn't just give one of the men a shot. And did I have any idea how I was affecting the family name."

"She leaves a lot of messages, huh?"

I swallow. "I don't pick up the phone that often."

The irony of the universe is a funny thing. I barely have the words out when Miles' phone, sitting between us, begins to sing. The word *Mom* lights up the screen.

And—he does answer.

Just seeing the name sends a shiver down my spine, but there is no hesitation for Miles.

"Hey, Mom."

"Miles!" I hear the woman shriek, though he's holding the cell to his ear. "I'm seeing pictures and... and... What's going on?"

"I'm on my way to your place. I'll explain everything."

He hangs up and I watch him.

"We're on our way?" I ask. "Do we know enough?"

"No way." His thick brows give one quick leap. "Let's go."

16

MILES

I am ten times more nervous to tell my mother what I've done than I was when Delaney and I were actually getting married. That can't be right—right?

There are sweat beads pooling at the back of my neck and across my forehead. There's a tremor in my hand that I just can't shake off.

"We'll need to touch," Delaney says, watching me as I putter around my house, gathering absolutely nothing. I'm stalling.

"Touch?"

"Yeah. Miles, we're newlyweds. That means we kind of like each other."

"I do like you," I say. I don't know her well. But I like her. As fake as this marriage is—she's real. And I wasn't crazy when I saw kindness in her on the television screen. She is kind. I see it. I feel it.

Her cheeks go pink with my words producing a grin of my own. I haven't figured out what it is that makes her blush, but I like it when it happens. She swallows and tugs at the end of her long braid. "Right. But like, *love*-like me."

"Oh." I clear my throat. "Right. Sure."

"Miles?"

"Just looking for my keys," I tell her.

She stands next to my door, next to the wooden plaque painted with miniature keys, cars, and houses. She lifts my keys from the small hook there.

"Ah, those are the keys to my Toyota. I'm looking for my house keys." Sure. Why not? I don't normally bother locking the door to my loft. Most people don't even know about the entrance through the gallery. The gallery is locked, so why lock my home?

"They aren't together?"

"No, I—" I pause with a pounding on my door.

"Miles Gavin Bailey, open up!" my sister bellows. The knob on my door twists but doesn't open. Delaney locked it after Alec and Bonnie took off.

Delaney cups a hand over her mouth and whispers, "Aww… I thought you said no girlfriend."

"That isn't a girlfriend."

"Stalker? Who else would sound so angry?" she says, flapping her hands to her sides.

I cough a little. "I do not have a stalker. That would be my sister. Though she should be at work."

"*Miles!*" Coco barks again. "I know you're in there!"

I speed walk over to the door and open it up for her.

"What in Charlie's Chocolate Factory is going on, Miles?" Coco says, pushing her way inside. Her green scrubs are anything but clean. I don't even want to ask what's on them. Her hair is pulled back, and there are lines around her glasses where protective eyewear probably pressed into her skin. I'd guess she just got out of surgery by the looks of her.

I swallow. I've never seen my sister quite like this. "Ahh—"

"I'm in surgery, and my tech keeps showing me photos of *you*. They're all over the internet. With this *girl*. They're calling her—" Her speech slows as her eyes see just past me. "Lane…

Jonas." She blinks just as a hiccup escapes her lips. She slaps a hand over her mouth, still staring.

I glance behind me to a closed-mouth, smiling Delaney.

"Aw, Coco, this is Delaney." I nod toward my sister. "This is my sister, Coco—she's a vet who may have skipped out early on her duties."

Coco blinks back to life and slaps my shoulder. "I didn't skip out on anything. It was a simple neuter. I finished up." She licks her lips, taking her eyes from Delaney to question me again. "*Delaney?*"

I nod. "Yes. Delaney Jones."

Her chest heaves and her words come a mile a minute. "The online gossip said Lane Jonas, and while that's completely insane, she looks—" Her eyes swoop over to Delaney once more. "She looks like her." She gives her head a small bobbling shake. "Ah, you, you look like her. You know that?"

Delaney tilts her head, still beaming. "I *am* her."

My sister's mouth falls. "But you—" she says, and with the words, her knees dip. I swoop one arm around her back, keeping her steady on her feet, though she doesn't seem to notice. "But—*Delaney.*" More rapid blinks, as if she's trying to see this scene clearly and it just won't come. It's a blur that won't focus.

"Delaney is my given name. Lane Jonas is a stage name. My real friends all know me by Delaney."

"Real friends?" Coco stammers. "Miles is a *real* friend?"

"I hope so." Delaney laughs. "He's my husband."

I grit my teeth and glare at my new *wife* just as Coco loses all feeling in her legs.

Thankfully, I'm already holding her, and she's easy to catch when her limbs stop working. I walk my sister to the couch, all while her eyes stay glued to Delaney.

"Husband?" Coco shakes her head.

"I wanted to tell my mother first," I say to Delaney.

She clamps down on her bottom lip. "I'm sorry, Miles. She's your sister, I just—"

"And I wouldn't have told her *like that.*"

"Wait." My sister's eyes find my face. "This is real? You're married? You—Miles Bailey—are *married?*"

I swallow and look down into Coco's kind, disbelieving face. "I am."

"To her?" Coco says, sliding her gaze back to Delaney.

Delaney holds out her hands as if she's a Price is Right model putting herself on display.

"You got married without us?" Coco suddenly has all the strength of a full-grown gorilla as she slaps my arm. "How could you do that? How could you date Lane Jonas and not tell any of us?"

"Oh! Oh!" Delaney waves her hands, calling attention to herself and jumping in to redeem herself. "That's my fault. I wouldn't let him. I was under contract with the network. Technically, it was pushing it for me to tell Miles that I was still single." She clears her throat with the lie. "So I made him promise not to tell." She zips her fingers over her full lips as if locking them up.

Coco stiffens as if remembering that we are in the company of someone she watched date a dozen guys on TV, someone *famous.*

It's funny.

I get it. But Delaney is *just* a girl.

Only, I suppose she's a girl who was hurt and humiliated in front of a million people. The thought hits me like a brick.

Okay, maybe not *just* a girl.

"That's why you wanted to watch the show with us." Coco's eyes zone out in thought.

"Wait, you watched *Celebrity Wife?*" The color drains from Delaney's face. It's easy to see that this thought horrifies her.

"No." I shake my head. "Once. I watched it once." I don't

want her uncomfortable—not because of that show and not because of me.

Yes, I want my building—more than almost anything. I want a studio for my students. This is going to change things for Walt, for Cinnamon, and so many others. But I'm also overwhelmed with compassion when I look at this girl. No one should have to go through the heartache she's suffered while others watched. No one should be treated the way those two men treated her. I want to help her for so many more reasons than my building.

It's a truth I'm just now coming to.

The realization turns me into a world-class actor.

I stand from Coco's side and walk over to Delaney. I slip my hand into hers as if it were the most natural thing in the world, though her soft palm and long fingers feel like an electric current lighting up my limb.

"I never wanted to keep anything from you," I tell Coco, and in my defense, it's one hundred percent true. I'd love to tell my sister the truth. "But I couldn't let Delaney get hurt again."

Coco's eyes drop to our fingers clasped together. With Delaney's other hand, she wraps her fingers around my bicep, holding to my hand and my arm like a lovesick newlywed.

"Holy *snowballs*." Coco stares at the two of us, her eyes ping-ponging from our faces to our hands. I can't tell if she's just in shock or completely impressed.

"Snowballs?" Delaney looks from my sister up to me.

"Coco dropped a curse the other day, and her daughter repeated the word. She's..." I draw out the note, trying to decide how to explain this, "experimenting with new words now."

Coco huffs, arms crossed, on the defense. "It wasn't my fault. I didn't even know Alice was in the room, and Princess peed all over my newly mopped floor. She's one hundred percent potty-trained." She throws up her arms. "One hundred percent! Turns out the poor girl had a UTI. But still, I work all day at the clinic, then come home and spend time with my girls before I have to put them to bed. Mopping my own kitchen is like a delicacy. And then Princess went and peed all over my delicacy!"

"Delicacy?" Delaney wrinkles her nose.

"That four-letter-word slipped out *one* time, and Alice had to repeat me in front of her father."

"Alice," Delaney says, remembering our short conversation about my nieces. "*Stepdaughter*, right?"

Coco's eyes turn into marbles. "*Crack bananas*, Lane Jonas knows I have a stepdaughter."

Delaney points at her. "And another daughter!"

"Peter pumpkin eater," Coco mutters.

Delaney tilts her head. "You swear a lot, huh?"

My sister scrunches her nose. "Actually, no. I'm just sort of on a roll with my made-up curse words. Jude challenged me and —" She waves a hand. "It's a whole thing."

Delaney smirks, then draws her eyes from Coco to me. Her hand inside of mine squeezes. She breathes out a small laugh. "I'm gonna like the Baileys."

17

DELANEY

"Should I be scared?" I say, looking at Miles, who has yet to open his car door. We're just sitting here like we've got targets on our backs.

"No. My mother is the sweetest human on the planet."

"Your face says otherwise." I can't look away from Miles' deer-in-the-headlight stare.

"It's just—we had to drive around for half an hour to ditch those photographers. And—" He shrugs. "This is all just strange. I'm sorry."

"The photographers will lay off some after the press conference."

"Are we really doing a conference—with as little as we know?"

"It isn't until tomorrow night," I tell him, hoping to ease his worries. "We've got some time to go over things."

"Okay, let's go meet Lucy," he says, pushing open his car door.

Miles told his mother we were coming—an hour ago. If the woman is anything like my mother, she's in full pout mode at this point. But then, from everything Miles has said, Lucy

Bailey and Claire Jones are on opposite ends of the mother spectrum.

We'll see.

Miles reaches for my hand, his eyes darting left to right down the street, but the photographers who've been following us are nowhere in sight. Still, his hand folds into mine, and while it's foreign, it doesn't feel wrong. He guides me up the stairs and inside of the charming little gray house.

"Mom?" he calls, but the end of his word drowns to a mere squeak as we leave the small entry to a sitting room. I'm guessing one of the people sitting in this small living room is Miles' mother, but she definitely isn't alone. Miles clears his throat. "Hey, everyone."

A dark-haired man sitting in the corner next to a little blonde folds his arms, his muscles flexing with the motion. The frown on his face is hard to ignore.

A little redhead sits on a blond man's lap next to them. She smiles—almost robotically—at me while he just stares, brows raised.

Coco, Miles' sister, is holding a plump little girl on her hip. She rocks side to side on her heels, bouncing the girl.

A dark-haired woman with eyes like Miles' and a soft grin sits in the armchair at Coco's right.

Miles' hand tightens around mine. He points to the scowling man. "Work." Then to the blond man. "School." He shakes his head. And then he rounds to Coco. "Clinic. You all have places to be right now. Why aren't you—"

"Coco called us," the scowler says.

I flick my gaze to the sister that I think I'm going to end up liking. She's got spunk.

"I've explained nothing, Miles. But I felt like this was important enough to call a family meeting."

Miles coughs. "At least Coop is—"

The redhead holds out her phone. "He's here."

Another man—who, while blond, still looks too much like Miles to *not* be a brother—waves via Facetime. "Hey, bruh."

Lucy steps forward. "We saw pictures online. Coco said you'd explain."

"Mom, I know this is a little unorthodox." He swallows. "And unlike me. But"—he dips his chin, tilting his head toward me—"this is Delaney, and we recently got married."

A girl gasps and the scowling man stands. "You did not," he says, cursing under his breath.

"Levi!" Coco growls.

"What? Alice isn't here and Lula can't talk yet. Miles is talking crazy. You know I have no patience for crazy!"

Miles waves for his brother to sit again—he doesn't. "It does seem crazy. To me too. But Delaney and I met, and one thing led to another. I don't know what to say, Levi, except that it just felt right." He's so sincere, so earnest. And *felt right*... Does he mean that? Everything else is true. In fact, somehow Miles Bailey confessed our marriage to his mother and his entire family without telling our secrets *and* without lying. The man has more skills than I realized.

"It felt right?" Levi says. "It didn't feel stupid? It didn't feel selfish? It didn't—"

"Sweetie." The blonde girl reaches for Levi's hand, pulling him back down beside her. "Shush. Be kind to your brother."

Huh. I'm gonna like her too.

"Mer, he's *married*. None of us even knew this woman existed—" He says the word *married* as if it alone were an insult. "And now he's—"

"Settle down, Levi," Lucy says, her tone less sweet and more commanding. "You can ask questions, but Meredith is right: you don't get to make judgments."

My heart flutters—no, it pounds. My eyes are glued on Lucy, and I can't look away.

"There's one other thing," Miles says, and I realize Coco

truly didn't share anything except that Miles had news. "The reason I never said anything"—his words are choppy, this is Miles lying—"Delaney is also known as Lane Jonas."

"Wait, what?" the redhead pipes up.

"Lane?" Levi's Mer says. "I knew you looked familiar!"

"Wait." Levi shakes his head, his eyes narrowing as if to see me better. "As in The Judys?"

I clear my throat. "Ah, yeah." My cheeks burn with an abnormal flush—people recognize me all the time. But this is Miles' family. And while they may not have seen it at first, they certainly do now. Not to mention, I'm still reeling from Lucy's compassion, but I have to help Miles out here. So, I find the words. "I'm the reason he didn't say anything. That show, *Celebrity Life Celebrity Wife*—my contract stated that I couldn't tell anyone outside my very small wheelhouse the truth."

"Lane Jonas!" The redhead hisses, and she snags onto Meredith's arm. "I saw you. And I know her. But *her* being in our living room. I never thought— I didn't think that could be real. I just assumed—" She locks her eyes back on me. "I'm a fan!" she whispers.

The angry wrinkles over Levi's face smooth out—not with approval but curiosity.

"Delaney?" Lucy says with kindness and patience. She takes control of the conversation again.

I nod. Suddenly I have no voice. My voice is my superpower, and all at once it's gone.

"You've captured my Miles' heart. Only someone completely and wholly good could do that. While I'm not a fan of missing any of my children's major life events—you're here. You're his." She smiles, and I think Miles might be right: Lucy Bailey is an anomaly. She might be the kindest woman alive. "Which means," she says, "now you're also mine." She holds a hand to my cheek, and I melt like butter in a microwave.

Is this woman for real? She has to be at least ten years Claire

Jones' junior, and yet she talks with love and wisdom as if she's lived a thousand lives or spent a year with the Dalai Lama.

A loud groan sounds from the scowling Levi, but everyone ignores him.

Lucy reaches for me, taking my hand from Miles. She cups her fingers around mine and steps toward her waiting family. "Delaney, this is Miles' brother, Owen."

My heart pounds. I can hear it in my ears.

Crap. I do not know enough about these people.

There's a warm hand on my back, and then Miles is on my other side. "The teacher," he says as if he's told me this before.

"Right." I nod. "Nice to meet you, Owen."

"His new wife, Annie," Lucy says, without one little jab about how Owen and Annie didn't disappoint her by eloping.

"I'm so *trilled*—" Annie laughs a shrill giggle. "Ah, *thrilled* to meet you," she says. I'm pretty sure her voice isn't normally that high. She holds out a hand and I shake hers, flooding her freckled cheeks with pink.

Levi snorts. "New?" he says. "Annie's been around longer than Coop."

"Hey. Not true," the man on FaceTime calls out.

"That's my youngest." Lucy motions to the phone Annie holds. "Cooper."

"Hey, Lane Jonas," Cooper says, and while he isn't in the room and I'm married to his brother, I still get a flirty vibe from the cute kid on the screen.

A breathy laugh leaves me. "You're trouble."

"He's sweet," Lucy says, only to sigh a second later. "And trouble."

"That's him," Levi says. "Cooper, the *sweetest* little troublemaker, named for Mom's favorite dog."

"A dog?" I say, unable to stop myself.

Lucy grins. "He really was the sweetest dog."

My brows lift as I remember that I do know something. I'm

MILES BAILEY GETS DOWN ON ONE KNEE

not completely oblivious. "And Miles was named after Miles Howard—who I totally know! I used to watch him with my grandma."

Lucy's eyes brighten. "What a small world."

"It's a worldwide television show, so not *that* small," Levi says.

"Levi, sweetie, simmer down." Meredith pats his leg.

Her words seem to bring Lucy back to the present. "This is our Meredith. Levi's fiancée." Meredith takes Lucy by the hand and they share a small squeeze before dropping the other's hand. "They'll be getting married at the end of summer. But then, you probably know all about that."

I don't. But their lives aren't a secret, so it makes sense that Miles would have told me. And with more time, I'm sure he would have. I grin like I know exactly what she's talking about. "August, right?" I assume, looking to Meredith for confirmation. She said the *end* of summer—August feels like a safe bet.

She giggles. "Yes. The twenty-seventh."

"And my Levi," Lucy says. Her brows raise at her son as if silently telling him to play nice.

Levi's jaw clenches, but he holds a hand out toward me. "What do we call you?"

"It's Delaney, Levi. I already introduced her," Miles says from beside me.

"But you changed your name, right?"

"You know who she is," Coco says to him. "You sing that one song of hers all the time."

Pink blooms over Levi's ears.

I tilt my head. "Which song?"

He gives a small head-bobbing shake. "I don't know," he mutters.

"Yes, you do," Meredith says. "It's in half of your playlists. The one about a thousand years, a thousand lives—"

"Right. That one," he says. "I've heard it before."

I hold in my chuckle but can't stop my grin. Levi listens to The Judys. "I helped write that one. And yes, I have a stage name. My PR manager thought Lane Jonas was punchier." I sigh. "Honestly, that particular name is just confusing. I can't tell you how many times people ask me about Nick—as if I know."

Levi grunts—or maybe that's a laugh. I'm not sure. But he doesn't look like he totally hates me.

"You've met Coco." Lucy continues down the line.

Miles' sister smiles at me while bouncing the baby on her hip.

"Alice is in school, but this is Lulabelle." Lucy runs a palm over the chubby baby's head. "And Jude, Coco's husband, is away for work. He'll be home tomorrow. You can meet him at our family dinner on Sunday."

Family dinner. Huh. Lucy doesn't ask, she just tells.

The rest of the afternoon is a mix of questions and Miles' siblings returning to work. Owen's the first to go—he got a friend to cover one class and spent that as well as his lunch break with us. Not long after, Levi decides he's needed at the shop he runs. Cooper has better things to do than sit on FaceTime all day long with us, so he's gone too.

"All this time, we were watching *Celebrity Wife* and betting on who you'd end up with and you were dating Miles." Meredith heaves a breath, her eyes on me.

"They must have filmed it weeks ago, though. Right?" Annie asks, looking to me for confirmation—at least all her words are coming out right now.

"Weeks and weeks," I tell them. "It's been hanging over my head. I just wanted to move on with life, and that show wouldn't let me."

Meredith's brows cinch and Lucy's hand finds mine. We sit on this couch together while Miles runs out to grab lunch. He was hesitant to go, but I promised him I'd survive. I'm certain I've survived worse—in the very home I grew up in.

And I am surviving.

I think.

Everyone is kind—a little smothering, but kind.

"So, where will you guys live? Miles isn't moving to California, is he?" Coco scoots to the edge of the couch—she's done feeling squeamish around me and ready for some answers.

Lucy looks semi-alarmed at the idea of her son moving and I'm not trying to cause a family meltdown. Miles clearly likes his family, and I do too. I don't want to turn my mess into his. He doesn't need any more drama.

"Ah—no. Of course not. I travel a lot. So, we decided Coeur d'Alene will be our home base." We never had such a conversation, but it sounds good.

Lucy lets out a breath I didn't realize she'd been holding.

"Where will you live?" Annie's eyes bulge. "I mean, that room he lives in is like... tiny."

"Well—" I swallow. Where *am* I going to live? I just assumed I'd extend my Airbnb for a time... but newlyweds would probably want to live together... "I have a house I'm renting. It does have more space." I clear my throat. "We may live out of both for a little while until we figure out a more permanent place."

There. That's smart. Then none of these happy little Baileys can fault either of us for spending time at either place.

18

DELANEY

"Whew. That was long. And a little draining." I peer over at Miles sitting in the driver's seat. "Don't get me wrong. I like them. A lot. Much better than my parents. Still, I can't believe you live so close to your family. You do that all the time."

He watches the road but smirks. "I don't normally bring home a celebrity wife. It's not usually that intense. I love living near my family."

"Really?"

"You don't miss yours at all?" he asks, glancing over at me.

"Nope." But that isn't completely true. "I miss my sister... and my grandmother." I haven't talked to Gram in so long. Long enough to make me ashamed. "And it's better now that my parents split. Together they're a ticking time bomb. But I'm either tracking down my dad only to fight for his attention—he likes to give it all to his addiction—or I'm counting down the minutes until I leave my mother and the lecture about the many ways I've disappointed her."

"What does she have to complain about?"

"Plenty. Don't you know? I am a horrid letdown of a daughter."

"I highly doubt that, Delaney. You're successful and smart—"

"And *beautiful*." I hold up my finger. "Don't forget beautiful."

His lips perk up in a grin at my sarcastic tone. "You *are* beautiful," he says with all the sincerity of a nun under oath.

My cheeks warm. I don't know why. My mother has been telling me I'm a *beautiful disappointment* my entire life. I've never really doubted that I'm pretty. Just that I use it incorrectly. Though using looks for any gain never felt right to me. But Claire Jones says I've wasted my best asset.

"Beautiful, but no beauty queen."

Miles' brow furrows as if he's not understanding, and clearly, he isn't. "You want to be a beauty queen?"

"Crack bananas! No!" *Oof*, I hung out with the Baileys way too long. I'm using Coco's made-up curse words.

"I'm confused. Should I drop it?"

"Good idea." My eyes wander out the window, then back to Miles. "So, wedding night—"

I don't mean to be so direct. And I'm certainly not implying anything, but my new husband goes cherry red, like a twelve-year-old boy who just walked down the ladies' undies aisle at the mall. Red is cute on an already pretty darn handsome Miles Bailey. I'm not going to forget this.

Sorry, Miles.

"Where should we spend it?" I ask, completely changing my statement of "I'll head back to the Airbnb" to a wide-open question just to see how deep that red will go.

"Aw. Well. I thought—"

"Oh, this is painful and fun all at the same time." I tap his leg. "Miles, I'll go back to my Airbnb. But how do we want to handle this? I'm pretty sure most madly-in-love newlywed couples would be sleeping in the same bed."

"That's a fair assessment."

"But you don't love me—"

He shakes his head, but his cheeks are still blooming that rosy shade of cherry red.

"Which is perfect. Because if you loved me, this whole entire thing would blow up in our faces." I smack his leg. "Keep up the good work! And tell me how we're going to handle this. People will notice."

"People?"

"Yeah. Sorry. *People*. All the people will notice. I promise you."

He stares out the car window, his eyes narrowed in thought. "We could do breakfast in the mornings—early enough that maybe *people* won't notice if we haven't been together all night."

It could work. Maybe. But is it worth the risk? "My Airbnb has a spare room."

"My loft has my food, paints, and my toothbrush."

I flick my eyes to the roof of his truck. "Fine. We can try early mornings. But we may need an excuse. I swear, paparazzi don't sleep." Still, we haven't been swarmed. I'm thankful for that. It's one of the reasons I chose this little Idaho town: there isn't a lot of action driving the paparazzi here. If I'm all that's offered—and if I'm not that exciting—maybe they'll all go away.

19

MILES

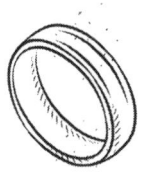

*L*ove? No. I'm not in love with Delaney Jones. She really likes pointing that out. However—*attracted*?

That's a completely different story.

I'm pretty sure I'd have to be dead or a monk to *not* be attracted to the woman.

Nope, a monk would still feel the attraction. Death is my only hope.

Does she not realize that?

She's lived enough life. She must. But she thinks I am some holy being, as she keeps referring to me as *super decent*. Even the most decent of men couldn't stop feeling stupidly attracted to her simply because love isn't a factor.

What about *like*? Is like a factor? Because I like her. And decent as I am, I can't help but notice her long legs, full lips, and a dozen other items I'm currently evicting from my brain.

I kick at the blanket wrapped around my feet.

This is an annoying problem to keep a man up at night.

Congratulations, Miles Bailey, you're attracted to your wife. You're also very much alone in your bed.

I roll over onto my side and force myself to play out that

staph infection documentary that Coco made me watch with her last month. The one all about veterinarians who aren't taking enough precautions and the effect it's having on animals and their owners. It was a delight. Or quite the opposite. It about made me ill.

If that doesn't get my mind off of Delaney Jones, I'm not sure what will.

20

DELANEY

The press conference is fast and productive. Miles is a quiet one, so I do the talking while he stands at my side—my little bit o' eye candy.

I may not be interested in love right this minute or having a family... ever, but I'm not a total loon. Miles is nice to look at. And he's an incredibly decent husband. He picked me up early, fed me, and listened to all of my press conference instructions until this evening.

Show time!

When it comes time for questions, I am pretty good at commanding the attention. Which Miles doesn't mind.

I answer the typical questions: Where did you meet? When was the wedding? Why so secretive? How long did you date? This last one is trickier because of the show. We finished filming in August. The show aired from February to May. So, I go with September. "Filming was over for *Celebrity Wife*, and while I was bound to silence, life doesn't stop. You can't stop love. Believe me, after the show and *not* falling for any of the men, I wasn't looking." I peer up at Miles. "But I couldn't stop seeing Miles." It's true—well, the last part anyway. Of course, I didn't meet Miles in September since I met him this very week. Lucky for me, after the show I went into hiding. The press had no location on me for a time. They can't call my bluff.

"Miles," says one man, hand in the air though no one has called on him. "You're pretty quiet. Second thoughts on this quick courtship?"

Miles clears his throat while I refrain from punching Mr. Baldy Badge in the back.

My new husband moves closer to the mic before I can swoop in and save him—which I would have had I not been taken so off guard. The press just loves a struggling Lane Jonas. Even now, with this "happy announcement," they like to pair me with *regret*.

"No second thoughts," Miles says. "Just grateful a mansion full of men didn't stop Delaney from being true to herself."

Anyone can Google and look up my actual name. Still, it's rarely something said or heard through a microphone, on a stage, or in front of the press. Not even the men in the mansion knew my name.

I inadvertently hold my breath. But Miles wraps one arm around my shoulders. I rest my head on his left pectoral, breathing in his pine and musk like he *is* the great outdoors. I'm thankful he's here. I'm thankful this whole thing fell conveniently into my lap. I'm thankful I convinced him to go along. Maybe he's thankful too. *No second thoughts.*

With my side snuggled up to Miles', a round of flashes light up the room.

"Did you watch the show, then?" the same man asks.

"Would you want to watch your girl date a bunch of other guys?"

"I'll take that as a no," the reporter says with a chuckle.

Miles' arm around me tightens and soft lips press at my hairline. "No. I didn't watch," he says, though he did confess to one episode.

We smile for a couple more photos, and then Miles' friend Nina ushers everyone out into the hall.

"You think we'll have less company now?" Miles asks, peering down at me. His hazel eyes are bright with green—especially today, with his contacts in.

"Umm, maybe," I say, thoroughly and ridiculously distracted. "You have nice eyes," I blurt.

Miles' brows pinch together.

"That's not a come-on." I swallow and straighten out my shoulders. I'm good at confidence. I can usually muster it, even when I don't feel it. "Just a fact. Very nice eyes." I smile, for some reason stupidly pleased with myself. And because my brain likes to jump into multiple conversations and categories at once, I say, "And just an FYI, you may have to kiss me one day."

"Excuse me?"

"We *are* married."

"In theory," he says.

"In reality, bud." I huff out a breath. "The public may want it one day. I'm just giving you a heads-up."

His brows lift. "So thoughtful of you."

I lift one shoulder. "I'm here to please."

"How about a late dinner? Would that please you?" He holds his arm out to me, and while I slip my arm through his, I'm also not my grandma. So I slide my fingers down his forearm to his hand and lace my fingers through his.

Nina's outside and she and her officer friends have done a decent job clearing the way to Miles' truck.

"You're so good at feeding me, Miles. Believe me, I appreciate that. But I think I'm ready for my bed."

"Already?"

"I know I sound like an old lady. But it's been a long week."

"Yeah. No problem. I'll take you to the rental."

Nina watches as Miles opens my door. I bat my eyes up at him. We have an audience; we might as well get that first awkward kiss over with. I slide onto the passenger seat of his small truck but keep my gaze locked on his.

He's a smart man.

He gets it.

He also leans in and kisses my—*cheek*. Oh, wholesome, decent Miles. It's *just* a kiss. You are my husband.

I bat my lashes at him. "Thanks, honey," I say as sappy as I can. Nina glances from down the street to Miles and me.

"You're welcome, *Baby Cakes*."

I lift one brow and watch as shy, quiet Miles walks around the truck and hops inside.

"Baby Cakes?"

"It just felt right," he says, his eyes on the road but his lips turn up in a wry grin.

21

MILES

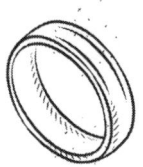

*T*here's a car across the street with a guy not even hiding in the driver's seat. "I'll come in for a minute if you don't mind."

Delaney sees him too. "That would probably be smart. Sorry, Miles."

"Hey, it's all part of the deal. Lars hired someone to clean out his building today." But this isn't about our deal or what the public thinks of me staying or going. Some creeper watching Delaney outside her house while she's inside alone isn't ever going to sit well with me. I won't sleep a wink unless I know he's gone.

"You mean *your* building, right?" she says.

I blink back to the present. "Yes, *mine*. I can't wait to tell Walt."

"He's the student I saw you with."

"He is. He could never get up to my current studio. The hall is narrow. Building a ramp isn't even an option. So, this—this is going to be great."

Her cheeks bloom with a grin. "Come in. You shouldn't have

to wait too long. We're lucky it's just the one guy. We can order some food in if you're up for it."

We exit the vehicle, and for the benefit of the man taking photos across the street—at least, that's what I tell myself—I slip my hand into Delaney's as we walk to the front door. Her hands are small and soft, except for her fingertips. I can tell she plays guitar; she's got calluses on the tips of her fingers. I mindlessly run my thumb over the end of her pointer.

She unlocks the front door and we walk inside to her pristine rental. It looks as though she hasn't stayed here at all yet.

"I don't hang out here much," she says as if I've spoken my thoughts aloud. "I like the master bedroom. And the hot tub out back."

"There's a hot tub?"

"Yeah, do you want to—"

"That's probably not a good idea." My wife might be the most beautiful being I've ever come across. I don't need to see her in a bikini. I'm trying to stay neutral after all.

She swallows. "Right. No swim trunks. Well, we can watch a movie or—"

A loud *thunk* sounds from the back of the house. Delaney jumps, her hand snatching onto mine once more.

"Cat?" I say.

"No. No pets," she says, her face pale.

"Stay here," I tell her, but she snatches a hold of the back of my shirt and moves herself right up behind me.

"You aren't going anywhere without me," she hisses.

We're halfway down the hall when her chest bumps into my back. I grunt with the hit. She snakes an arm around my middle and holds me with an iron grasp.

"Delaney, I—"

Another *thunk*.

I pull her hand from my stomach and turn, bending a little

to look her in the eye. "You aren't coming with me," I whisper. "I'll be right back. Stay."

Her throat bobs with a swallow, and her steel blue eyes glitter with unshed tears.

"Do you have any pepper spray?" I ask.

She nods, her hands in fists at her sides.

"Get it out. Get it ready. I *will* be back." Holding her head in my hands, I kiss her forehead before finding her eyes again. "Right back. Okay? Trust me."

I let her go and she scrambles a hand into her purse for a small pink can of pepper spray.

She nods me on with courage, but I can see the fear in her eyes. This isn't something she's simply used to because of who she is.

She's a young, single woman—and idiots from all over now know where she's staying. Why did I ever think she could stay here by herself?

My feet are quiet and quick as I walk to the back of the house. I listen, not knowing what I'll find or what I'll do when I find it. Maybe it is a cat—one Delaney didn't know existed in the house.

Another low thump at my left tells me this is no four-legged creature. The door is shut tight, and I crack it open as if I were James Bond himself.

A bedroom. It must be the master suite because this space is definitely lived in. Clothes and dishes are strewn about the place, two guitars lean against the far wall, and a suitcase lays open and empty on the ground. Delaney's bed is unmade and there's a turquoise bra hanging from another door within the room.

I inch over and open up the door to a man looking through a small bag that I can only assume belongs to Delaney. There's a breeze flitting in through the window above the tub, the lock broken, and the glass opened wide.

"Hey!" The word bellows from my mouth as if I could attack with that one syllable. The man jolts, standing straight, and whips around to face me, just three feet away. And then I do something I have never done in my twenty-seven pacifist years: I ball up a fist and hit another human.

Not just hit—I wallop this man with one punch to the face. One pain-exploding punch that snaps like a firecracker causing blood to burst from the man's nose. Stabbing pain shoots down each of my fingers and up into my arm, but I'm in a lot better shape than the guy holding Delaney's lipstick.

The man cries out in pain and crumbles to the ground, holding his nose that I think might be broken.

I shake the sting from my fingers and grunt with an ache that refuses to leave.

"Miles?" Delaney calls, her tone panicked.

"Call Nina!" I yell.

The creep has a small camera, and in my adrenaline rush, I bring my foot down on the thing, crushing it.

"Hey." He moans, his hands still up around his nose and eyes.

"You're lucky it was the camera," I growl, heart racing. I may need to reevaluate my claim as a pacifist.

"Miles?" Delaney says again, this time closer.

"Stay outside the bathroom," I tell her. "Did you call Nina?"

"She's on her way."

"Okay, stay there. I'm just going to wait right here to make sure our friend gets out the front with the correct ride."

She's quiet.

"Laney," I say, giving her a nickname on the spot—one I'd never thought about. Is this what high-pressure situations do to a man? Force inner caveman violence and intimate pet names?

A small whimper sounds outside the room.

"It's okay," I tell her, comforting her while keeping one eye on our intruder. "Okay?"

"My grandma calls me that," she says, her voice small.

"Oh yeah?" I say, trying to keep calm. If I'm calm, doesn't that tell her there's no reason to panic?

The man on the ground moans in pain but he doesn't attempt escape.

"Laney?"

I wait for her to answer just as a faraway voice calls, "Miles?" Nina's at the opposite end of the house.

Delaney gasps in a breath—that doesn't convince me I've helped anyone stay calm. "We're back here!"

In less than a minute, Nina and her partner barge into the room, and I gladly let them take control. I hurry out to find Delaney in a heap on the floor, just outside the bathroom door.

"Delaney?"

Her watery eyes look up to find mine. I reach out a hand and pull her to her feet, but she crumples in my arms. Her arms clasp around my middle and she buries her face into my chest. Hot tears seep through my shirt and onto my chest.

I rest my head on hers. A small wisp of blue hair flies up and in front of my eyes. I take her in—small and smooth, roses and sweetness, strong and scared. Then I remind myself that I'm not allowed to fall for my wife. It's against the rules—the very special, specific rules that Delaney laid out for us *yesterday*.

Still, I hug her back, babying my right hand. *Crap.* Well, this isn't going to be great for my career.

"Come on," I tell her after Nina's dragged the intruding man out of sight. "Let's go."

"But, where—"

"You think I'm letting my wife stay here? Without me? Not happening. Time to go home, Laney."

22

DELANEY

$\mathcal{T}$his place is dead quiet. Eerily quiet. I can't decide if it's calming or maddening.

Miles walks me up the stairs to his apartment, an arm around my waist, though no one is around to see us. I'm grateful for the support. Those times on tour, when we had loony fans trying to get a little too close, we also had bodyguards. We never had anyone get closer than allowed, or if they did, at least we saw them coming, like cameramen and reporters out in public.

This was my rental. My bathroom. This was hidden breaking and entering. If there hadn't been a guy across the street, Miles and I would have said goodbye at the door.

I shudder and hug myself closer to his side, to this man who, in all sense, should be a stranger. But he doesn't feel like one. I trust him.

We cross the threshold of Miles' tiny apartment. The smallness feels like safety. No one could hide in here—not without being seen.

"Go sit down. I'll get you some tea."

I don't argue because Miles' kitchen is legit inside his living room, which is inside of his bedroom. He can't escape me. He must think I'm ridiculous. People are around me, taking photos all the time.

"He was in the house," I say in defense of myself. "I've just never had one in the house before. I'm used to the crowds and the cameras. I promise. I—"

"Delaney, do you think I'm judging you for being afraid of an intruder? Believe me, I am not. Any sane person would have been afraid." He sets a red teapot on one of the two electric burners in his kitchen. "I was afraid."

He was? Why does that make me feel better? I rub my hands together, creating warmth where his fingers once cradled mine.

"Please tell me this isn't the norm for your life."

I swallow, feeling better by the second. Miles Bailey doesn't judge—if anything, he validates. "It's not," I say. "Cameras and paparazzi, but we only ever needed bodyguards on tour."

"So tonight was different?"

"*Very*," I say, releasing all the air in my lungs.

"That makes me feel better."

Another minute passes and Miles brings me a hot cup of chamomile tea and a small bowl of candy. "Gummy bears?" I say, looking up from the bowl. When did he have time to buy me gummy bears? Haven't I taken up all of his time the last couple of days?

"Just in case," he says, his arms at his sides.

"Oh, no." I blink, taking in the red-and-purple blotch forming in front of my very eyes. "Your hand."

"Oh." He stretches out each of his fingers—it doesn't help how they look. "It's fine."

"Miles," I say, and my voice cracks. He's an artist. His hands are his livelihood. "You're hurt. You hit that guy and now you're hurt."

"It's just a bruise." He attempts to shove his hand into his pocket, but I can see that the action pains him. He leaves it awkwardly dangling at his side.

"It's not. Let me get some ice." I start to stand, but Miles sets a hand on my shoulder, pausing my undertaking.

"I'll get the ice. You drink your tea." His uninjured hand gives a little shove to my half-standing body, pushing me back to the couch.

I sip my tea, stir in my seat, and watch him single-handed as he fills a plastic bag with ice cubes and wanders back over to me.

"Sit down," I tell him. "Please."

He does, and I reach for his hand. His knuckles are split and bleeding with an ugly bruise blooming. I breathe out a sigh. "I'm so sorry."

"None of this," he says, nodding to his hand, "is your fault."

But it sure feels like it is.

Gently, I take his hand in mine, cradle it in my left while my right moves the ice back in place. "What a crazy night," I mutter, my nerves hypersensitive to his soft fingers and the feel of his skin on mine.

"Rock star Lane Jonas hasn't had a crazier night?"

"I didn't say that. Still—*pretty* crazy."

"Yeah." He blows out a breath and slips his hand from mine. With his other, he snatches the bag of ice and adjusts it back on his hand, hugging it close to his abdomen.

Picking up my mug, I gulp down the rest of my tea.

"I'll take that." Miles stands, retrieving my cup. A second later, he's back, holding a hand out to me. "You're tired. But I can't give you a bed to sleep in unless you get up."

"Oh." I glance down at the pull-out couch. "Right." I set my hand in his uninjured one and let him pull me up. My chest bumps his in this small space. The contact sets my heart racing. I scoop a strand of my long hair behind one ear and step to the side, out of the way.

But Miles doesn't start disassembling the couch. He moves

over to the tall dresser in the corner of the room and opens the top drawer.

"Here," he says, holding out a button-up pajama top. There are tiny Christmas trees scattered over the light blue. "I only wore it once. Mom bought us all matching pj's a couple years ago. The bottoms," he says, glancing down toward my hips, "would fall right off of you. But at least it's something other than your jeans."

I swallow. "Thank you."

"You can change in the bathroom or the studio. Both have a door that locks."

I blink up at my incredibly moral husband. "I appreciate it. I'm not exactly worried about those doors locking." I run my teeth over my bottom lip. "I'm not afraid of you."

He gives a curt nod, his mouth in a tight line.

I disappear into the tiny space that Miles calls a bathroom. A twelve-by-twelve-inch mirror sits above the smallest sink I've ever seen. Seriously, who knew they made them this small? I can just see my face in this thing—how does he ever get ready with that? A toilet squeezes between the sink and stall shower. It's tiny but clean and smells of the outdoorsy pine scent that I breathe in every time I'm near Miles.

I'm not sure what possesses me, but I dig into my purse and pull out my liquid eyeliner. I stand on my tiptoes until I am certain I'm almost the same height as Miles. I look at myself in this mirror, imagining Miles looking into the small glass. With the wand of my liner, I draw a handlebar mustache onto the glass, right where I'm certain Miles' lips would appear.

I smirk, imagining Miles looking into his mirror tonight. It's a lame prank—I should probably wash it off. But I don't. The thought of Miles looking in this mirror and seeing a mustache on himself keeps my head calm and sane at this moment.

I strip off my jeans and shirt, wishing I had a brush to comb out my long hair and a toothbrush to freshen up. But I left everything back at the rental. I needed to leave.

Tomorrow I'll find a new place and hire someone to grab all my things. But tonight, I am brushless and emotional. I'm not sure what it is about being completely terrified that makes me want to vandalize Miles' bathroom... but then, I think the mustache will make him laugh.

Will my bra on his door handle and my jeans on his floor make him laugh? I cringe before snatching my things and rolling them into a ball to go out with me.

I exit the room in his nightshirt. The ends hit my thighs, and while I'm not a shy or overly modest person, I feel exposed in this moment.

Miles has a bed all made up for me—and with the tiny bit of space left on the kitchen linoleum, he's laid out a blanket and pillow for himself.

I'm not even sure there's five feet of space in there—for my six-foot-something husband.

I swallow. "Miles. You cannot sleep there."

He meets my eyes, not even glancing down at my bare thighs —this man is an angel. I swear he is. "There's nowhere else. My studio is full and—"

"No, you can sleep right next to your wife." I tilt my head and offer him an apologetic smile. "I'll take the right side beneath the sheets. You can take the left on top. We'll have a good foot of space between us, and I promise not to spoon you."

He breathes out a laugh. "I guess. If you promise."

"I do."

He snatches the pillow and blanket from the kitchen floor and walks back over to the pull-out bed. "You're sure?"

"Yes."

Miles lays his things down, then heads into the bathroom himself.

I settle beneath the sheets on this thin mattress and listen... waiting to hear the moment he sees the mustache in the mirror.

But... *nothing*.

Maybe I drew it too low and it looked like a *chin*stache.

I'm up on one elbow, watching the bathroom door and barely breathing so that I can hear the minute Miles sees it... But the door to the bathroom opens without a chuckle or a yelp or *anything* from Miles.

Huh. How thoroughly unfortunate.

Maybe I read his sense of humor wrong. I was so sure he'd find that funny.

I fall onto my back and pull the sheet up to my nose. I am innocent. *I didn't convince you to marry me, force you to lie to your mother, and then vandalize your home... that was another Judy.*

I keep my eyes on the ceiling. Silent.

Maybe he didn't see it.

Maybe the man doesn't look in the mirror when he brushes his teeth.

Maybe I'll hear that quiet, masculine laughter in the morning.

I feel Miles sit on the bed. He adjusts his pillow in half, then lays down overtop all of the blankets on this bed. He's making certain there is more than a sheet between the two of us. I'm unsure if that's a good sign or a bad sign.

"Do you need anything?" he asks, and I can tell that he's looking at me.

I roll onto my side toward him. "No, I—" A snort escapes my nose and lips. I clamp my mouth closed and move a bent arm beneath my head for support.

Even in the dimness of this moonlit room, I can't miss the handlebar mustache Miles Bailey has drawn on his face.

"Anything?" he says, displaying the largest smile I've yet to see his lips produce.

A bubble of giggles sneaks through my clamped lips. "Nu-uh.

I'm good." I purse my lips to the side, reining back my grin. "You got a little—" I circle a finger in front of my face.

"Aw. You're impressed with my ability to grow facial hair so quickly. I get it. It *is* impressive."

I can't control my smile anymore. "So impressive." I stare at the artistic work of that mustache—it's a thousand times better than my own. "Where'd you get the—"

He turns to face me, his curly brown hair flopping to the side in the process. "I'm an artist. I always have a marker in my pocket."

I cram my eyes closed and giggle again. "You should stitch that on a pillow. And seriously consider growing a mustache."

"Oh, I am—now."

I sigh, calm and content for the first time since we left the Airbnb. "Am I screwing up your life?" I ask. I don't even mean to, but it's a question I've been trying very hard to avoid.

"Because you drew on my mirror? Was that permanent marker or something?" This time Miles is the one to laugh, low and quiet, but joyful nonetheless.

"No, not permanent marker. That mirror is a joke, by the way. Replace it as fast as humanly possible." I swallow and hold his eyes once more. "You know, because I conned you into marrying me and being a part of my craziness for the next year."

"You didn't con anyone, Delaney."

My head goes back to the moment he called me Laney. Just like Grandma. Just another reason I feel like I can trust Miles Bailey. All I can do is stare at the man across from me. He should be a stranger, but instead, he's my husband.

"We made a deal. You bought me a building. Even if I could have afforded it, I never could have talked Lars into it."

"Yeah, he did seem pretty annoyed when he realized it was for you."

Miles laughs. "I'm sure he did."

"That building is really worth being stuck with me?"

His eyes narrow, breaking our contact. "Yeah. I mean, I don't consider myself too stuck. But yeah, that building is worth a little drama. Tomorrow, if you have time, I'll take you with me when I tell Walt—you'll see."

"It's a deal." It's not like I have an actual job to get back to... just a semi-thought-out plan that I can work the day *after* tomorrow.

The moon must rise because it's not streaming through the window like before. The light in the room has dimmed, but my eyes are adjusting along with it. I can still see Miles. He's awake. He's watching me back.

"You don't mind putting off your personal life?" I ask.

"Are you trying to talk me out of all you talked me into? Too bad, Laney. It's a done deal. We're married."

My chest warms with the nickname. "No—just learning a little more about my husband."

"What about you? You don't mind putting off any personal romantic connections for a while?"

I smirk a little. "I *really* don't."

"Because..." he starts, waiting for me to finish.

"Because my job is my life right now. Maybe one day I'll be ready to find love. But I was literally gifted twenty of the most attractive, talented bachelors in the country, and none of them stole my heart." I don't talk about the show lightly. But Miles is a safe place; he's a friend. However new he might be. He won't make me relive or suffer through anything just for gossip's sake.

"I get that." His forehead wrinkles. "Okay—not the twenty attractive bachelors part. But the work part. It's hard to split your focus."

"Exactly. I only did the show because after I left The Judys, Ash thought it would help my image. And who doesn't want to fall in love? At least, that's what Ash said. Surely one of those guys would have been a right fit had it been the right time."

"And they didn't hurt you?"

I scoff. I can't help it. It's just so far from my truth. "No, Miles, they didn't hurt me." I sigh, thinking of Patrick and his lies. "Okay, maybe scratched, but not scarred. The thing is, I just don't want it yet. Why does the world think that every twenty-seven-year-old needs to be planning a wedding? There isn't one prime age to fall in love. Why can't I get married and fall in love at forty?"

"Forty?" His turn to scoff. "So, kids? They're not in your future? Or maybe they are. I don't know."

I blow out a breath. "*Kids...* I don't dislike children. The only one I was ever around was my sister. I was eight when Eryn was born. And then ten years later, I was gone. I escaped the clutches of Claire Jones as quickly as I could. Every time I think about kids, I think about my mother. Would becoming a mother turn me into her? Because I really, really don't want to be like my mother." But then Miles' mother is quite the opposite of mine. I'd turn into Lucy Bailey any day.

"I don't think there's one recipe for becoming a parent. I think you get to decide. I don't think you'd be like your mom. Because you don't want to be. And for what it's worth, I think you'd make a great mom."

That makes me grin—and I don't even know why. "Do you? Because you've known me *so* long."

"Long enough to marry you."

My chest rumbles with a giggle. "That's true."

Miles lays flat on his back, his gray T-shirt melting into the color of his comforter. He stares at the ceiling, and when he closes his eyes, I think he's done talking and ready to sleep.

But then he says, "Why The Judys? The name. That always confused me."

"Miles Bailey, are you a fan?"

His eyes open, and he glances my way while staying on his back. He takes up a lot of space in this bed—there isn't the foot of space between us I thought there'd be. I'm guessing this isn't even a queen. I'm so used to my king at home and when on the road—but then I'm not a large person, so how much space do I need? Somehow, I don't feel crowded with Miles next to me.

"Honestly?" he says, referring to my question.

"Of course," I tell him. I don't care if he's not a fan. Okay... maybe I care a little. He is my husband, after all, pretend or not.

"I was a fan of your first album. I haven't listened to much since." He scowls as if he might be in trouble.

"The first one is my favorite too." I sang more on the first album. We all did. Then Serena became our permanent lead. I played bass guitar, Astrid played acoustic, and Dawn has always played the drums. I sigh. "The Judys. That's my grandma's name. I was kind of running away from my mother when I met up with Serena and Astrid. Dawn came later. My grandma has always been a sanctuary for me. She was proud of me, no matter what. When I put out that first album, she beamed with pride. Rock was so far from her genre of music and yet she knew every word to every one of my songs." Goosebumps bloom over my arms and neck with the memory. "She told me I could do it when others told me I couldn't." I swallow past the lump forming there. I haven't seen Grandma in a year—the same amount of time I've been avoiding my mother. But then, Gram lives in the house behind Mom's. I can't see Grandma without seeing Mom. "Anyway," I say, remembering why he asked. "I adore my grandma. Astrid had an Aunt Judy that she loved—though spelled with an "i"—and Serena's mom, who died when she was little, was also a Judy. It felt too ironic. Too right. So we went with it. Later we found Dawn, who had zero Judys in her life, but she was committed to the band and the name."

"Is that common knowledge?"

While I've fallen over onto my back, Miles is turned, watching me again.

"Aw, Serena mentioned it in one of our very first interviews.

But the story didn't circulate. My grandma knows why. That's the only thing I cared about." And now, I've abandoned The Judys—more like I moved on and they didn't want to move with me. How does Gram feel about that? I wouldn't know. I haven't spoken to her since it happened. The thought of ever disappointing her makes me sick—I shudder at the thought.

"What?"

Oh, that's right. I'm not alone.

"What is it?" Miles asks again.

I press my lips in on one another. "I—I just haven't talked to her since I left the band."

"From what you've said, she'd be proud of you for following your dream."

He isn't wrong. It's easy to believe when Miles Bailey says it.

In fact, I'm calling Grandma Judy tomorrow.

"Night, Miles."

"Goodnight, Delaney."

23

MILES

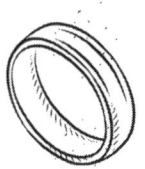

I'm hesitant to leave. We stayed up late talking, and I know last night rattled Delaney. It rattled me. But I'm also certain this girl will want her morning drink as well as a toothbrush. There's a gas station on the corner. I wouldn't even have to drive...

I peer over at her—even breaths, pouty lips, hair strewn out like a Chinese fan.

Nope. I can't do it.

I can't leave, not when she's asleep. Not when she might wake up and fear being alone. Not after last night.

I know two people who are also up this early, both would be willing to help me.

I shoot a text in my group with just Coco and Owen:

Me: Hey, I know it's early.

I pause my writing... I have to get creative. How long am I really going to be able to go without telling my family the truth? A year... I doubt it.

I resume typing and add:

Me: Delaney hasn't moved her things in yet. We had a scare at her place last night. We came back here in a hurry. She doesn't have a toothbrush. Any chance either of you'd be able to grab one and quietly bring it by this morning? Possibly with some type of caffeinated morning drink?

Coco: Me! I call it! I'll do it!

Owen: Did you even take four seconds to read through the entire text, Coco? That was lightning fast. In the texting Olympics, you get the gold.

Coco: I know. I read lightning fast too. I'll bring a toothbrush by for my new SISTER in a blink.

Owen: Wait. Scare? What kind of scare?

Owen: And Coco, you aren't allowed to like Delaney more than Annie just because she's famous.

Coco: Hey, I resent that. I love Annie. As far as I'm concerned, Annie is just sister—while Delaney is a NEW sister. Does Annie need a toothbrush? Because if so, I'm on it.

Coco: Wait? Scare? Confession, I did not read that text all the way through.

Me: Everyone is fine. Just a break-in at her Airbnb. Nina got him.

Coco: Holy spitballs!!! Someone broke into her place?

Me: Alice isn't reading over your shoulder, is she?

Me: Also—yes, as said above: Nina got him. All is well.

All is well—and it is. The night is over, everyone is safe, and Delaney Jones is tucked safely in my bed.

Whoa. That's a sentence I never thought I'd conjure. Lane Jonas—of The Judys—is in my bed. I peer over at her; a strand of long blue hair splays over her lips and neck.

I have one job—and that's to *not* fall for my wife. Surely I can do that. We're on day three—this shouldn't even be a question at this point.

There's a string of texts on my phone when I look back down, but nothing I really need to respond to. Coco will be here in less than fifteen minutes—and hopefully, she won't wake Delaney.

I'm dead-on—sure, my sister may have been adopted at birth, and she's only been in our lives the past three years, but I know her.

The quiet tap on my door at 7:12 in the morning couldn't be anyone but Coco. Only my family, myself, and Lars know the code to open the gallery door, and Lars doesn't come up here. He is also oblivious to the fact that my family knows the code. It's a good thing the Baileys are honest.

I crack the door open. Coco's already in her scrubs. She's got a City Drug bag in one hand and a cardboard carrier with four drinks in the other.

"I didn't know what she'd want," she says. "I tried texting you and asking, but you never responded."

Oh—maybe there was something I should have paid attention to. Either way, I don't know her drink. I wouldn't have had an answer.

I shrug. "Your guess is as good as mine."

"You don't know her drink?" Coco's forehead wrinkles, and she looks at me as though maybe I've grown a third eyeball.

Ah—*shoot.* I probably should know that. "Well, we aren't often together in the mornings. Just schedules. And stuff."

"And stuff?" she whispers, giving me the smallest of eye rolls. At least she isn't looking at me like I am what I am: a big fat liar.

I just smile. Anything else I say will only incriminate me.

Coco takes one more step inside. "Can I just take one look at her?"

"She isn't a sleeping baby, Cora." I first-name her—she needs to hear it. "You aren't going to go look at her. That's creepy."

She presses her lips together. "Sorry." If she were a puppy, her tail would be between her legs.

I reach for the bag and drinks and leave her with a kiss on the cheek. "You're the best," I tell her—because lecturing anyone, but especially Coco, is not my thing. "Thank you. I'm certain the two of you will be friends."

The right side of her mouth quirks up in a grin. "You think?"

"I do."

"Because I feel like I already know her from *Celebrity Wife*. Now she just needs to get to know me. I think you're right, Miles." She shakes her head. "This is crazy. All this time I was trying to set you up and you were seeing Lane Jonas."

"Yep. *Crazy*." Because she's not wrong, it's more than crazy—it's bonkers.

My sister lengthens her neck and tries her best to see over me and into my house. She's still looking for Delaney.

"Cora," I lecture.

"Fine." She grunts and flaps her hands at her sides. "I'm sorry. What are you guys doing later?"

I glance back at Delaney, making sure we haven't woken her. I shrug. "I don't know."

"Good. No plans. I'll call you after work. Because Jude and I will not be telling your niece that she didn't get to be the flower girl at your wedding. You have to do that—so bring Delaney by later."

"Coco—" I hiss, but she gives me a quick hug, and then she's gone without even trying to sneak one more peek at the woman in my bed.

I exhale a tired breath. Holding the drugstore bag in one

hand and the drink carrier in the other, I knock the door closed with my hip.

"Wow, you really do see your family every day. Don't you?"

"Whoa!" I jump, spilling hot coffee onto the back of my hand—thankfully not my beat-up hand.

"We do too have plans today. We're visiting Walt and checking out the building. I offered Lars cash and my lawyers are all over it, so the whole process should go through fairly quick."

I heave a sigh. "*Delaney.*" I set her toothbrush and drinks on my square of kitchen counter. "You're awake."

"Yeah, well, your sister isn't as quiet as she thinks she is." She lays with one arm bent behind her head and one leg peeking out from beneath the blankets.

I divert my gaze. "Sorry. But I did have her bring you a toothbrush."

She bounces into a sitting position, the blankets gathering around her and her back against the couch cushions. Her hair poofs out in all directions and her pale cheeks are pink. "Bless you!" she says.

"And coffee—or some variation."

Delaney scrambles from the bed, her legs and feet bare. She pads the two steps across the floor to the counter, where four cups sit in the to-go carrier.

"Which is yours?"

"I'm pretty sure they're all yours. Neither of us knew what you liked."

"Chai tea with cinnamon and vanilla, but anything with a little caffeine will work."

I make a mental note—I'm supposed to know this, right? *Chai tea with cinnamon and vanilla.*

Each cup has the contents written on the sides. "Take your pick," I tell her. "I'm going to shower."

"Sure," she says, sipping from cup number one only to move

on to cup number two. "Ah, hey, do you have a phone charger? I just need to make a few calls. I don't have a lot of stuff, but I can't leave it at the Airbnb. You really don't mind if I have my things brought here until I find a new place?"

A new place? I just assumed she'd stay here—at least until she went back to California. With the break-in and the act we're keeping up, it seemed to make sense.

I clear my throat. "Yeah. My side of the bed."

"Thanks." She presses her full lips together, then sips from cup number three.

"Delaney," I say, nerves coming alive in every part of my body.

Maybe it shows because she lowers the cup and gives me her full attention. "Yes?"

"You're welcome to stay here. If you want. Or not." I shrug like it doesn't matter. "I thought it might make sense with our situation. And then—" I swallow. "You wouldn't be alone."

She thinks for a minute, and the nerves inside my body begin to thunder in my ears.

"You don't have to—"

"No, it's a good idea." Her head tilts my way, her expression soft. "Thanks, Miles."

I nod, clumsy and foolish-like. "Sure," I say, and before I can turn for the bathroom, she picks up cup number four.

24

MILES

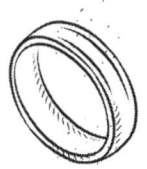

*D*elaney's things come sooner than I expected. The girl does not mess around. She doesn't have her hairbrush, which is apparently vital to her life. I offered her mine or to grab one from the drugstore on the corner, but she quickly declined.

I've talked her into calling her grandmother and telling her about me. She has to tell her family too, doesn't she? Though after yesterday and the press conference, I'm guessing they all know. Still, if her grandmother is her favorite person and she hasn't personally told her, she needs to.

I sit in my studio, giving her privacy while men bring her things up to my loft. And sure, she isn't moving in an entire household, but the girl has stuff. And a lot of it. My studio is full of work, so I point them in the direction of my apartment. They can set it wherever they can find room.

The paintbrush in my hand is on automatic as men carry things in through my propped-open loft door. Delaney is on the phone, and while I am not an eavesdropper, I know that she's talking about me, about us, and I'm too curious to not pay attention.

With my less dominant hand, I paint who-knows-what and hear her words without even straining.

"I know. It's been so long—too long. I'm sorry and—" She pauses. Grandma Judy must be commenting. I hope I'm right. I hope the woman she spoke of will accept and forgive her instantly. She sounded like the kind of person who would do that.

"But I should have called," Delaney says. My brush is on pause but picks up again with the positive note in her voice. "Miles—" Annnd, we're on pause again. "You'll love him. He's an artist and just a really decent human."

I swallow. *Decent*. I mean, she isn't wrong, but she uses that word a lot.

"Oh!" Delaney pipes. "And wait until you hear who he was named after." A short pause, and then she's speed-talking again. "No, you *will* know. I promise. Grandma, listen—who is your favorite hottie from your favorite soap?"

I shut my eyes. *Thanks, Mom*. Because of you, I'll get grandma-approval from my sort-of-wife's family.

"Where do you want this?" a man asks. We've told them to put everything in the loft. So, I'm not sure why he's asking. Until— "My songbird painting. Where did you get this?"

"The guy downstairs said to bring it up. You want it in here with the others?"

Lars. He's mad I'm getting my building so he's kicking out my watercolor?

I swallow, my jaw clenched. "Yeah. In here is fine."

He sets it down, propping it against a stack of more unfinished canvases, and exits. I'm ready to seethe when I hear Delaney say, "You do too remember their names. Stop being silly. It was your guilty pleasure. We both know it." She sighs. "Fine. I'll tell you. Miles Howard."

A giggle from Delaney makes me forget all about how I'd like to introduce my not-so-pacifist fist to Lars' face—actually no, I wouldn't. My hand still hurts from last night, and I am indeed a pacifist. Last night was not the norm.

"I told you!" She listens for a minute, and I keep dabbing with the yellow paint on my brush. "I'll visit soon. I promise. I've got some time now." Her voice cracks. "Ah, yeah. I'll see if Miles can come. He wants to meet you too."

There's a quiet, short goodbye—and then, all at once, I'm pretending I'm *not* listening as she steps through the open studio door.

"How'd it go?" I ask though I'm pretty sure I could guess.

"Good." She exhales like she's endured some straining physical activity. Her hair wisps out of place in a way that makes me smile. "So much better than I thought. You were right, Miles. She was totally understanding." She plops onto the stool next to me. "I mean, I know she's not my mom who understands nothing, but I just couldn't disappoint her. You know? She's the one person who's always stood by me."

"You haven't disappointed her," I say, then, for some reason, I lay a hand on her knee. I shouldn't be touching her—it does things to my insides. "And you aren't lying to her either. I *am* excited to meet her."

She cringes. "You heard that."

I remove my hand from her kneecap—maybe she didn't notice my momentary insanity. I rub at the back of my neck and clear my throat. "Just that last part." But I'm not the most skilled liar; she sees right through me. Ironically, it's exactly what makes me wrong for her, for this kind of marriage. It will be a miracle if someone doesn't find us out.

She scoffs out a laugh. "Sure. Okay." Standing, she steps over to my songbird painting, leaning against a pile of others. She tilts it forward to look at it better.

I grunt. "Yeah. I guess Lars is tired of having it on display. He told the guys to bring it up with your stuff."

Her manicured brows pinch. "Lars didn't tell them that. I—"

She lifts one shoulder. "I bought it." Her head tilts, giving the smallest of shakes. "Lars didn't mention that it sold—"

"You bought it?" I blink... and I can't seem to stop.

"Well, yeah. I like it." Her eyes fall back to the watercolor. "I like it a lot, actually, and I couldn't let it go."

"Oh." She likes my work. She *bought* my work. My head spins. My *wife* bought my painting. I swivel on my stool, facing her. "You know, I would have given it to you. You didn't have to buy it. You're—"

"Miles." She drops the painting back in place and stands in front of me, hands on hips. "That isn't how it works. You're doing a service, an artistic service. And you're selling that service. It's called making a living. You sell. I buy." She grins.

"Right. Only usually not many buy."

"Is that because you're always giving things away?" Her hands reach out, one holding to each of my shoulders. Her lips quirk upward, drawing my eyes there.

She told me I'd have to kiss her one day.

I told her I didn't think so.

Today—I might not argue with her...

What hope is there for me if we are on day three of our marriage and I'm already considering giving in?

"I don't give everything away," I finally say—but my mouth has gone dry. Unfortunately, my wife is pretty much a bombshell, which actually wouldn't affect me so much if she weren't so real, so down-to-earth, so kind-hearted.

I don't think I've ever met anyone like Delaney Jones.

Delaney smothers a laugh and drops her hands from my shoulders. "Give me ten minutes. I'll be ready to meet Walt."

Twenty minutes later, my left-handed painting has some sort of direction and Delaney is ready to go. Her hair falls down her back like a waterfall, the blue barely visible. Her jeans are light and whitewashed, and her shirt just hits where her high-waisted jeans end. When she moves, I get a peek at her slim, tan tummy—except that I'm not looking. Why would I look?

"How's your hand? You were painting, so—"

"Better this morning." I peer down at the purple bruise forming over my right fist. It hurts like crazy, but I can move it; nothing is broken. I'm just babying it for the day—and apparently getting an abstract piece of art in the process. Left-handed painting is interesting. "I'm fine."

"I'm glad, Miles." She rocks on her heels once. "Are you ready?"

I study her. I know that we're conning the world, but— "You don't have to do this. You don't have to spend your vacation this way."

She swallows, those blue eyes peering into my soul and making me do things I've never considered before. "I know that," she says. "If it's okay with you, I'd like to. We may not stay married for life, Miles. But I think we could be friends. If you're okay with it, I'd like to meet Walt."

I run a hand below my chin and blink away from her piercing gaze. "Yeah, I'm okay with it."

"Good! Should we run by Target? Should I bring Walt a gift? How does this work?"

I chuckle. "We're headed to his group home. If you buy Walt a gift, you'll need to get something for everyone. Or you'll have a revolt on your hands—rock star or not."

No matter my insistence that we don't need to come with gifts—because a visit is a gift in itself—we head to Target. Delaney insists. She only gets stopped twice—one of the women even recognizes me, which weirds me out to no end and sends Delaney into a fit of giggles. Once we find a nice hiding spot down the stuffed animal aisle, she picks up a gift for all six men who live in the group home with Walt.

"Are you sure stuffed dogs are the way to go? We could have

looked at watches or video games or—" She tilts her head, staring at the brown stuffed pug in her hands.

"Most of them wouldn't care about a watch or a game, but they'll love the dogs. Yes, these men are grown, Walt is forty-two. But you have to remember that his mind isn't forty-two."

"Right." Her grin is kind and small when she returns her eyes to the pug. "Good. I'm with Walt: the dogs are much cuter than a lame-o man watch."

"Lame-o?"

"Yeah." She nods. "If you're going to be married to me, Miles, you have to understand that at times I revert to a thirteen-year-old." She shrugs like this is just a fact and she's passing on information.

"Thirteen?"

"Mm-hmm."

"I think I knew that already."

"Hey." She moans as if she were offended, though she's the one who said so.

"What?" I glance over at her. "Do you have any idea how long it took me to scrub off that marker mustache?"

"You drew that on yourself! I had nothing to do with that particular mustache." She laughs, her lips parting into a huge grin. "It's strange. We haven't known each other long."

"Less than a week." I fill in that fact not only for her but myself.

"And yet," she says, and my heart drums, beating out the word *y-e-t*. "It feels longer. Doesn't it? Like we've been friends a while?"

"Yeah. It does." It really, *really* does.

25

DELANEY

The group home workers give me a double take—but bless them, they do not make a fuss. They clearly know Miles as he greets everyone he sees. None of the residents seem to know who I am, and most stay busy with the tasks the workers have them on.

We walk through the living room and into the kitchen, Miles introducing me to each man as we go.

Eddy might be the youngest of the bunch at thirty-three. He sits with one of the workers, planning a menu for the week. He takes a break from his task and gives me a light handshake, happily taking the pug I brought.

Arnold and William work together on a hard wooden puzzle of farm animals but happily give me a minute when I offer them each a gift.

Tuff, gray-haired with the eyes of a little boy, draws a picture with markers, the large mat beneath his paper marked up where he's missed his coloring sheet. He drops each of his pens and looks from me to the dog I'm holding out to him.

"It's a gift, Tuff. From Delaney," Miles explains.

He smiles, one of his front teeth missing and takes the stuffed animal from my hands.

Mikey sits in a recliner, rocking back and forth, staring at a gameshow on the TV screen. All men have taken a minute to say hello to us—except for Mikey. He stays silent. I set the dog next to him and with his eyes glued to the screen he pays the plush Rottweiler no attention.

"Where's Walt?" I ask. We've yet to meet Miles' friend.

"He must be in his room."

Tuff has decided to leave his drawing behind and follow us down the dim hallway. "Deeee-laney," he says, shaking out his hands.

"Hey, Tuff," Miles says, glancing back at the man. He's clearly not worried about our tag-along. "Is Walt in his room?"

"In his room," Tuff answers.

"Is he having a sad day?" Miles asks as we meander down a dim hallway.

"Sad day," Tuff says, stuffing his poodle under his armpit and shaking his hands towards the door.

"Thanks, buddy. Can you go show your dog to Jo and Denise? They'll want to meet him."

"Jo," Tuff repeats. He turns around and heads for the kitchen, where Jo helps Eddy with his menu.

Miles peers back at me as if to check on my comfort level.

"He's sweet," I say, letting him know that I'm good.

"He's a good guy."

Miles taps on the door at our right and waits. When there's no reply, Miles taps again. "Walt, I brought someone who wants to meet you." Still no reply. "And she brought you a gift."

There's a rustling inside the room, and then, "All right."

I knew a gift was a good idea. I bounce my brows at Miles, saying as much.

He lifts one shoulder, and while he hasn't said a word, this means he agrees with me. He opens the unlocked door and peeks inside the room before opening the door wider for me to enter. Walt's room is small, with a bed, a small dresser, and a desk against the wall. Above his desk hang a dozen paintings—his own, I'd guess from looking at them.

His head, brown hair with sprigs of gray, bows low with his chin tucked in. There's a children's book on the desk he sits by, but he's looking at his lap, not the book. His hair is thin on top, and what little there is left is combed over the top of his head. The wrinkles around his eyes and lips tell me he's lived a few years. But when he looks up, finally meeting Miles' gaze and then mine, he grins, and those eyes and that smirk are youthful and sweet.

"You brought a gift?" he says, looking at me. "For me?"

"She did," Miles says, "but first, can I make introductions?"

Walt sighs like it's a big inconvenience for him to meet me—and already I like him. "Okay."

"This is Delaney," Miles says, glancing back at me. He returns his eyes to Walt, waiting for the man's reaction. Then, unlike with the others, he adds, "My *wife*."

Walt does not disappoint. His mouth drops to a gaping O, and his eyes turn to sweet little moons as he giggles uncontrollably. "Wife. Wife." He shakes his head. "Miles has a wife!"

"I do." Miles chuckles. "And she brought you something because she knows we're pals."

Walt's brows raise, wrinkling up every bit of his forehead. He looks at me and then down at the stuffed dog in my hands.

"Oh, right." I giggle, suddenly nervous. Walt is Miles' friend. While we aren't exactly *married* married, I want him to approve. "Here." I hold out the bulldog with a blue-and-yellow collar. "It's so nice to meet you, Walt."

Walt is still grinning like a schoolboy. He holds out one hand, his fingers thin and stiff. Miles takes the dog and helps Walt to grasp the thing. Walt giggles again, looking into the face of that smiling bulldog.

"He needs a good name." He nods, his chin jutting out, then looks up at me. "What's her name again?" he asks Miles.

"Lane," I answer, giving him the easier version of my name.

Another giggle slips through Walt's lips. "Lane." He pats the dog's head, then drops him in his lap, that mischievous grin still blooming on his cheeks. "Good boy, Lane."

"I like it," I tell him. I give him a thumbs-up—but for some reason that only sets Walt into another fit of laughter.

Miles shakes his head, but he's smiling like Walt and I are two troublemakers, and yet he can't help but adore us. "Hey, buddy, Delaney and I come with news." Miles sits on the made bed next to his friend, setting a hand on top of Walt's. "We got the building."

Walt's bushy brows jolt upward, saying so much more than words ever could. "We got it?"

"With Delaney's help, yes, we got it."

"No, the credit goes to Miles." My eyes blur with unshed and unexpected tears.

Walt's grin explodes now. "We got the building!" He howls. He pushes on the knob of his electric wheelchair, and I stumble back and out of the way. He straightens out his chair and faces it toward the door. "Let's go."

"Whoa. Whoa. Whoa. Break there, stud." Miles taps the arm of Walt's chair. "We got the building all right, but—" Miles lifts Walt's hand from the go button. "Lars has to move his stuff out. We need some time to get it ready."

Walt blows out a raspberry, spittle spraying over the front of his shirt and lap. He knocks his head against the headrest of his chair and groans.

"Can you give us two weeks, Walt?" I ask. "I think I can pull some strings and get some help to speed up the process."

Walt's clear blue eyes stare into mine, his lips in a flat line. "Two weeks," he says to me, his tone serious. Swiveling his head back around to Miles, he giggles. "Miles, your wife is hot."

26

DELANEY

*A*lice Taylor stares at me like I have stolen her pink unicorn backpack and lit the thing on fire.

Weird. Kids usually like me.

I pat the top of her golden retriever's head. At least Princess likes me.

"You are kidding me right now. Because there is no way I missed my flower girl debut."

"You were Owen's flower girl," Miles tells her.

Her little blue eyes turn to giant marbles. This is clearly the wrong thing to say. "And I had to wear *green*!"

"Alice," Jude says, one hand on her shoulder, though the man looks nervous. "Miles didn't get married to hurt your feelings."

"Only it did, Dad. It did hurt my feelings. Big time. Uncle Miles got married and it hurt my feelings real good."

"Sweet pea," Coco pleads.

One tear trickles down the girl's face, and I'm pretty sure it breaks Miles. His screwed-up, worry-filled face falls to pieces with that one single tear. He crouches, then sits on the hardwood floor in Jude and Coco's living room, holding out his arms.

Alice falls into them, and instead of giving her an excuse or blaming me—which is totally warranted by the way—he says, "I'm sorry, Alice. That was selfish and thoughtless of me. I'm so, so sorry."

"And what about Lula?" Alice says, ignoring her uncle's heartfelt apology. "She never got the chance to walk down the aisle!"

"She isn't walking yet," Jude says. "She couldn't have—" He grunts with an elbow from his wife.

"You're right," Miles tells her. "*Poor Lula.* How can I make it up to the two of you?"

She thinks for only a second. "I'd like one wedding, please. I will wear pink and walk down the aisle, and as the main attraction, I will throw red rose petals to the crowd right before Lane Jonas comes on down!" She sings that last part like she is the new voice of *The Price Is Right*. "Unless she would like me to carry her dress's caboose—and then I am willing to save the best for last. Otherwise, I prefer first." She nods, her words final.

"Oh. Umm." Miles peers up at me. "I don't think we're going to do another wedding. We kept it small for a reason because Delaney—you know," he whispers, "AKA superstar Lane Jonas is my new wife, and we didn't want a bunch of cameras and people crashing the wedding."

But Alice is unimpressed with my stage name or anything Miles has said. She sits in her uncle's lap, folds her arms, and stares into his eyes, her bottom lip trembling.

She is good.

"But you said you wanted to make it up to me," Alice says.

"I do. Laney and I could take you to the zoo or the park or—"

"Disneyland!" I offer.

Jude and Coco peer at one another with my over-jubilant response. I really don't want to be the bad guy here.

Alice nibbles on her lip, reminding me a little of her mom

—*err*, stepmom. I keep forgetting those girls aren't blood related. While Alice is fair and blonde—the opposite of Coco—they still remind me of one another.

She isn't buying what we're offering. And yet, the girl says in the world's smallest voice, "Okay."

"Miles, why couldn't we do a family celebration? We could have a small ceremony. Alice could be your flower girl and—"

"I like it. I'll take door number three—" Alice says, pointing to Coco.

"But we don't want guests or gifts—" Miles says.

"Yes, what he said." I point to Miles, my stomach churning at the thought of a ceremony with actual guests. Plus—as new as Miles is to me, I can tell that the thought of kind people bringing us gifts for our sham of a marriage sits as well with him as it does with me—*terribly*.

"So, not a ceremony, no gifts… but a celebration. The family would like to celebrate the two of you," Coco says.

"Yes, we would." Alice smacks her hands to Miles' cheeks, then kisses him on the nose. "Grandma Lucy would appreciate that plan as well. I know it."

Miles looks up at me from his seat on the floor, but then he looks at Alice sitting in his lap, and I've lost the fight before it's begun. "Yeah. We could probably do that," he says.

27

DELANEY

I'm ignoring Miles' apologies by staring at the texts on my phone. My sister is done being quiet.

> **Eryn**: I'm not mad.
> **Eryn**: Okay, I'm a little mad. But mostly because I still haven't heard about any of whatever it is that's going on from YOU.

"It's my sister," I say to Miles as he pulls up in front of his new studio.

He nods, zips his apologetic lips, and gives me quiet and time.

> **Me**: I'm sorry, E. I haven't had a second to call. It's been crazy here. And I want to talk. I do. I'll call soon. I promise!

Against my better judgment, I ask:

> **Me**: How did Mom take the news?

> **Eryn**: Oh, you know. How does Cruella feel about her stolen dogs escaping?

I slap a hand over my mouth—it's the most ruthless thing my sister has ever said concerning our mother. Eryn knows how difficult the woman is. And yet she never seems to have issues with her. It helps that my mother's life goals for Eryn aligned with Eryn's own goals. Still, my sister is very much aware of how our mother treats me and while she is one hundred percent against it, she's also nineteen and trying to maintain a civil and somewhat good relationship with the woman.

I don't blame her. I never have. I love my little Eryn, who will always seem little in my eyes. How can she not? When I moved out, Eryn was barely eleven.

My phone pings with another text.

> **Eryn**: You know—her life is unfair, and the world is out to get her. But now her daughter is too, so the world is falling to pieces.
> **Me**: That bad?
> **Eryn**: I could lie to you… but what good would it do? Besides, I've told her again and again that you must have had your reasons. You aren't unkind by nature and there has to be a reason for this.
> **Eryn**: There is. Right?

I steal a glance at Miles, who's patiently scrolling through his phone, waiting for me to finish my conversation before going into the building he's only waited—oh, I don't know—*forever* for!

> **Me**: There is.

Though I can't exactly tell her the true reason.

Eryn: And that fabulous reason would be?????

I swallow. "My sister wants to know why I got married without her."

"And you gave me a hard time about Alice," he says. But he's smiling. There's no I-told you-so in that grin.

"Well, none of you can say no to her."

He breathes out a heavy breath. "It's a problem. I know." He studies me, then his eyes drop to my cell. "So, what are you going to tell her?"

"I don't know." My brow furrows. "This is harder than I thought it would be. How about you're dying, and we decided we couldn't wait another second."

"I'm dying? That's the best you got, Jones?"

I clamp down on my bottom lip and stare at my sister's name, her "awaiting message" bubble. "Or your grandma was dying, and we had to hold the ceremony before the Good Lord took her."

He blinks, long and slow, his head doing that mini shake it does from time to time. "Could we possibly come up with something that isn't death-related?"

My lips purse, and my heart pounds while I ponder that question. "I don't think so."

Miles coughs out a laugh. "Delaney, come on. We told my family—my very close-knit family—that we just couldn't wait. And with all of your"—another head bobble—"celebrity stuff, it seemed right."

"It seemed right."

"Didn't it?" he asks.

The green in his eyes seems to spark. It did seem right. Very right. "Yes. It did."

I turn back to my phone and type.

> **Me**: E, all I can say is it was the right thing to do. But I am sorry my baby sister wasn't by my side.
>
> **Eryn**: I guess that'll have to do. For now.

I reread her message one more time before stuffing my phone into my bag. "Come on," I say to Miles. "You've waited long enough."

With the key in hand, we walk up to Miles' new building.

"So, a party?" I sigh. It's fine. I'm still working on writing songs, and Ash is getting copyright approval on a few covers to remake. Recording will come much later. It's not like I need to leave Coeur d'Alene this minute. But a party? Neither of us wanted that. It's easier to focus on that truth than disappointing my sister. "You know it'll just be a big show. And I think a show is easier for me than you."

Miles clears his throat. "It'll just be my family."

Right. If my mother were planning a celebration, it would be with everyone she'd ever met. I shut my eyes and stand in front of the glass door. Miles' family is not my own. If I've learned anything this week, it's that.

"And your family, if you want?"

"Mine?" I scoff. "Um, no thank you. Nope. They aren't invited."

"Not even your sister?"

The key is in the lock, but he waits for my answer.

I exhale a strained, deranged laugh. "No. Not even Eryn." I mimic Miles' head shake and say, "I'm sorry, I'm not trying to be difficult. The whole thing just caught me off guard."

"Same," he says, hand on the door handle. "I'm sorry."

"No more sorries. Let's go inside. Yeah?"

He nods, unlocks the door, and pushes his way into the building.

Honestly, it doesn't look like much to me. But then, the bass guitar Dad won me when I was a kid didn't look like much to my mother. But it was everything to me.

The floors are cement, and the paint is peeling, but the windows are wide and tall, letting the light shine in. The ceiling is covered in wooden columns—that, with some work, could be decent looking. But right now, it looks abandoned.

"What's your plan?" I say, looking about the wide-open space. At least Lars' things are gone.

While I see a ton of work, Miles is all smiles. He glances over at me, seeing the unimpressed look on my face. "I know it isn't pretty. But it will be. And look at those windows. And that curbside entrance. Walt will have no issue getting through that door." He walks farther in, and I wonder for a second if Miles Bailey is real.

Just like me, he's invested. His work is his life. It means so much. Not many people know Miles Bailey the artist, though the man is skilled. I know exactly where that songbird watercolor is going in my L.A. apartment. Still, he's happy. This place, Walt being able to be here—it makes him happy. It's worth fighting with Lars. It's worth the manual labor of readying the place. And it's worth being married to me for a year.

My throat constricts. I swallow past the lump forming with Miles' pure goodness. "What do you need to do to get it ready?" I ask.

"Well, I'll need more than two weeks," he says, referring to the timeline I gave Walt, "but Walt could probably visit next week." He rubs his hands together, circling the space and peering all around once more. "I need to stain the beams." His eyes dart up to the ceiling. "Polish the floor. Paint. I'd love to add a wall—" He walks farther in, beaming like a kid on Christmas day, motioning with his hands. "—here. You know, for my own personal workspace. And then, of course, it all needs to be up to code for me to hold classes here. My brothers should be able to help me. We've all been renovating Owen's house, picking up construction skills along the way." His eyes take in every nook and cranny. "It'll take time but I'll be able to more than double my current class size. I've always wanted to offer different classes for different artistic styles, rather than the one style, three-person class I have now. And there's so much I could do with my children's classes—you know, for Alice and friends. She'd love that."

"You know, it's a good thing you don't plan to have children," I tease. "You're so incredibly whipped by that niece. I can't imagine you with an actual daughter." Though the thought makes me grin. Any girl would be lucky to call Miles Bailey her dad.

"I never said that," he says with a sheepish grin, glancing at me and then back around to the space in front of us. "You're the one that said you didn't want to have kids."

"Right. We're both all about work and—"

"And I want kids one day." He shrugs. "I'm not looking for my lifelong partner right now, Laney. But one day I will. And one day, I'll have a kid or two."

My insides scramble like eggs in a blender. Of course Miles would want kids. Why did I assume that just because they aren't on my radar they wouldn't be on his? I bite my inner cheek and walk farther into the building. With my stomach gnawing away from the inside out, I change the subject. "Paint, stain, a wall, and up to code."

"It's more than it sounds like."

"I'm sure," I say, making a mental note of all he's said. Hopefully, that's all he really wants because I'm making another call today. *Money does not make you happy*—my grandmother always told me that. *Don't let it change you. Don't let it rule you. Don't let it dictate your joy.*

She was right. But money does get things done. And technically this building is still in my name. I promised Walt he'd have his studio in two weeks. I'm going to do my best to keep that promise.

Besides, this surprise is going to bring the sweetest smile to my husband's face.

28

MILES

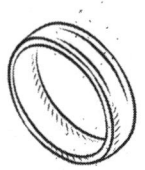

*D*elaney spends the rest of the night organizing her things and finding a place for her luggage. My loft is tight—there isn't a lot of room—but she figures it out. I think this means she's staying. Neither of us has brought up her finding a new place again.

I've been alone for a long time. I never had a roommate after I left Mom's. And I surprise myself by not minding having Delaney around all the time. She's quiet at times—I think when she's writing music in her head. I've paused to watch her scribble in her notebook more than a couple times during her cleaning process.

Tonight she has her own pj's, though I've given her the button-up pajama top. I never wore it anyway, and I won't be able to look at it without seeing her in it. She might as well take it.

She exits the bathroom—makeup-less, teeth brushed, and hair in a bun on top of her head. I swallow and blink and remind myself not to stare. She is beautiful.

And more so like this than all made up.

I scan away from her as I head into the bathroom myself.

There's a teal bra hanging from the inside of my bathroom door handle, a purple toothbrush next to my blue one, and a pink bag with a monogrammed *L* on the front of it sitting on the back of my toilet. And the entire room smells of roses.

Delaney Jones has officially moved in.

I don't hate it. Her things take up hardly any space, and I like the rose scent.

I brush my teeth and wash my face, splashing cold water over my eyes and neck again and again before leaving the Lane-infested bathroom.

She's tucked in bed—*my bed*—but her eyes are bright like sapphires as she scans over to me.

"Hi," she says.

"Hi."

I lay next to her, on my back, hands beneath my head, and stare up at the ceiling, making sure in this tight space that not even my arm brushes hers.

I can hear her breathing; she isn't asleep.

And I'm curious. So I ask, "Why Coeur d'Alene?"

I feel rather than see as she rolls onto her side to face me. "Hmm?"

"I get that you needed somewhere quiet to get away after everything with that reality show went wrong. But why Coeur d'Alene? How did you pick this town?" I glance over at her.

"Um." Her teeth clamp onto that bottom lip—possibly just to draw my eyes there. I'm not sure. But I do think Delaney enjoys seeing me squirm. "Well." She swallows and squirms a little herself. "I have one memory of a happy family. No judging mother, no gambling father—just a mom, a dad, and two girls on vacation. My dad won this work trip"—her eyes widen a little—"back when he still worked. And for some strange reason, I was too young to identify the why—why we came without anyone arguing or belittling or hurting the other. We swam in the pool, played golf, stayed up too late, and ate too much food.

We just had fun together. It was the strangest, most beautiful day of my life." Her tone is whimsical as if reliving a dream. Her eyes flutter at nothing in the dimness and then over to me. "I never understood why we couldn't be like that all the time. When the show aired, kicking up all the dirt and drama with it, I needed some peace. I needed somewhere I felt safe." She rolls onto her back. "Someplace the media wouldn't suspect me to be and where I could shut out the world. Coeur d'Alene came to mind and just seemed like it could be that place. *Again.*"

She's done and I'm processing her words. I never had the father I should have. But we always had Mom, and she took care of us. She loved us more than enough for two parents. We weren't the perfect family, but we were happy.

"It's silly," she says.

"It's not," I say. "Besides, it's a great place to get married."

Quiet laughter spills from her lips. "Well, yeah. Of course there's that."

29

DELANEY

Miles' loft isn't exactly my music room back in L.A., but I have writing tools, my guitar, and—time. We spend the entire day with Miles painting in the small studio attached to this loft and me writing and strumming on my guitar in his apartment.

A message dings on my cell, and I glance away from my music notebook to the device next to me.

My mother.

> **Mom**: So, which is it, Delaney—are you married or not? I'm getting conflicting messages. None from my actual daughter. Shocker.

I purse my lips and close out my messaging app without a response.

I *should* be sharing this news with my family, with my friends, with my online following. That's the point of all this, right—to get the word out?

I set my guitar to the side and walk into Miles' space. I don't want to interrupt him, but I don't want to share anything without telling him first.

I knock on the frame, the door opened, and peek my head inside. "Hey," I say when he turns to face me.

"Hey." He runs a hand through his hair, smearing black paint over his forehead in the process. "Are you hungry? Did I miss dinner? Sometimes I get lost in the project and lose track of time."

"No—no, you're fine." My eyes draw to the mark on his head and my lips twitch with an unspoken giggle. "Um, I'm going to post about our... *big news* on my social media. Okay?"

"Oh." He clears his throat and shuffles in his seat. "Sure. I mean, you wanted to reset your image with your fans. This is part of that. So, yeah. That makes sense."

"What's your handle?"

"Mine?" he says, eyes narrowed. I wait for the classic Miles head bobble... but not this time.

"Yeah. Can I tag you?"

"Ah, sure. I guess." He smiles, his lips closed and just turned up. He sets one hand in his curls and scratches, giving me an urge to touch his short brown hair. "It's @miles.bailey.art."

"Direct and to the point. I like it." I clasp my hands together in front of me, and then, because I can't seem to help myself, I step into the room and walk until I'm standing directly in front of Miles. He peers up at me from his stool as I completely invade his space. I stand so close that I'm right at the center of him, his legs on either side of me.

"Delaney?"

"You just have a little—" I say as pine and musk fill my senses. I drag my thumb along his head, scooping up as much of the black paint as I can. Then, I lean in, pressing a kiss to my husband's head as he has mine a handful of times in the past few days. It's soft and slow and more intimate than I intended. Then again, did I intend to kiss him at all?

He takes my wrist, holding my hand to see the black smudged over my finger. "Thanks," he whispers. With the tail of his flannel shirt, he wipes the paint from my thumb. There's a tinted outline showing exactly where the paint had been, but he's wiped it dry.

"Knock, knock," a voice calls from the hall.

My heart pounds like a teenager caught. Then again, Miles is my husband, and it should be perfectly normal for me to stand this close to him. But is it normal for me to feel this sparking attraction every time he's near?

"Come in, Coco," Miles says to his closed door.

I swoop an arm around Miles' neck and plop down onto his left leg as if we had choreographed this scene.

He grunts in surprise at my new position, his cheeks blossoming that pretty pink I love, but he doesn't have time to question me as Coco enters the room.

She freezes in place when she sees us, a grin plastered to her pretty face. "Hi," she says.

"Hey." Miles' arm dangles at his side, and I wish he'd wrap it around me. I'm guessing if I fell backward, the man would catch me on instinct. But we're supposed to be *newlyweds—lovers—in love*. Does he need a refresher?

I'm still pondering how to get my husband of less than a week to touch me when—

"Are you free tonight, Lane—*err*, Delaney? I'm not really sure which to call you."

I swallow, blinking over at Miles' sister. "Ah. Either. I go by either." I pinch my brows. "Free?"

"Yeah, well, if we're going to throw you and Miles a reception, the girls and I thought we could have a planning meeting. Sort of a bridal shower-slash-planning-slash-celebration night."

"That's a lot of slashes," I say. It sounds like a lot packed into one night. A lot of unnecessary things filling up a night I'd already planned out with writing, picking, and creating a list of all the things I can do to make Miles blush.

"Sure. We want you to have a say—it's your party—and we'd all love to spend more time with you—as Miles' wife," she adds quickly, "not because you're a rock star. I know you're both. But we aren't being—"

"I get it. I know what you're saying." I do. They love their brother, and they want to know his new wife. It's normal. It's nice. It's welcoming. It also sounds like a big family outing—something that is a little out of my comfort zone. But I'm the one who started this. So, I slap on a smile and look at my new sister-in-law. "Sure. What time?"

"Really?" she says, her shoulders straightening. "Great. Seven. Is seven okay? We'll pick you up. And it'll be cool." She steps backward toward the door, her eyes still on me, and backs right into a standing easel. "Whoops!" A nervous giggle floods from her mouth. "Okay. See you then. I'll see you then—which is tonight."

"Yep." I smile and wave as she stumbles her way out the door.

"Girls' night," Miles says, turning his head to look at me. He is so close and so deliciously musky.

I register his words and cringe. "Girls' night?" And not just any girls' night but *family* girls' night.

My clear discomfort only makes him chuckle.

So I tip myself backward, betting on Miles. Betting he'll catch me and betting that blush will bloom again, twice in fifteen minutes. And—

Miles swoops his arm around my back in half a second. His other scoops beneath my knees, lifting my legs. In two seconds flat, he is standing, and I am a sack of flour scooped up in his arms.

His clean-shaven cheeks do not disappoint—they're as pink as Alice Taylor's backpack.

30

DELANEY

I force Miles into a few selfies of the two of us in his studio and then leave the poor man alone. I retire back to his room, spread out on the couch, post a pic with a simple hashtag #hangingwithmyhubby, and then I find myself in a rabbit hole down Miles' Instagram page.

He has three hundred followers, less than a hundred posts—all of his work—and he's following a hundred and one people. I would bet money that each and every single one is a blood relative.

He is completely underutilizing his social media.

So… I tag him in my post and share half a dozen of his posts to my stories. Then I take a picture of myself holding the songbirds' painting, posting that this is my favorite Miles Bailey creation of all time. By the time I'm ready to exit the rabbit hole, he's more than doubled his following.

Mental high five for me!

Before I can get too excited, I remember that Coco will be picking me up for who-knows-what tonight. I should probably change my clothes and brush my hair and look semi-presentable for this outing with my… *sister-in-law*.

I set my phone down, grab my bathroom bag, and shuffle off to that water closet Miles refers to as a bathroom.

I've only been in here for ten minutes when I hear Miles talking to someone. I twist my wrist and check my watch—I still have twenty minutes. Coco is early.

I finish up my lip gloss, adjust my Milano silk blouse, and head out for the girls' night I never asked for.

"Um, an artist," Miles says to *no one*. "And a teacher, I guess. Though not a schoolteacher."

Wait. *Not* to no one. He's holding out his phone, looking at the screen. *Nope*, wrong again. He's holding *my* phone. Looking at *my* screen. He's talking to someone on *my* phone.

I speed walk to his far left side and see *Claire Jones* staring back at him, studying him and *judging* him for all he's worth.

Miles glances at me, but thankfully Mom doesn't see me. I didn't make it into the camera lens.

I stand where only Miles can see me, and I mouth, "*My mother?*" I slap a silent hand to my forehead. He's talking to the one person I avoid at every cost.

His eyes glance past the phone to me.

I throw up my arms and mouth, "*What are you doing?*" It's a silent fit, an Oscar-worthy performance.

He gives a small shrug just as Mom says, "That can't pay much. Even successful artists struggle for a time, and I have never heard of *you*."

"Well, no ma'am, it doesn't pay much, but it pays enough."

"Enough for what?"

We've only just begun with her put-downs, but I can't. *I can't —I can't*. I leap to Miles' side and wrap one arm around his waist. "Enough, Mother. You don't need any more explanation. Miles' finances are none of your business."

Mom's short golden hair wisps back and her red lips— thanks to L'Oreal's Rose Garden— smile sardonically back at me. "But it seems they are yours." Her tattooed brows rise to the tippity-top of her head. She sighs—more dramatic than necessary. "Well, look who it is. Alive and well. My prodigal daughter hasn't come home, but she can show her face on a phone call. She *can* say hello to her mother. It's good to know that not all of my teachings were lost on you."

Say hello? More like asking the woman to back off.

"Not all. But most," I say, and Miles stiffens next to me.

I don't mean to make him uncomfortable with my Mother issues.

I stopped apologizing for who I was years ago. I stopped believing her judgments years ago. Still, Miles is clearly uneasy beside me. It's not my fault. I never planned to introduce the two of them. But then, I didn't answer the phone.

"So, you are married, Delaney Sage?"

I clear my throat and unapologetically answer, "I am."

"You don't look very married."

I flap my arms at my side, but it's lost on her. I'm not even sure she can see it. "What does married look like, Mother? Would you like me to put on an apron and make Sunday dinner? Or maybe I should make out with my husband here and now to prove to you we're married?"

Miles turns his head and stares at me.

"Are you a child?" Mom says, her eyes slits. "What would that prove? You've kissed plenty of boys, Delaney. And we both know you can't cook." She huffs. "I want to see the certificate."

"Oh," Miles pipes up. "We have that—"

"We do, but she doesn't need to see it. We don't have to prove anything to her." I tighten my grip around Miles' waist, holding him next to me.

"Tell me you were at least smart enough to get a prenup."

We were—but that's another piece of information she doesn't get to have.

"Knock, knock," calls a voice from the studio. Coco steps into Miles' home, two more women behind her.

Does no one *actually* knock in this family? I mean, saying "knock, knock" isn't knocking; they know that, right?

"Kiss your husband goodbye, Lane Jonas, it's time to party," Annie says, making her way into the loft with a dorky dance that no one should be doing.

"Who's that? Who's there?" Mom says as if we're under attack.

And maybe we are.

Attack of the self-appointed bridesmaids.

"Oh, phone call," Coco whispers, pointing toward the phone Miles holds, then snatching onto Annie's wrist and hushing her up.

"Sorry," Annie says, just above a whisper.

"No," I say, my nerves on edge and ready to end this conversation. "You're right, Annie! It's time to go. Kiss me goodbye, Miles." I look away from my mother, and up to Miles, ready to put on a show.

"Right." As if he were a high school actor playing a really bad version of Romeo, Miles squares his shoulders and turns to face me.

Mom is still watching. His sisters are staring. We are, in fact, the latest showing at the movie theater. And I am all hyped up.

Typical Miles leans in—and I know where that kiss is going. My forehead is officially a snogging station.

Bouncing up on my tiptoes, I surprise him by tipping my head back and letting his lips land right on mine. I swing my arms around his neck and hold him there for two seconds and then three.

Our harsh beginning melts away as my lips take over and explore his. My mind forgetting everyone around us as I focus in on Miles, and only Miles.

His empty hand cups the back of my head, cradling me there, holding me close, while his mouth responds to mine, kissing me back with urgency. His right arm is a frozen structure, still holding out my viewing mother.

But I can't worry about her. Not with Miles so very close.

His soft lips part with my tease, like butter—smooth and sweet. I can't get enough. Miles Bailey—accidentally making me flame with touches and words—can kiss. He could kiss a girl into oblivion.

Seconds later, he breaks free, clearing his throat and peering down into my eyes. Saying so much—without saying a word.

"*Delaney*." My mother groans out my name as if I were a child causing a scene at one of her garden parties.

In the corner, some member of Miles' family sighs sweetly. I'm not sure who.

Despite the audience we have—one appalled, the other awed—I take in the sparks tingling over my skin and lighting up every corner of my body. I embrace them, listen to them, and hold onto them. This feeling is new and beautiful and I don't want to forget it.

Just a kiss, I'd told him before. It's not a big deal, just a kiss.

I might have been wrong about that.

31

MILES

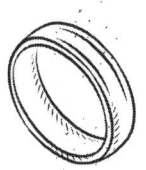

I just kissed Delaney Jones. Aka Lane Jonas.
Wrong—she kissed me.
Either way, kissing happened. The buzzing in my lips won't let me forget it. After which I promptly hung up on Delaney's mother. Not on purpose—it was an accident. I was caught off guard and... it just happened. Of course, I let her watch me kiss her daughter before I hung up on her.

Delaney didn't seem to care that her mother got a show or that I hung up on the woman. She just hopped up to peck me once more before saying goodbye and taking off with my sisters.

As she left, I spouted something really suave like, "Call me!"

I am suddenly back in high school with a huge crush on Fara Frame and no idea how to behave around her. Except that, I'm not afraid of Delaney or talking to her. I'm all grown up—sort of. And a little concerned about my new bride. She's going out in public when she just had a break-in this week. She likes to act like she's fine, but I've seen her startle. And maybe breathing exercises are a part of her daily routine, or maybe they're new due to the trauma she's experienced.

I bounce a nervous knee and stare at my painting—but I can't see what's next. My head won't clear.

Delaney knows what she's doing. She's been living this rock star life a whole lot longer than I have. Besides, I told her to call me—and I meant it and not in a pining-after-Fara-Frame way. So I'm just going to assume that's how she took it.

There's a knock on my door, and I pop my head up like a jack-in-the-box. "Delaney?"

The door opens to my three burly brothers and one brother-in-law. They let themselves inside, filling the space of my studio.

"Miles!" Owen says, a big smile on his face. "Bachelor party?"

"He isn't a bachelor anymore." Levi crosses his arms, peering down at me on my stool.

"Ah, shut it, Levi," Coop says.

"Coop?" I say, realizing my youngest brother should be in Boise for school. "What are you doing home?"

"You announce you're married—to a *rock star* of all people—and I'm supposed to stay at school for the weekend? I'm here to celebrate. Sunday dinner is gonna be fun." He chuckles, smiling that award-winning grin he's had since he was a kid.

My brow sits in its constant furrow. "So—"

"We're going out. Celebrating." Jude holds a fist out to Levi, and when he is denied, he turns to Coop, who happily bumps fists with our brother-in-law.

"The girls aren't the only ones who get to party," Owen says.

His joy is contagious.

"Annie came up with that line, didn't she?" Levi says. "This whole thing is Annie's idea."

Owen bumps his shoulder to Levi's. "It was mine. Of course we want to celebrate our brother. This is a big deal."

"Where are we going?" I scratch the back of my head. I'm not sure I'm up for a night out. But then, what else am I going to do? Stay home and stress about Delaney, replay that kiss in my brain—again and again, and again? At this point, it's like Grandma Bailey's record of the *General Hospital* rap anthem: broken and repeating the same line over and over.

Owen points a finger at me. "Pickleball—"

"In the dark?"

"It isn't dark yet," Cooper says. He pulls his phone from his pocket. "It's only seven. We've got an hour of light."

"Yep." Owen's finger redirects to Cooper. "And then we'll hit Twigs."

"The martini bar?" Levi says, unimpressed—clearly he wasn't a part of the planning committee.

"They serve food too. We'll feed you, we promise," Cooper says, slapping our oldest brother on the back. He may be the youngest, and Levi may be the most bearish, but Coop has never been afraid of our big brother.

This is my bachelor party? Apparently, my expression speaks for me.

"Yep, kinda lame," Levi agrees.

"I had no time to plan," Owen complains.

Cooper is the first to laugh. "Come on, Miles. Get your shoes on. I gotta hear how you met Lane Jonas."

But I don't want to talk about that—those are lies that I don't want to tell. "We already told you. The gallery," I say.

"Yeah, but how does a woman like that decide to talk to a guy like you?" Coop laughs. "I mean, she's Lane *Freaking* Jonas."

"Can we just play pickleball?" I stand and grab my shoes in the corner. "To me, she's just Delaney. I don't really think about the fame part. I'd rather not let it get to my head."

"You married the girl after how long?" Levi says. "I'm not sure there's a lot going on in your head."

"He's smarter than me," Owen says. "Better to jump at the chance to be with the person you love than wait around forever."

I ignore my brothers' bickering and head back to my loft to

change. It takes me an entire two minutes to get ready for our night out. Joggers and shoes on, I open the door to find Coop in a headlock, courtesy of Levi.

"Hey." Coop smiles from his throw, red-faced position. "Ready to go?"

We head out, playing and talking like this is any other night until the sun sets and most of our light is gone before heading off to Twigs.

Before anyone can ask me a question about Delaney, I ask Coop about himself. That'll take up time. "So, Coop, only two more years before the bar exam and you're official. Do you think you'll come home?"

"Home?" He scrunches up his face. We all know Mom is banking on our little brother coming home to practice law. "I don't know. There's a big wide world out there, Miles."

"That's true."

"You don't want to take over for old man Holmes? Mom is planning on it." Levi twists around in Owen's Buick to glare at Cooper smashed between me and Jude. The only person Levi might want to protect more than Meredith is our mother.

"Mom knows it's not a done deal," Cooper says. "I'm twenty-four, Levi. Don't make me decide on forever right now, okay?"

Levi faces forward and the air is thick with Bailey men's nerves and aggression.

"So," I say, ready to ease the tension, "my wife's pretty hot, eh?"

Cooper cracks a grin and Owen belts out a laugh from up front.

32

DELANEY

"How often do you get recognized?" Annie asks me.

"Um." I slide onto the chair in the private back room of this bar and grill. "I don't know. Often." We had more than a handful of people stop us at the bowling alley, but thankfully no photographers.

"That's why we booked this back room," Meredith tells me. Her pink dress hits her mid-thigh and is super cute—I need to ask her where she got it.

I look from Meredith to Miles' sister. "Thanks."

"Yeah. We want you completely comfortable," Coco says, leaning her body closer to me. The table is a barrier, though; as she sits across from me, she doesn't make it far. Annie sits next to her and Meredith next to me.

I don't tell them that I'm never completely comfortable. It's like a job hazard. But out with my fake husband's family for a night of fun—yeah, *so not* comfortable.

Our waiter enters the back room, and his grin is too wide for his face. "Well, *hello*, ladies."

Annie smiles up at him. "Married," she says, holding up one hand. "Married." She points to Coco. "Engaged." She points to

Meredith. "And married." She lets out a sigh as she points in my direction. "Don't spend too much time on us unless it's to refill our drinks. Okay?"

"Holy bologna, Annie," Coco says, eyes wide, but she's trying not to laugh.

Annie holds up both hands. "Just making this picture perfectly clear for him."

Our server, Kevin, clears his throat and nods. "Can I take a drink order?"

I chuckle despite my discomfort. These girls are funny. And in another life, we would have been friends.

But then, why not in this life? I'm not running off on tour at the moment. My bandmate, Astrid doesn't have a minute-by-minute schedule planned out for The Judys. Ash isn't even here to coach me on my next PR move. I might actually be able to take a hot minute and make a friend.

We give the man our drink order and send him off, tail between his legs. Annie does not mess around.

"Tell me this," Coco says. "What is the first thing you noticed about Miles?"

"Ah." I think back to when I first saw him talking to Lars. "His passion. Even from afar, his passion for his work was evident. And then—" I clear my throat, feeling like it's breaking all the rules to talk about or even to think this. "His eyes. I've never seen eyes like his before. Hazel and green and shining, like glass."

Coco smiles. "Miles does have nice eyes. They're like Lucy's." She beams as if she loves that she sees her mother every time she looks at her brother. Then again, Lucy is a sweetheart; maybe she does love this.

"Yeah, but have you seen Owen's eyes—"

Coco raises her brows. "*Newlyweds.* You'd think she'd be over his eyes by now; she's been looking at them for most of her life."

Meredith chuckles. "Levi's eyes are like Hershey's kisses."

MILES BAILEY GETS DOWN ON ONE KNEE

They are a bunch of lovesick puppies—all three of them. It makes me laugh. "You're all so whipped," I say.

"We aren't the only ones." Annie laughs right along with me. "We saw that kiss back at the loft. You're fairly whipped yourself!"

Except that I'm not. Yes—it was one hot potato kiss. I can only imagine the heat level had we actually been alone—you know, without Miles' family and my mother watching. But whipped? *Nope.* I'm pretty sure you have to know a guy longer than a week for feelings to be determined as whipped.

I'm right, logic says I am. Yet my nerves are exploding inside like a mini firework show.

I can't be crushing on my not-so-real husband. That'll never do. I made him promise not to fall for me.

"I've never seen Miles kiss anyone," Coco says.

"He had a girlfriend once back in high school." Annie makes a face. "It didn't last long; she wasn't right for him. She kept trying to change him." She scrunches her face disapprovingly, making me like her all the more. Miles does not need to change —for anyone.

"Has he dated anyone since you met?" Meredith asks Coco.

Coco shakes her head. "No." She glances at me, offering a smile. "Not that I knew about, anyway."

"*Wait.*"

Coco is the sister. Annie is Owen's wife. Owen is the brother... and Coco is the sister. I'm sure of it. I do not have this mixed up.

The women stop talking and look over at me.

"Sorry." I clear my throat. "Ah—confused."

"Wait." Meredith's nose wrinkles. "You don't know about Coco?" Annie tilts her head and they're all looking at me like I'm the crazy one. I'm not. It's not me! It's *them.* They're the crazies. I've got my facts straight!

"Miles didn't tell you?" Coco says.

I swallow. "You know, our romance really has been a *whirlwind*. We still have a lot to learn about the other." It's true and false all at the same time. I like it. I make a mental note, reminding myself to inform Miles of my brilliance.

"Oh." Meredith's lips part in a grin. They all seem appeased by my answer.

Coco sits straighter, her eyes on me. "I was adopted as a baby. I just found my biological family three years ago. So"—she shrugs—"Annie's actually known Miles longer than I have."

Well, I hadn't expected that. *"Shut up."* I slap my hand onto the table just as our waiter makes his way over with our drinks.

My scene makes him do a double take. He stops, not serving any of us. "Hey, I recognize you," he says, shaking a finger at me.

Annie stands and points at each of us in turn. "Married, married, married, engaged. You *don't* recognize her. Go away."

He blinks, afraid of the little redhead. He doesn't even serve us; he just sets the tray down, eyes wide, and off he goes.

"That was vicious. I might love you," I tell her. Who needs a bodyguard when Annie's around?

Meredith sighs. "I wanted to order." As if on cue, her stomach growls.

"One of us could go out to the main restaurant and order for all of us," Annie suggests. "That might be better for Lane, anyhow."

"Yes! Me! I'll go," Meredith says, raising her hand. We all give her our orders, and then she's out the door, heading to the main area of the bar and grill.

"Okay," I say, turning back to Coco. "Tell me more."

And she does. She's very open about being adopted. About Lucy sending Jude to go find her. About not wanting to meet the family at first. And about feeling nothing but love and gratitude now.

"Maybe I was adopted," I say. "Maybe I have secret parents out there who... aren't mine."

"You don't get along with your family?" Coco asks.

"Ah, I mostly don't get along with my mom. And my dad is... not exactly dependable." I swallow; I don't say those things out loud often. Talking to the press, you learn to hide all those skeletons away, making everything look hunky-dory. I rarely share about my rocky relationship with my mother. Or my trust issues when it comes to my father. "My grandma is wonderful. And my sister and I get along well even though we're eight years apart. Yeah—I don't need the whole adopted family, just the new mom."

Coco smirks, and I'm glad she knows I'm not mocking her situation in any way. "Well, in a way, you do have a new mom. *Lucy*. And she's the best."

Annie nods. "She really is. Those Bailey boys are so lucky."

I plaster on a smile, all the while singing in my head, *"No attachments, no attachments."* I can't get attached to Lucy Bailey just to leave Miles a year from now. What good would that do?

"We're lucky too," Coco says, reaching out and placing her hand on top of mine.

"Right? Who knew Lane Jonas would become our new sister. Oh man, Kayla flipped when I told her." Annie grabs her drink from the tray and sips from the fancy glass. "That's my actual sister," she tells me.

But I'm stuck on—*new sister*? I blink down at Coco's hand over mine. These women have shown me more acceptance and love than Serena did after six years with The Judys. Or after twenty-seven years of being Claire's daughter.

My eyes sting—*new sister*—but I suck those ridiculous things back into my head because *no attachments!* *Holy bologna*, these Baileys!

Meredith wanders back, arms swinging at her sides like she's discovered gold. "Apps are ordered, but I might have been followed."

"Ah, snap," I mutter. I pull out my phone, Ash is too far away, and no bodyguards on duty... Who needs them? I've got Miles. He's the only one I need.

But then—broad, curly, and handsome pokes its way around Meredith.

Miles.

33

DELANEY

*C*oco stands, hands on hips. "You're crashing?"

Jude cups a hand to his wife's cheek. "Not crashing. *Eating*. We were eating when Meredith found us."

"How'd you guys get a room back here?" Miles asks, peering around the table and four chairs.

"If you slip the host fifty bucks, you get a little privacy," Annie says, lifting one shoulder, her eyes on Owen.

I am surrounded by a bunch of yuppies in love and it's starting to suffocate me. We are outnumbered!

"Delaney!" Miles' youngest brother beams. *Wowza*, that kid is handsome. His long arms stretch out wide, and I am pulled into a giant Cooper bear hug.

"Coop." Miles groans.

Coco smacks Cooper's arm. "Stop suffocating her."

"I'm welcoming her," Cooper says, though all their voices are a little muffled as the kid is legit smothering me.

He lets go and I can breathe once more.

"I'll ask for more chairs!" Annie disappears behind the door, and she's back with a frowning Kevin.

Our waiter isn't shy about his annoyance. "What happened

to married, married, married, engaged?" he says, pointing to each of us as Annie did before.

Annie tilts her head, grinning, so proud of her cleverness. "Husband, husband, husband, fiancé," she says, pointing to each man. She pauses when she gets to Coop. "And, ah, brother."

"Single!" Cooper says. "And ready to mingle. Feel free to share that with any ladies you might serve tonight, Kev."

Kevin might be a foot shorter than Cooper and half his size, but he looks at him like he could possibly take him down. He will not be telling any single woman that Cooper is back here and ready to mingle. Still, he says, "I'll be sure to do that."

We spend the next two hours eating, talking, and laughing. I watch Annie, Coco, and Meredith. I even mimic them from time to time. Annie grabs Owen by the chin once and I attempt the same action, dabbing some nonexistent sauce from Miles' lip. Coco slips her fingers through Jude's on the tabletop and I do the same to Miles.

Levi has an arm around Meredith at all times and I sort of want to elbow Miles and tell him to step up his game.

"So you're on this show, looking for a husband, and then suddenly you meet my brother." Cooper pops another French fry into his mouth—Levi's French fry. His are long gone.

"Did you watch *Celebrity Wife?*" Meredith asks him.

"Oh yeah. Didn't miss an episode." Cooper runs a hand through his dark blonde hair.

"You're kidding," Levi grumbles. "You watch that junk?"

Meredith pinches Levi's side—we all see it, it's no secret. He jumps but doesn't call her out.

"*Show*. I meant *show*." His lips fold in on one another. "Sorry," he mutters to me.

"I call it junk too," I say with a sardonic smile. "No worries."

Cooper just laughs at our exchange, then goes on like we haven't just called something he watched every episode of *junk*. "Delta Zeta watched it every single Thursday and I was the only guy invited." His mouth spreads into an ear to ear Bailey grin.

Coco and Annie glance at one another. Annie's eyes roll back, but Meredith giggles. "Pretty smart," she says.

"Thanks, Mer. It *was* smart. I got multiple dates out of the deal—I mean, until the ladies realized multiple dates were happening and then I got uninvited, but by then I was invested. I finished it out with some girls in my apartment building."

"Are you in law school or at a constant frat party?" Levi asks him.

"Hey, I work my butt off ninety-five percent of the time."

"So, you make that remaining five percent really count, huh?" I ask.

"Exactly. Lane gets it." Cooper nods. "So, how did this happen?" He waggles a finger between his brother and me.

Miles is quiet—too quiet. I opt for mostly true. "The show wasn't my idea or my plan. My manager thought it would help boost this newish image I'm going for—"

"New image?" Cooper reaches for another one of Levi's fries. Levi flicks him on the wrist, but Coop doesn't seem to notice.

"Yeah. I'm officially no longer a Judy." I swallow—it's still a strange thing to say.

Annie gasps, but Coco doesn't look surprised. Miles must have told her. "No more music?" Annie asks. She's practically sitting in Owen's lap. Do those two share a hip or something?

I clear my throat and look away. "Of course, music. I can't quit music. I just want to go in a different direction. The Judys didn't want to come, and I never should have expected them to—" It's a realization that hits me as I sit here explaining myself. "So, with the recent rejection in my life, my manager thought some good PR, some acceptance"—I lift my brow—"some very public romance would help. Only I wasn't into it. I wasn't ready. In the end, it all blew up in my face and only made things worse—my career is at an official all-time low."

"I don't know. That show may have still helped your image—more than you realize. I know a lot of people who respect your honesty," Coco says.

I appreciate her grace. But most people don't see it that way. They see my *dishonesty* from the very start. I didn't want to be there. I never truly embraced the concept, and now that everyone is looking back, that's fairly clear.

"So then—" Cooper looks at Miles beside me. "What happened?"

"Miles?" I turn my head and peer at my stupidly cute husband. "Miles wasn't planned. Miles wasn't calculated. Miles was completely unexpected."

As if on cue, he presses a kiss to my forehead, sending small shoots of electricity throughout my limbs and jarring memory sparks to my lips. Yep, they recall Miles' kiss, very well.

Oh, Miles.

Quiet but deadly Miles.

34

MILES

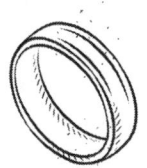

It's late when we get back to the loft. But Delaney isn't tired... and since there are no other rooms up here, I'm apparently not tired either.

"We could play poker," she says, kneeling on my bed, her hair in that big bun on top of her head. Her pajama shorts hit her mid-thigh, and I'm doing my best to be a gentleman. While I'm not looking for a relationship, I'm also not blind.

"Sure. Okay." I pull a pack of playing cards from my top dresser drawer.

"Cards in the sock drawer. I like your style, Bailey."

"It's the only place for them, *Jones*." I toss her the deck and tug off my T-shirt, ready to put on one that doesn't smell like the bar and grill we spent three hours in. I slip the clean shirt over my head in time to see Delaney watching me. She's staring.

I tug my shirt down—I'm not used to an audience. I probably should have changed in the bathroom.

"Miles Bailey, you've got hidden abs?"

I scoff. "I don't exactly hide them. I just don't walk around shirtless all day."

"Hm." The right edge of her mouth curls upward. "Too bad."

My cheeks warm with a blush, one that only Delaney can produce. I'm not normally a blushing school kid—unless I'm near my wife, that is.

"Okay," she says, sliding the cards from their case and shuffling. "Texas Hold'em or Five-card draw?"

I sit on the bed across from her. "Texas Hold'em."

"What are you betting?" She shuffles and deals, her eyes drawing up to mine with the question.

"Ah—" I shake my head. "I don't own any chips."

"We don't need chips. My dad taught me to play, and I lost my favorite guitar pick to him. You can bet anything. But be wise." She lifts one brow. "You *do* have to bet."

My brows furrow a little. "What are you betting?"

"I've got twenty-two dollars in cash and a package of gummy bears."

"You mean you aren't betting that?" I point to the rainbow charm around her neck.

"This? No way! This necklace is my lucky charm, Miles Bailey. It doesn't leave my neck."

I laugh, happy that I can rile her up every now and then. "Wait a second—the package of gummy bears I bought you earlier today? You're betting that?"

"Only one gummy at a time." She lifts one shoulder. "They're mine."

I grab Alice's bag of M&Ms and open them up. I pay my ante and she offers hers, starting with dollar bills rather than gummy bears.

I peek down at my two of diamonds and six of clubs. "Your dad really took your guitar pick?"

"Oh yeah. Robert Jones does not mess around when it comes to cards. It doesn't matter if you're an eight-year-old girl."

She ups the bet and I toss in three more M&Ms.

"When did you first start playing?"

"The guitar or poker?" She grins.

"Guitar," I say, though I'm sure she knew what I meant. I'm learning that my wife likes to tease.

"Dad won my first guitar at one of his gambling nights. Mom was so mad." My eyes go wide. "In fact, I'm not sure I would have picked the thing up except that it really ticked her off." She breathes out a small laugh. "What was the big deal? It was a guitar. I couldn't figure out why she cared so much. So, I watched YouTube and started playing. I quickly fell in love—I no longer needed the motivation of annoying my mother. I moved on to the bass a couple years later. I fell in love with Bill Lee."

"Who?"

"He's a bass player. Danny Thompson made me love folk, though." She stares off, one card in her hand, ready to flip. A small, pleasant sigh escapes her with the memory before she throws down the next card—queen of hearts. "Danny plays bass too."

"So, you've always liked folk?"

"Always," she says. She lays out another card—jack of hearts. "When did you start painting?"

"I'll raise by two," I say, tossing in my M&Ms, bluffing all the way. "I don't remember not painting. Mom said I used to paint with my baby food as a toddler in my high chair."

She smiles, her full lips parting so sweetly. Lips that are easy to recall the sensation of. "I believe that," she says.

We play and talk until midnight, until my king-size bag of candy is empty and Delaney has eaten half her package of gummy bears.

She's won it all. I am candy-less. I have to go to bed before I end up gambling away something I'll regret.

35

DELANEY

It won't be long now before Miles' building will be ready. I've spent days fibbing, telling him what a jerk Lars is—that we aren't allowed back in the studio yet—when I'm actually remodeling the place. Hey, he already dislikes Lars, so what's the harm?

My husband and I have fallen into a fairly decent routine. He paints. I write and strum my guitar. He's in one room, I'm in the other. We eat together. We sleep in the same bed—and I am so not blind to him hugging the edge of that bed to keep from touching me.

I've gotten two, maybe three, more forehead kisses.

Okay—it's three. I might be counting. I can't help it. Miles Bailey can kiss—and yet he insists on sending all that love to my *forehead*. Which ironically makes me swoon each and every time.

I'm checking on an email from the painter—they should be done with Miles' studio tomorrow—when a text comes through.

Coco: I realized we never talked about your

reception last week.

"Miles," I call from my seat on his couch.

He appears in the doorway, barefoot and broad, making my heart flutter like butterfly wings. It's a simple human reaction, completely natural—nothing more.

No crushing on your husband, Delaney!

"Yeah?" He leans against the open doorway.

"Did you give your sister my phone number?"

"Yeah. Is that a problem?" He's in glasses today and somehow four eyes make the man even sexier than two. How is he still single?

Oh, wait. That's right. *He's not.*

I press my lips together. "I don't normally give it out. That's all."

"I'm sorry. It's my sister. You're her sister-in-law. I thought it might be weird if I didn't share it when she asked."

"No, you're right. It would be." I turn back to my phone and away from Miles' smoldering sorry eyes. Since when does Miles smolder?

I shove away the thought and respond to Coco.

> **Me:** We can count the other night—the bar and grill. Or even Sunday dinner. Your mom did bake a cake.
>
> **Coco:** We can't count the bar. Ew. Besides, Mom wasn't there. And that cake was for Cooper. She makes it for him every time he comes to visit.
>
> **Coco:** And what about your family?

"She's asking about my family and the reception," I say, though Miles has gone back to his room.

He wanders in and sits next to me on the couch. "That

sounds like a normal question to me." But he's timid, looking at me like he knows it isn't normal for me but not really knowing at the same time.

"My family won't come, Miles." But that isn't completely true. They might. But I don't want them to. This place feels like a sanctuary. All of that would go away with Claire Jones' presence. I'd love to see Eryn and Grandma, but bringing them here, so far away, for a reception that's a lie... I don't want that. I can't do that. "I don't want them to come."

I'm not sure what I look like, but Miles voluntarily cups a hand to my cheek, forcing eye contact with me. "They won't come, or you don't want them to come? Those aren't the same thing, Laney."

I melt a little. *Laney.* Is it weird that Miles calling me by the same nickname as my Grandma turns me on a little? It is—I know it is, but I can't turn off the firework show inside of me.

"Right." I close my eyes and breathe like Dr. Baker taught me to.

The minute I could afford therapy—I got it. It saved me from my mother's ruthless judgements. I remember Dr. Baker's counsel—*she's one person, not the world, breathe.*

Blinking, I flick my gaze up to Miles' hazel eyes and speak. "I don't want them to come here."

"Okay. Can you elaborate?"

"I've told you—my mother is difficult. This place—" I peer around Miles' tiny home, at the small TV in front of us, the two-burner hot plate on his small kitchen counter, the door to his miniature bathroom. "It's not difficult. It's peaceful." I'm not sure I'm making any sense. "I'm not ready to lose that."

Miles dips his head, smiling at me as if maybe we're supposed to be married. Maybe this is real and not a stunt. Maybe he loves me, he's here for me, and he'll help me. *Always.*

It's a fantasy.

One that isn't even mine—*usually.*

But in this moment, it's nice to think about Miles saving me from all the anxiety that Mom creates. I've never had a savior before.

"Hey," he says, being *that* man. "You don't have to lose that. Ever. If ease goes away with an invitation to her, then that invite is getting lost in the mail. She *isn't* invited."

I nod, small, quick bobs. "Okay."

"Is she—" he says, then stalls. "I mean, she's that bad?"

"You talked to her." But I can see he still doesn't get it. To Miles, a mother is the equivalent of love. And I'm so, so glad that's how it is for him. I sit up straighter, keep eye contact with the man, and explain. "Miles, I have an extremely healthy self-esteem. I know my worth. I have fought for my worth. I'm far from perfect, but I have talent, and I'm trying. I want to leave my mark on the world and be a good person. But when my mother walks into the room, all that worth transfers into the toilet. She convinces me that I'm no better than the fleas that covet her garbage."

One hand cups my cheek, his thumb tracing below my left eye. "You don't believe that."

I huff out a deep, tired breath. "No, I don't. But she makes me fight for my self-worth every second we're together."

Miles lifts my phone from my grasp and begins to type.

I don't object; I simply watch as he texts back his sister as me:

> My family won't be coming. No matter the day or time. Miles won't allow it.

Three little bubbles bounce on my screen, but no message from Coco comes through. All at once, his cell back in the studio room begins to ring.

He stands, winks down at me, and then, as if he can't help himself, leans in and presses a gentle kiss to my head.

36

MILES

*M*y hour-long lesson with Walt is canceled the minute I arrive. The poor guy is sick. So, not two minutes there, I'm back in my Toyota, driving home, with Owen on speakerphone. My mind is running—Walt, work, online shop, and Delaney. Always Delaney.

I stay in the safe zone and talk about the newest confusion in my life. "I don't get it," I say. "My little online shop has had zero to two customers a month for the past year—and this week I've sold out of everything I have. I even have people asking for prints of originals. They're willing to pay me for a copy."

"Wow. What's new?" Owen says. I'm stealing his prep period.

"I don't know."

He goes silent, and then— "You don't?"

"No." I really don't. I haven't tried any new tactics. "My Instagram has blown up. I have no idea why. I post maybe once a week. I wouldn't even have realized it, except that Delaney made me look up a video."

"Delaney," he says, his tone urging, as if he's feeding me a clue.

I move on, my mind skipping to its next worry. "Speaking of—she thought she was going to have an hour or two without me, but Walt's sick. No lessons today. Do you think I should go find something to do? Give her some time."

"Time for what?" This answer comes quickly. My brother with a heart of gold thinks I've gone crazy.

"I don't know. To be alone," I say, trying to explain, to help him see that I'm not crazy. In fact, I have a legit reason for thinking twice.

There's a pause on my brother's end. "I don't know, man. Annie and I are pretty happy being together. I mean, you've been working, right? You haven't stopped just because she moved in?"

"We both work. I just—" I let the word trail off. I'm asking Owen—my newlywed, madly-in-love brother—about giving my wife space. Of course, this sounds like a dumb question to him. "You're right. It'll be a great surprise."

And while Delaney and I get along—and I've strangely enjoyed having her around all of the time—I know she's used to some alone time. And space. My place doesn't have a lot of that. She might be missing it. We work in separate rooms, but we're never truly alone.

And yet, if I'm being honest—I feel kind of excited at the thought of an extra hour with her. One that doesn't involve me working or sleeping or trying my best not to touch her. Well—I might have to work on that last one. She is a very difficult woman not to touch.

She's also interesting and fun to talk to. She's down-to-earth and passionate.

"Miles? You still there?"

"I am. Yeah. Sorry—still getting used to married life, I think."

Owen laughs. "Go home. She'll be happy to see you."

And while Delaney and I aren't Owen and Annie, I head for home. It's what I want to do.

"Also—dude, your wife is a rock star. People have now googled *you*. They know your name."

"Uh—"

"Your sales, Miles. Your work is getting out there. It's being seen by new eyes. And apparently, they like what they see."

I'm still thinking about Owen's words minutes after we've hung up. Why hadn't I ever considered that? I appreciate the way Owen suggested that these new buyers are simply finding my work for the first time and liking it. But I can't help but wonder if it's that—or if it's Delaney. They like her, and by association, they like me.

My mood has dimmed with the idea. I don't want my work to be revered due to who I'm married to. I want my work to be appreciated because of the time, effort, and emotion put into it.

I trudge up the stairs to my place, my steps louder and heavier with my sour mood. I reach the landing and set my hand on the doorknob. Groaning, I knock my head to the door. I never foresaw this problem—being successful because of Delaney. Anyone else would be happy, grateful even. But somehow this doesn't feel like success to me.

The door is locked—which isn't the norm. But then, maybe Delaney locked it. Or maybe she went out.

I sigh. I don't have a key on me—I rarely do.

I fiddle with the handle, then knock. But Delaney doesn't answer and no noise sounds from the other side. She must have gone out. I jimmy the handle, using my pocket knife to wiggle the lock mechanism. It clicks, making it way too easy to break into my place. If my house weren't inside of a locked-up gallery at night, I'd be nervous.

I cross the threshold, my head and heart in defeat mode. I've sold all these paintings—but did they want me, or did they want Lane Jonas' husband?

One more step and then—I'm hit. *Scorching, searing, blistering pain hits me like a hammer.*

My worries over my work are gone. I'm being attacked—in my own home. "Wha—" I bellow with the never-ending burn. My eyes, my throat, my nose—pain explodes all over my face.

I squint and jerk my head away from the attack, covering my eyes and trying to make sense of what is happening.

"Miles?" Delaney says, her voice small as a bird. "I—I didn't know. I thought you were— I thought someone was trying to break in and—"

It hits me all at once. Wasps haven't infested my house with the intent to attack me. Nope. "You pepper sprayed me?" I say through the throb and the flame.

I'm an idiot.

And prideful.

I've been so busy worrying about idiotic things, I didn't even think to text her or alert her that I'd be home early. After our scare last week—of course she's on edge.

I move two feet forward, my hands at my eyes, blind, but I need to get to a sink. I need water. I walk right into a standing easel.

"Crap. I'm sorry. I'm so sorry!" she cries. Her soft hands find mine and pull my fingers from their protecting position at my head. I'm guessing she isn't going to spray me again, so I let her. "Come on," she says. "I'll help you."

She leads me along, her hands in mine, and while I can't see, I feel the warmth of her body near mine.

"Okay, going through the doorway," she says, and on instinct, I duck.

I've lived in this for loft three years; I know I don't need to duck to get inside. But it's a defensive reaction.

"A few more steps and we're at the couch."

"Nice aim," I tell her, feeling for the couch arm and sitting myself down.

"I'm sorry, Miles," she says again.

I breathe out a low, painful chuckle. "I know."

I feel her sit next to me, and while I try not to be a total baby in front of my wife, this hurts—a lot. I hiss with the pain and bring my hand back up to my eyes.

"No, don't rub them," she says, pulling my hand down. "I'm googling what to do. The first thing it says is to not rub your eyes."

"And then?" I'm ready to do it. I cram my eyes tighter, but it only makes them burn more. *Gah*—this stuff is in my mouth and throat. I'm really wishing I'd sprayed Delaney's intruder with this junk rather than punch him. My hand is still healing from that hit. He deserved this pain much more than I do.

"We need to wash your face and rinse your eyes if we can. Come on." With her hands back in mine, she leads me past the couch and into the bathroom.

My loft is tiny—I should be able to get around blind without killing myself—but I've bumped into multiple things, and with Delaney's hands snug in mine, I let her lead.

The bathroom is tight, though. Unless she's willing to step into the shower, she's going to be stepping on my toes.

"Let me see if I can do it." I attempt to open my eyes to see myself, but I can't.

"Stop that," she says, pulling my hands away from my face again.

"I just—" My chest bumps hers, and in her stumble, a chuckle leaves her lips. "You think this is funny?" I say. "I thought you were sorry."

"I *am* sorry." And yet, she laughs—again. "I'm so sorry," she says, and while it sounds like a whimper, I know what it is—it's Delaney trying very hard not to laugh at me. "It's just when you tried to look in that pathetic excuse of a mirror just now—"

"Now you're making fun of me?" I'm not really offended. In fact, what I am is thoroughly distracted.

"Shush. Let me help you already, okay?" She sets a hand on

my back. "Bend down a bit; I'm going to splash water on your face."

I bend, hear the rushing of running water, and then a splash of cool water rinses over my eyes and nose. There's an instant relief, only to have the boiling sensation start up again.

"I'm happy you know how to use that thing."

"I mean, it's pointing and spraying. It's not that—"

I groan with another onset of stinging pain.

"Never mind—" she spats. "Sorry."

I move my hands over Delaney's. "I can do this," I tell her, feeling my way to the faucet and cupping my hands beneath the water. I splash water over my face again and again, rinsing off the sting only to have it come right back.

I cup a handful and gulp down the cold liquid, spreading the sting down my throat, though it's fading.

Delaney's warm presence stays right next to me, with an occasional caress over my back. If I weren't in so much pain, I'd laugh. It's ironic that in the short time I've known this woman, I've hurt my hand and my eyes—two things that are pretty vital to my job—all while selling more pieces than ever before.

After drowning myself over and over again, the stinging in my eyes begins to fade. I might even be able to open my eyes. I pause and breathe, then stand up straight.

"Okay, where's my couch?"

Delaney laces her fingers through mine and once again walks me to the couch. Her hands slide up to my shoulders. "All right, sit. Need a drink?"

"I don't have a single beer. I don't drink." I laugh without humor. The irony. "Man, I could use a beer."

"Should I run out—"

"No. Don't go." I feel around for her hand, finding her leg, then her stomach, before she slips her fingers through mine. "Water will be great," I say.

"Water. Got it." She pulls herself away from me and I hear her bustle into the kitchen.

Soon, she's pressing a cool, hard glass into my palm.

I sip, then press the thing to my face.

She rubs my shoulder. "Ooo, I'll get you a cold compress too."

I don't argue with her. I chug the water she gave me, then lay my head back against the couch cushion, pressing the cold glass to my forehead while I wait for her.

Her fingers brush mine as she takes the glass from my hands and lays a cold washcloth over my eyes and head.

"Miles, I'm so sorry."

"Please stop apologizing," I say. "I should have told you I was coming home. If someone ever tries to jimmy the lock on that door and enter unannounced, please spray the crap out of them with pepper spray. You did nothing wrong."

"I should have looked."

"You shouldn't have," I say.

"I should have answered when you knocked."

"Nope." I blindly look for her with my hand. I find her fingers and press her palm to my lips. "You did exactly what you should have. Now we just need to get you into karate so next time you can spray, then kick."

A muffled laugh sounds from her lips. "Oh, Miles."

"No more apologies," I say, blinking my eyes and squinting them open to try and see her. She must be sitting on her knees on this couch because I can make out her smile, peering evenly over at me. Her eyes crease through my blurred vision. She *is* sorry. But I can also tell she finds something humorous.

My eyes bite in pain, but at least I can see—sort of. It's getting better by the minute.

Delaney scoops a strand of hair behind her ear, wiggling until she's two inches closer to me, and peering up.

"I'm a lot of trouble," she says.

"You're not," I lie. She's very much *trouble*. Apparently, I like trouble.

"I'm glad you're back." Her hands find mine.

"Me too."

Loosening her grip on my fingers, her right hand trails up my arm until it reaches the back of my neck. Long fingers swoop through the curls at the back of my neck, sending small shivers down my spine.

"Miles, why are you so good?"

"I'm—" I'm not sure how to answer that. I'm not that great. I'm normal. But then, I don't know that Delaney's had a lot of normal in her life.

Maybe she doesn't want an answer; she doesn't press. Her fingers tickle my skin on either side of my neck. And though my vision isn't perfect in this moment, I see, feel, and hear as she moves until her breaths, sweet and hot, warm my cheeks. She inches ever closer... until her lips are a centimeter away from my own. "Miles," she whispers before closing the gap, her lips colliding with mine.

Blindly, I find her hips with my fingers and hold her next to me. Kissing her back, I follow her lead. Her lips are the guide, and I am here to ensue. I match her desire and attempt to ignore the burn and throb that refuses to completely disappear. She moves, and I move with her—heat and desire coursing between us. Only—*a lot* of heat. A whole lot of heat in my eyes. And unfortunately, I'm human and hurting, all while trying to enjoy the best kiss of my life.

I grunt—on accident—and not the sexy kind. Nope, this is the kind of grunt that says, *"Hey, remember? You sprayed me with pepper spray less than an hour ago. And sure, my face is melting, but I'm more than willing to fight through the pain to keep kissing you."*

Delaney freezes with my pathetic moan.

Her hands slide down to my chest. She pushes herself back. "Well, that was dumb," she mutters, her head falling forward and knocking into my chest. I'm not sure if she's talking to me or herself. She lifts her head and, with one finger, taps my chest. "Ah, I'm gonna go out and get you that beer. You wanted one, right? I'll grab it and maybe a meatball sub or some jerky... some kind of meat. You like meat, right?" Her body scurries up while she rambles a mile a minute.

Half blind, I reach out, but she's too fast and I'm too blurred. If the girl ever has to use her pepper spray on an attacker, I think it will do the job.

I know I have no chance of catching her.

37

DELANEY

"Holy spitballs, Delaney Sage. Are you an idiot? You can't go falling for your husband. Stupid. Stupid. Stu—" I suck in a breath, gasping as I run smack into Lars Simon.

"Ms. Jonas." He smiles, and it somehow reminds me of a snake. I expect a long, split tongue to come slithering out of his mouth any second. "How's the building? I'm assuming you've pleased your..." His nose wrinkles and his eyes widen. "Husband?"

I clear my throat. "Ah, yeah. I have. Thanks. It's in renovations now." I'm saying too much, but my nerves are shot, and they've taken with them my good judgment. I cram my eyes closed and clear my head. "Only Miles doesn't know about the renovations. It's a surprise, and I'd appreciate your silence," I say as a warning, not a request. Something I learned from my mother years ago.

"And I'm assuming you're referring to me paying you to keep quiet about where I've been sleeping at night. Yes, I am pleased."

At least we haven't had any photographers near the loft. "Thanks."

"Absolutely," he says, and I picture the single word slithering out of a snake's jaws.

I peer around the room once, not caring about this man or what he thinks as long as he keeps quiet. "Do you have any more of Miles' work down here?"

He smirks. "One."

"Perfect. Can you have it mailed to this address?" I pull a notepad from my purse and write down my grandmother's address.

"You don't want to see it? It's pathetically predictable."

It's Miles. It's not pathetic. It'll be perfect. "You can bill the same account as the last piece," I say, ignoring that he ever opened his mouth, let alone spoke.

Lars takes the note from my hand and reads Grandma's name. "Judy Jones?"

"Yes, my grandmother."

"How nice for Miles to finally be a success—that is, as long as his wife is purchasing all of his work."

I am anxious. My nerves are shot, and I think I kissed a little pepper spray down my throat. There's no stopping what is about to happen. I plant both hands on my hips. "Excuse me, you do get a commission from this sale, correct?" All at once, I am Julia Roberts in *Pretty Woman*—without all that messy prostitute business. I clamp my jaws shut, stopping myself from yelling. *Big mistake! Huge!* Nope, it's not time for that—yet.

Lars clears his throat without bothering to answer the question.

"If you'd rather, I can always ask Miles to paint something specific for her." That would take a while and I'd like to send her something now. But I don't mind taking the opportunity to put Lars in his place.

"No need," he says. "The piece is yours."

How has Miles put up with this joker for so long? "By the way, please don't diminish what my husband does." My hands are fists at my sides. And then I say *it*. I become Julia. "That would be a *big* mistake! His heart and soul go into his work, and just because you're too small-minded to understand it doesn't mean he isn't brilliant. So, he isn't known around the world *yet*. He will be. Wouldn't you rather be known as the man who gave him a chance rather than what you are—the imbecile holding him back?"

Lars' shoulders push back and his neck straightens, long and thin. His lips purse into a tight line, but he says nothing.

I am ready to storm off—ready for a Julia Roberts grand exit—when I remember. "Ooo, can you tell me where to get beer and meatballs?"

38

MILES

I don't bring up the fact that she kissed me and neither does she. The next day Delaney acts as if nothing happened. As if we're just two people—sort of friends, who happen to be married.

Until—

"I have something to show you."

We've shown each other a lot of us in the past two weeks. I've learned a lot about Delaney, and I think it's rare for either of us to open up the way we have.

I can't deny her this. Not that I want to. But especially not when she's been so vulnerable with me.

I wonder if I could deny her anything.

Of course I could.

What a ridiculous question.

"Yeah, anything," I say, regretting my word choice instantly. I just told myself *anything* was not on the menu. Man, when Delaney asked me to do this with the one stipulation being that I do not fall in love with her, I never dreamed it would be this difficult.

I swallow and stir cream into my coffee, staring deep into the dark pit of that mug.

"Great. Get ready and we'll head out."

"Great." But I'm unsure if any of this is great. I'm having feelings I'm not allowed to have.

And yet, I'm showered and ready to go in less than fifteen minutes. Reaching for my keys, I have one eye on Delaney. Her hair is pulled to the side in a long braid over one shoulder, just like the day I met her. Her eyes are bright and excited.

Something is definitely up.

"You won't need those," she says. "We're walking."

I follow her down the stairs, into the gallery, and out the front door. My building sits waiting for me, waiting for all the changes I have planned. Waiting for Lars to give it up. I'm sure I'm the reason he's causing Delaney so much trouble with her cash purchase.

"Ready?"

"For?" I laugh. "I have no idea what we're doing."

Her lips pucker and screw over to the side. "Come on." She laces her fingers through mine, and we walk out into the warm spring sunshine.

We cross the street, right over to the new studio.

"Did Lars finally give it up?"

"Something like that," she says, winking at me.

Every now and then, I am brought back to reality. Lane Jonas just winked at me. Delaney is known all over the place for her music, for her ability on the bass guitar, for her voice—and she's standing here with me, holding my hand.

And, oh yeah, she's married to me.

I blink, trying to bring myself back to reality. The fact is, I'm not imagining the smoothness of her skin or the length of her fingers. Or the callouses on two of her fingertips. I'm not imagining the sweet scent of roses in the air, though there isn't a garden anywhere near us.

She is reality.

We stand in front of the doors—all blacked out with paper or paint, I'm not sure which. When did Lars put that up? We can't see inside at all. He's covered the best part of this place: the windows.

Delaney releases my hand, digs into her purse, and holds out the key. "She's officially yours."

"Officially? As in, we're done with Lars?"

"All done." She bobs her head from side to side. "On this end, anyway. He's still your landlord."

I turn the key and step inside, my heart pounding as if this too is too good to be true. But Delaney and this building are both very tangible, each right beside me. The lights are dim, and yet the space feels different. It doesn't smell like dust anymore. In fact, it smells like new paint and *strawberries*. Is that a thing?

I'm squinting and staring when a ripping noise sounds just behind me. Light spills into the room, giving the space new bones. Delaney tears away at the black paper covering the windows and doors, letting the sun stream through.

The space is different. There's a wall—right where I showed Delaney that I needed one. And the walls are blue and crisp.

I walk over to the next picture window lining the east side of the wall and rip the paper from the glass.

"I had to keep the place dark so you wouldn't see the renovations happening," she says.

"Wait. You?" I turn to face her. "You did this?" Paint, stain, the wall, the flooring—it's all in new condition. I shift in a circle, taking in the space. There's room for my students to learn and mounds of wall space to display, just opposite the floor to ceiling windows. I jog to the new wall in the middle of the room and peek through its open doorway. There's space for me to work, double what I have now in this one section of the building.

"I know I'm at my two-week max," she says, leaning against

the door frame. "But I wanted Walt to get his lesson here sooner than later."

My heart pounds in my chest. I love my work, the craft of creation, the blessing of painting. But I love to teach even more. My students—from a full class to the one-on-one lessons—are where I find my joy. Art is my job, but for them, it's a gift. A gift I experience whenever I teach. One that I get to give them. They help me keep passion and perspective every single day—and this space, this beautiful place, is only going to amplify that.

My eyes blur with unshed tears. I start for her, knowing I shouldn't but unable to help myself. I scoop her up, hold her tight, and bury my head in her neck, taking in the sweetest sensation my body has ever experienced—roses and warmth, softness, and curves.

Delaney.

I am in so much trouble.

"No one has ever done anything like this for me before." I swallow, memorizing the feel of her. "Thank you, Delaney."

Reluctant, I pull back, my lips grazing her neck as I set her back on her feet. There are tears on her cheeks. She nods her welcome, unable to speak. It takes everything inside of me to rein in my self-control and *not* gather her back into my arms. I am so tempted to return the gesture she began last night.

A joyful laugh spills out of her. "Come on! We have work to do."

We spend the next several hours moving my current studio into my new one. Delaney adds a decorative touch to the already warm indigo walls and gray cement floor. We laugh and talk, and for a short time, I forget that our relationship is a bargain. For a moment, in my head, she isn't famous and I'm not a nobody. We really are together, and the idea of marriage between us isn't something laughable.

"Do you like Chinese?" I ask. We've already missed lunch, so we might as well have an early dinner.

"Yeah. But you better order a little extra. I invited a few people over." Her eyes go wide, and she presses her lips tight. They're pretty and pink and silently say they have a secret.

I scoff out a laugh. "Who do you know here?"

"Your family, *silly*. I knew you'd want to share this with them." She walks to the middle of the spacious room, her sandals tapping on the cement floor. "This place has great acoustics."

"Yeah?"

"Mmm-hmm." Then, without reservation, she opens her mouth. She sings. And I think maybe an angel has graced us. Her voice is sweet and high and sounds so different from what I've heard from her in my headphones the past few days. But then, there's no guitar or piano, and the beat of this song is slow without her regular rock anthem. "*It was summer. But it was cold. The day he went away. Mmm-mmm.*"

I don't know the lyrics. I don't know the tune. And I've listened to every Judys song ever recorded in the last two weeks. I've never heard this before.

I stand frozen, watching, heart pounding. I'm listening as her voice rises and falls, bouncing off the walls with the sad, soulful lyrics.

When her voice and tender cry go quiet, I am dizzy. The silence is tangible.

"What was that?" I say.

Her cheeks bloom pink as her eyes find mine. "Just something I've been working on."

"It's sad," I say.

"It is."

"It's good." I walk toward her, slow, afraid my angel will disappear.

She brushes a stray hair behind her right ear. "Yeah?"

"Yeah." I stand in front of her, cupping my hand to her cheek.

I've never wanted to kiss her so badly. As if she's cast a spell over me. "That's your folk?"

Her throat bobs with a swallow as her eyes fall to my lips then dart up to find me again. "Yes."

"I don't think you need me, Laney. You're going to be fine no matter what the press decides to say about your image. That— that was—" My nostrils flair with my exhaling breath. "Mesmerizing."

She tilts her head, peering up at me, her eyes drinking me in as if there were nothing left in the world to see. Could she possibly see me as I see her—unplanned, unpredictable, and absolutely captivating?

My body is successfully convincing my head that we've known one another longer than two weeks. That the chemistry bubbling between us is very real—and not this dangerous game of pretend. That I'm somehow worthy of her.

"Knock, knock!" a voice calls—no, my *mother* calls—as the doors to the studio push open.

Delaney blows out a breath she must have been holding. "So, that's where she gets it."

39

DELANEY

That's right, I invited all of Miles' family over—to be kind. I had no idea I'd regret it the second they showed up.

Okay... that's a bit harsh and untrue, but I'm not imagining it. Miles was about to kiss me. I'm certain.

"Oh, Delaney!" Lucy croons. "Look at this place. You did all this?" She holds her hands to her heart, tears in her eyes. "Sweet girl." Then she wraps me in a hug I don't expect. "This is Miles' dream. His life goal, his—" The tears fall freely now. "But then you know that."

Levi and Meredith, Coco and Jude holding little Lula, Owen and Annie, along with little Alice, all file inside. They tour about the open space, peeking in every drawer and every cupboard. They ask questions—some that I answer, others that Miles only knows the answer to.

Miles sets up a station just for Alice, and the girl paints the very first masterpiece of the studio.

"Miles, what are you going to name the place?" I ask.

"Oh. Umm, not sure yet. There was so much to do before,

weeks and weeks worth of work, I hadn't even thought about a name yet."

"And then your fairy-wife swooped in and did all the things," Coco says, tilting her head my way and grinning at me.

They all grin at me.

They love me; even Levi has nothing grouchy to say to me. But they love me because they love Miles, and if I'm showing him kindness, they're going to love me.

They won't find fault with my efforts, not when I'm trying to do something good for their Miles.

"All done," Alice says, holding up her rainbow and sunshine on canvas.

"Beautiful. Are you keeping it, or is it staying in the studio?" Miles asks her.

I expect her to take it home—like any kid, surely she'll want it for herself. Then again, I haven't been around kids all that much.

"It could be the first painting we hang here," he tells her.

Okay—I'm changing my vote. She'll leave it.

"Can you give it to Walt when he comes?" She lifts her bright blue eyes up to her uncle, and I dissolve—just a little. I've never wanted children. And I still don't... at least, I think I don't. But this is better than a Hallmark commercial.

"Sure," Miles says. "I can do that. We're supposed to have his makeup lesson tomorrow. He'll be excited when I tell him to come to my *studio*."

Alice pumps her fist, dancing in a circle around her uncle. "He'll be *so* excited! Can I come?"

"You'll be in school, silly," Coco tells her.

Alice tosses her head back. "Ughhh, Mama! Not if you take me out for this very special, one-time occasion. That would be so smart of you, I think."

Ahh—she is a normal kid after all. A smart one, but normal.

"We should grab some tables before the food comes," I say to Miles.

"I can help him," Jude says. And then the man hands me his baby.

His baby.

As in the child he co-created.

Why would he do that?

I look around the room to see who else is seeing this. Has the man gone crazy? But everyone is talking and laughing and... no one looks appalled to see me holding the little girl. I'm doing a not-so-terrible job, I might add. I've got one arm around her back and the other just under her chubby thighs and bum. She's sucking on her own fist, her other hand swinging wildly.

Huh.

Lula grabs a fistful of my hair and tugs—it doesn't hurt, not really. Her lips are pink and pouty, and her hair a curly brown—a little like her uncle's. She's so pretty—like, *beautiful.* Have I ever noticed how pretty this baby was before? Are all babies this pretty? Her eyes are as blue as her mother's, and she seems to sing as I jostle her.

Maybe she likes the noise my bounces create because she's smiling and her singing only grows.

I watch her little face, feeling the soft skin of her chubby legs. Then I hum with her. Her sapphire eyes flick up to mine, and her grin only widens.

Whoa. My heart thumps in the strangest way. In a way I have never ever felt before. Something in my gut stirs, and I just want to keep that smile on her face.

Lula sings and I sing along with her, making up the tune as I go. She loves it.

It isn't until Miles and Jude return with a long table that I realize the room has gone quiet. That it's not just the baby and me.

I'm too busy having a mind-boggling moment with a one-year-old to have noticed sooner. Miles' family watches the two of us, listening to our song. I'm used to being listened to... but the baby part is all new. I shut my mouth up quick.

I swallow, but my mouth has gone dry; it's like sending sand spittle over my sandpaper tongue. When Miles walks by, I pass Lula off to him, shoving my hands into my pocket and telling myself the whole thing was a freak incident.

"Hey, baby girl. Who's having a birthday?" he says, and his tone is so light, so child-like, it makes my chest bloom like an onion from Outback Steakhouse. "You, that's who," he tells her, and I am lost watching the two of them.

"Wait until you have one of your own," Lucy says from beside me.

I jolt on the inside but somehow keep my composure.

"They change everything and make everything else in life seem futile." She smiles as if she's giving me great news. I refrain from blurting that I won't be having one. She wraps an arm around my shoulders. "Although, my children by marriage are loved just as much, just differently."

I stare at her, trying to make sense of her words. Me? Is she talking about me? "You don't know me very well," I say, unable to stop myself.

"And yet, I love you." She smiles and it reminds me so very much of her son. "Thank you for making Miles happy, Delaney."

"He deserves this building," I say.

"He does. But it's more than the building. He's lit up since you've been here. Somehow I missed it before—when you dated in secret. But these past couple of weeks, it's like a light has turned on inside him. That's you."

40

DELANEY

I'm not creating the light in Miles. *Nooo*. I can't be. That's crazy. We barely know each other.

And yet, here we are twenty-four hours later, and I am still thinking about Lucy's words. Still thinking about her arm around my shoulders and the motherly way she told me she loved me too. It pierced me. The only other woman to have ever looked at me like that is Grandma.

"With that wide brush, you're going to paint over the white acrylic paint with any color you want for your sky." Miles weaves through his six students and me, winking as he walks past me.

"He's very, very, *very* handsome," Cinnamon says. She's the tiniest person I've ever met. Her auburn hair is pulled back in a low ponytail, and while I don't ask—and no one tells me—I can see that she is a beautiful girl with Down syndrome.

Her eyes flutter Miles' way as he walks over to Walt.

"Mr. Miles," a man named Eric says. "The sky is blue. It's blue. We need blue."

"You're right, Eric. The sky is often blue." His brows bounce as if he's about to share a secret with Eric. "Have you ever seen the sky at sunset?"

Eric closes his eyes and shakes his head, muttering to himself, "The sky is blue." The aide who stayed to assist Eric hops over, patting his back and whispering in his ear. There are two more aides, both on their phones, waiting out the lesson, but Eric's aide never leaves his side.

Miles continues. "Guys, look at this." He pulls out his phone and walks around to each and every member of his class. "This is a picture of the sunset last night. Delaney and I were walking home after a night with my family, and this is what we saw." He walks around showing off the photo he took. I don't need to see it. I can picture it in my head.

I dip my brush in the pinkish-purple color on my palette.

"What color is the sky here?"

"Purple," Walt says.

"Pink and orange," Cinnamon chimes.

They're both right. Last night the sky was beautiful—pink, orange, and purple.

Miles holds the phone for Eric to see. The man's bushy brows furrow and both of his hands at his sides rotate at his wrist. "The sky is blue," he says again.

Miles taps Eric's palette. "Do you see a blue you like?"

Eric's hands pause their movement, and he points to a color, his head nodding with the action.

"I love it. Use that one."

Over the next thirty minutes, we discover that Cinnamon is a hundred times better at painting than I am. Her canvas has a pretty pink sky, a low, setting sun, and a tree. Mine is covered top to bottom in the pinkish-purple hue I've mixed up. I kept trying to get my sky right and never added anything else.

"Has everyone finished up?" Miles asks, peering about the room. Lucy wasn't wrong; he does look like there's a light bulb within him shining from the inside out.

Cinnamon's eyes dart to my canvas, and she says, helpful and loud for all to hear, "Nope. Not her." She points at me with both pointer fingers.

"What if we ended our lesson with a little show?" Miles holds out his hands in question. "Huh? What do you guys think?"

"A show?" Cinnamon beams at Miles, making me a little worried that I've got competition. Though the gold band on my finger—the one Ash's friend brought with her when she married us—reminds me that he *is* my husband. I've got that leg up on Cinnamon.

"Did you guys know that Delaney sings?"

I swallow. My throat goes dry—though I'm not afraid of a crowd.

"She plays the guitar, the banjo, the piano, and she sings like an angel."

An angel? I mean, I'm good. But an angel?

Cinnamon swivels her head to look at me. I'm ready for a question, or even her disdain, but she only grins and claps those tiny hands together. "He is so handsome."

A laugh bubbles from my lips. "You're right, Cinnamon. He is."

"Laney?" he says, peering at me from across the class.

I walk over to where he stands and wrinkle my face, pretending only for a minute to be put out.

"Do you mind?" he says, picking up my guitar that leans against the wall. I practiced here early today before everyone came, and maybe Miles liked what he heard.

I sigh—dramatically—but let him off the hook all too quickly. "I guess not."

Miles grins, and Cinnamon is not wrong—my husband is a looker. He leans down and softly pecks my cheek. The stubble from his five o'clock shadow grates my cheek and tickles my skin. I'm so tempted to pull a Grandpa Vaughn on him again and whip my head about, surprising him with my lips.

But I don't. Not in front of his students. Not with Cinnamon watching. She might fight me for him. And as tiny as she is, there is something fierce inside of her. We'd fight and I'd lose.

Though his sweet blush might be worth the fight.

Instead, I sit on the stool that Miles pulled up for me and strum a chord on my guitar. I don't have a mic and I'm not hooked up to any amp. I also don't pick a Judys song. This audience isn't going to stone or judge me.

I try out one that's newly written, one that I finished last night after spending all evening with Miles' family. And right before I fell asleep next to him, breathing him in and feeling the warmth from his body only inches from mine. It's all strangely fueling my writing.

I'm not even sure I'll remember all the words or notes—it's so new. But I strum the first chord and feel the folk in my soul.

This is right.

This is what I'm supposed to be doing.

I don't even care that the two aides in the back have their phones raised and are surely recording this free show. I just sing. I sing about love and loss and finding love again. And when my voice cracks, I feel the anguish and hope of each and every word.

My small audience claps enthusiastically. Walt even gives me a "Woot! Woot!"

But I look for Miles—he stands to the side, tears in his eyes, and somehow that pleases me more than anything. I wrote this song with my whole heart and soul. Singing it now, I feel the music and lyrics to my core. And so does he.

"Ash, that was literally an hour ago. You're saying—"

"I'm saying whoever posted that video of you should be sent a great big thank you bouquet." She pauses. "It's blowing up, Lane. And people are liking what they see. This is working. You and Miles. Even the studio—it's out that you helped him, that you're helping his students."

"But how? I haven't told anyone, and I know Miles hasn't either."

I didn't do any of that for my image. I helped Miles so that he got something out of this deal too. Simply being seen as married, loved, and wanted was supposed to help my image.

"I don't know," she says. "Things don't stay quiet. You know that."

"I guess."

"Either way, I'm in the process of booking you a recording appointment. Afternoon Records wants a sample."

"The indie label?" My heart starts to thud. This is what I've wanted. I just hadn't expected it to come so fast.

"I'll need at least one other song, two if you can. Let's get you back on the radio, girl."

I blow out two short puffs and pull in one long breath through my nose. "Okay, then. Let's do this."

41

MILES

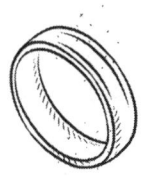

Delaney's hand slips easily into mine after two and a half weeks of marriage—and, *oh yeah,* knowing one another.

I walk through the back gate of my sister's home with Delaney in one hand and a baby doll that Delaney picked out for Lula in the other. For a girl who doesn't want to be a mom, she's got some maternal instincts.

"Ash has a recording appointment for me in L.A. next week," she says.

I'm thrown. "L.A.?"

"Yeah. I have a label interested in my folk. It's an indie label. But I've listened to their work, and I like it. It's the route I want to take. After that video went viral, Ash said we needed to move forward and fast while momentum was built. I've only got two songs written, but I think they'll do them justice."

She's leaving? I mentally smack myself in the head—*to do exactly what she wants to do. This is the plan. The goal.*

I nod—I tell myself to do so. "That's great, Laney." I bite my tongue and don't ask if she'll be back because that might sound like a man a little too attached to his wife. And I am *unattached*. I'm indifferent. I am not going to miss her at all.

I am also one hundred percent lying to myself.

"When do you go?"

"Three days. I'll be here for Walt and Cinnamon's next lesson, though. I wouldn't miss it."

I'm grateful for the sidetrack—and I take it. "I think I finally have a name for the place." We step into the yard and open up the back gate, the grass smooshing beneath our feet. It rained yesterday, making everything green and fresh for Lulabelle's outdoor birthday party.

Delaney pauses. "Wait. You have? I've been waiting!"

I swallow, wanting her approval on this. "Coeur d'Alene Creations Studio."

Her head tilts, and I can tell she's thinking as she peers up at me. "I like it. It's good... I like Miles Bailey Creations Studio better."

"That feels pompous."

"It's not!" She tugs on my hand, and we start our walk again.

We round the house to a parade of pink balloons arched over the high chair where Lula will destroy her first birthday cake. There are tables and chairs, pink streamers hanging from the awning, and stuffed giraffes decorating the entire space. Members of my family and a small handful of Coco and Jude's friends are scattered about the place.

"What does every musician name their first album?"

My brows lift. "Ah—"

"Self-titled. Always. Well, almost always. This is your first building, Miles. It's *your* studio. You're just getting your name out there—"

"Thanks to you," I interject. Though, I'm trying to check my pride and just be grateful that I'm finally selling my work.

"Thanks to *you*," she says. "You just needed eyes on the prize,

MILES BAILEY GETS DOWN ON ONE KNEE

Mr. Three-Hundred-Followers. That's all my posts did. People are finally exposed to your work and, no shocker, they love it."

I loose my fingers from hers and wrap an arm around her shoulders. "Maybe," I say as Coco's adopted mom walks our way.

"Miles," Heidi Coalfield says. "I haven't seen you in months."

I drop my arm from around Delaney and give Heidi a quick embrace. "Heidi, this is Delaney. Laney, this is Heidi—Coco's mom."

"Coco said you got married! And so suddenly." She holds out a palm to Delaney, who shakes the woman's hand. "She also said your wife is a famous musician," Heidi whispers, though no doubt Delaney has heard her. "I don't recognize her though."

"That's okay," I whisper, reaching back for Delaney. Her fingers wrap around mine, and in some strange foreign way, this is natural. It feels natural; it happens naturally. Our lie has become the norm. "Have you seen Alice?"

"She was in the bouncy house," Heidi says. "I'm sure she's still there. Here, I'll take your gift in." She takes the wrapped doll from my hand and gives Delaney another smile.

"Alice?" Delaney asks.

"Yeah, I just want to check on her. I'm sure she's good. She's just been *our* little star for eight years and today is all about Lula."

"Maybe that's good for her."

"Says the literal superstar." I perform my best eye roll for her and walk her to the bouncy house. "Shoes off," I tell her.

"Wait. I'm not going in there." Delaney shakes her head and drops the hand I hold.

"Sure you are. You are young and healthy and you'll love it." I slip off my shoes and tug her toward the entrance.

At the last minute, she tosses her sandals onto the grass and follows in after me.

The bounce house ground is soft and unsteady, like walking on a cloud.

"Hellooooo!" Alice calls, the only person inside this house at the moment. "Uncle Miles came to play!" She hops her way over to me and throws herself into my arms.

With the waves, Delaney is on her backside. "How do you stay standing in this thing?"

"I use ballerina balance. Were you ever a ballerina, Laney?"

Delaney huffs out a breath, trying to stand. "Ah, no. I wasn't. My mom had me in singing lessons from the get-go. No dance."

"Well, there you go. There is no hope for you then. I'm sorry to tell you." Alice gives her a pitying glance.

"Of course there's hope," I say, peeling Alice off of me so I can help Delaney. Her fingers grapple for mine, and I pull her to her feet. "There's always hope." I return my gaze to Alice. "How's my girl?"

"I am lovely—only there are really only babies at this party, so who is supposed to play with me in here?"

I tap my chest. "Me, that's who. I'm glad you're excited," I tell her, and I am. She seems good. She's her happy little self.

"And you were worried," Delaney says, her hip bumping mine.

"You were worried?" Alice repeats, her head bobbing from Delaney to me.

Delaney's face pales as if she's just spilled all the beans—though it isn't that big of a deal.

"Not really. Maybe a little. I just didn't want you to feel left out today," I tell her.

"Oh. Well, Uncle Owen did bring Lula *and* me a gift. While it is not a necessity—I understand it's not my birthday—it is much appreciated." She looks from me to Delaney expectantly.

Of course Owen thought of that.

Alice smiles but still says nothing. She's waiting.

And I have nothing.

"Ooo," Delaney yips. "We brought you this." She holds out the charm around her neck, her lucky tri-colored rainbow attached to the gold chain. "I bought it after our first song hit the top ten. There was a rainbow outside, and I was pretty sure it was there just for us. It's my good luck charm."

"Good luck?" Alice says, watching as Delaney unclasps the necklace from around her neck.

My eyes draw there, to every curve, every color, every texture of that soft, slender neckline. And all I can imagine doing is pressing my lips there and testing if it's really as soft as it looks.

Whoa. I swallow, blink, then cough down the thought—bringing both girl's attention right to me. "Sorry. Ah—*bug*, flew right into my mouth," I mutter.

Delaney giving my niece her personal necklace should not translate into me kissing her neck. Someone has got to knock some sense back into my head. Of this fifty-two-week marriage, we still have forty-nine-and-a-half to go. If I can't straighten myself out—I'm going to be certifiably insane at the end of those weeks.

"That's very thoughtful of you, Delaney. You don't mind giving me all your good luck?"

Delaney holds out the rainbow charm for Alice to see. Gently, she touches it with the tips of her small, eight-year-old fingers.

"I think your uncle Miles is my good luck now." She lays the charm around Alice's neck and latches the clasp in the back.

Alice folds her chin in and holds the charm up, trying to look at the thing. "This is the best necklace I've ever seen in my entire, whole long life." She hops onto Delaney—who cannot stay on her feet in this place. They tumble over, but Alice doesn't seem to notice. She hugs Delaney close and presses three kisses to her cheek. "I have to show Daddy!" she bellows and hops her way out of the bounce house. "He needs to know that I'm the lucky one in the house. So when he goes to Vegas, I need to come!"

"Vegas?" Delaney laughs, still on her back.

I watch Alice leave. "You didn't have to do that," I say. "Do you need help getting up again?"

Her long hair fans out over the yellow bottom of the bounce house, showing off the strands of blue more than ever before. She doesn't answer, and when I look closer, tears are swimming in her steel-blue eyes.

"Hey," I say, sitting on the bounce house floor next to her. "You okay?"

"I know why you want a family, Miles." She turns her head to look at me; when one of those tears escapes, she swats it away and faces the ceiling again. "I never understood before why anyone would want to take on the work and responsibility of making sure another human survived. Not knowing what that might turn you into, or how it would change you, or if they'd even like you in the end. But your family..." Her nose wrinkles, and she sniffs. "These past weeks." She peers at me again, blinking, another tear escaping. "I get it."

"And that makes you sad?" I'm unsure what to say here—or how she feels about this.

"Yes." But two seconds later, she's shaking her head. "No. It makes me confused," she says.

"Confused?" I think about all she's told me; she's never wanted a family. "It's okay to change your mind, Laney. Maybe you felt one way before, but things change. You are allowed to feel differently."

She stares up at me. And if one more tear falls from those eyes, I might do something drastic. *You want a baby, take my first-born. Whatever you want, Delaney Jones.*

"I feel confused," she says, pressing her lips together. "About *you.*"

"About me?" I'm officially on repeat. I can only echo her words while making zero sense of them.

Snatching a hold of the front of my T-shirt, she tugs until I lay right next to her.

"Yes." She rolls onto her side, her eyes still piercing through me. "You make me feel things."

I resist the urge to repeat, yet again, the last part of her sentence—all while feeling quite a few things myself.

"I kissed you four days ago, Miles."

"Yes," I say, remembering all too well her lips on mine. Didn't she make me promise not to fall for her? She's making it really difficult.

"We never talked about that."

"No."

"You haven't kissed me again."

"You made me promise not to fall in love with you, remember?" I move a loose hair over her eyes from her face, my fingers trailing over the sweetness of her cheek. "I've been working pretty hard on that."

Her long, dark lashes flutter, and she presses her lips together. "And how's it going?"

I swallow, my eyes locked on her. She is so much more than a rock star. So much more than a girl with a gift. And she's here with me. "Not great," I admit.

Her lips perk up in the smallest of smiles, and she breathes out the tiniest of sighs. Soft and timid, she says, "Kiss me, Miles."

42

DELANEY

Miles lays on his side, sweet pine filling my senses and making me dizzy. His hand finds the clavicle at my neck, sending shivers down my arms and heat into my chest as his fingers move to cup around the back of my neck. My eyes flutter closed and then his lips, warm and soft, connect with mine. His mouth moves and I follow along—a puppy at his beck and call.

Lacing one arm about his neck and finding a fistful of his T-shirt, I pull him closer. I wind one leg around his, refusing to let him go. Not that Miles is attempting to flee. He moves his arm between the bounce house floor and my back, cradling me closer.

I might run out of air. I'm not complaining; it's just a fact. When Miles breaks free of my lips, I'm ready to protest. But then, his lips press to the corner of my mouth, trailing kisses from my lips to my jaw to my throat.

Whether I want to admit it or not, I've had a crush on my husband for a while now—it's nice to know it wasn't unreciprocated.

Did I once tell Miles a kiss was just a kiss—no big deal? That had to have been someone else. Someone certifiably insane because this is poetry in motion. This is art at its finest. Kissing Miles Bailey might be pure bliss. To call it *just* a kiss is probably a crime.

"Time for gifts!" I hear someone outside the protection of our bounce house call.

Can't we just move in here? It's roomier than the loft without all the furniture crowding up the place. We could just stay *here* forever...

All his blissful kissing stops, and Miles blinks down at me. "We should maybe—"

"Do we have to?" I say.

"Has anyone seen Miles and Delaney?" Lucy Bailey asks from somewhere outside the safety of our little bounce house.

Miles sighs, rolling his neck to the side.

Yep—we're moving in. I like it here.

"I did!" Alice bellows.

"*Whoop*—time to go," he says, standing on uneven feet and holding out a hand to me. And just like that, all my fantastic real estate plans go out the bounce house window.

I breathe out a sigh. And I was just starting to love Miles' family. "Okay," I say with a groan. "Let's do this."

I slap my hand into Miles' and he yanks me to my feet, grunting when my chest bumps his.

"Um, your—ah—" His hand circles above his head.

"My what?"

"Your hair—it's kind of—" He stretches both hands out wide as if motioning to a giant invisible explosion.

"It's what?" I lay my hands on top of my head, but I can feel it —no need to ask. The static electricity in here and my head full of hair have decided to join forces and create one heck of a science experiment. "Great," I mutter.

I pull out the newly added brush from my crossover bag. Jostling on the unsteady ground while Miles holds me upright at my waist, I comb through my locks—but they really don't want to lay down.

"Miles?" Lucy calls, closer now.

"Ah, in here. We're coming."

I have one choice—I braid my hair into a quick knot, leaving it to hang over my shoulder. It's the only way to keep it from flying away.

"You aren't exactly neat and tidy," I say, seeing Miles' mussed curls and wrinkled shirt.

But before Lucy can open the curtain to our new private quarters, Miles snatches my hand and pulls me through the exit.

Levi stands not six feet away, Cooper at his side. With Miles' grand appearance, their conversation halts and they turn, gawking at us.

"Geez, Miles." Levi grunts. "In the bounce house?"

My hands automatically run over the length of my braid, making sure I have no flyaways.

Cooper chuckles, giving Miles a thumbs-up.

Miles runs a hand through his already mussed hair, doing it zero favors.

I smile enormously—and most likely obnoxiously—for Lucy. "We'll be right there. I promise."

"Sweetheart," Lucy says, pointing to my button-up top. I peer down to see two buttons open wide and my lacy lavender bra showing through.

I gasp, horrified, and pull Miles behind our yellow-and-red, air-filled oasis.

"I did not do that," he says, pointing to my shirt.

My fingers fumble over the buttons. "My hair you tell me about, but not the cleavage I'm suddenly sporting at a toddler's birthday party! *Miles!*"

"I'm sorry," he says—but the laugh that comes out with the

words makes him difficult to believe. "They must have popped open in... our shuffle."

I cram my eyes closed. I am a married lady—who didn't do anything in that bounce house, by the way. I mean, almost nothing. I blow out a breath and gather my composure.

"You okay?" he says, and for all his quiet, shy attributes, he doesn't seem fazed.

Pulling out my brush, I comb through Miles' curls, straightening him out a bit. I tuck one curl behind his ear, my fingers lingering on his cheek.

"Do we need to break up? Like, get divorced now?" My eyes search his—I'm not sure what happens after you're discovered making out in a bounce house at a Bailey family party, with everyone presuming more.

But more than that, I've broken every rule I set up when we started this. I told him a hundred times this would work *because* we didn't love each other.

I can't hurt Miles.

I can't hurt the Baileys.

"Excuse me?" he says. His hands snatch mine by the wrist, pulling it down from his face. "Confused."

"I like you, Miles. And you like me—" I swallow. "That kiss back there meant you like me, right?"

A curt laugh falls from his chest, and a crooked smile forms on his face. "Yes, Delaney. I like you."

"But neither of us was looking. Neither of us was ready for this."

"Ready or not, I like you." His forehead wrinkles. "And I *like* that I like you."

"So should we divorce? You know, so we can date."

Miles blows out a tired breath. "I know this wasn't the plan." His thumb traces the edge of my bottom lip. "And full transparency—I don't know what's going to happen. But here's what I do know: I don't *not* want to be married to you."

"So—"

"So," he says, scooping a stray hair behind my ear and cupping my cheek. "I think we just keep doing what we're doing."

"Doing what we're doing," I repeat.

"Yeah." He rests a hand on my shoulders, his finger tracing my skin there. "We'll figure it out along the way."

The next hour is filled with strange fireworks in my stomach, extra touches from my husband, and foreign thoughts from myself.

Lula sits in her high chair with Miles' family and a few friends standing around watching her as she investigates her pink unicorn birthday cake. She pokes it once, then twice, without ever trying the icing.

All the while, visions of curly-haired brunette babies fill my head. They all have Miles' eyes. I've never once dreamed of *babies* in my twenty-seven years.

I blame the Baileys.

"Just eat it, Lula!" Alice moans. She's the only child at this party. There are a couple of infants—babies of Jude and Coco's friends—but she's the only child. Which makes me think Coco really did rent that bounce house for Miles and me. Can we take it home?

"Here," Lucy says, scooping a small amount of the pink frosting onto Lula's own finger. She helps the little girl find her mouth, and then she lets her be.

Lula's eyes widen, and both of her hands reach for the unicorn, crushing it between her chubby little fists. Heidi stands next to Lucy and the two laugh, looking at one another as if they share some kind of grandmotherly secret. Maybe they do.

Coco watches with Alice and Jude, tears streaming down her cheeks.

This is motherhood—messy, exhausting, crying over birthday cake. Why would I want that?

MILES BAILEY GETS DOWN ON ONE KNEE

But in this moment, with Miles beside me, I do.

And as Coco holds Alice's hand and stares at her Lula, I see something I've never seen in my mother's eyes. Coco will never judge her girls or force on them the heavy burden of disappointment—not the kind that has followed me around my entire life.

She will be like Lucy. And her girls will be loved.

I squeeze Miles' fingers entwined with my own and he peers down at me. He will be like Lucy too—full of goodness and grace and love.

For whomever he loves.

I was wrong before—wondering why Miles would want a family. He *has* to have a family. There's no other option. Anything else would be tragic.

43

MILES

*T*hree glorious days and then—goodbye.

I replay my goodbye with Delaney in my head. She'll be gone a week, maybe longer. I don't know. She kissed me when she left, but she was so happy to be going. And I can't fault her for that. I don't want to, and I'm not trying to.

But dating—*err,* being married to—a rock star is strange, though. I like her more than I should—and it's doing weird things to my brain.

I know this has been her dream, her goal, for a long time, even before she voiced it. So many things have gotten in the way, and now it's time to record.

I'm happy for her.

And yet I don't feel all that happy.

The blank canvas in front of me has yet to paint itself. Instead, I'm replaying the morning and looking up things on the Internet. Things I *never* look up. Gossip. Will the gossip pages tell me when she's landed? Or will she call and tell me? Or will I just wonder forever?

The glass door of the studio opens, and Coco's voice calls

out in the open space. "Miles?" She's got Lula on her hip and Princess, the golden retriever, on a leash.

I step out from behind my blank page. "Hey. What are you three doing here?"

"We were in the neighborhood and thought we'd check in on Uncle Miles." She bounces the baby. "Hey," she says with a big smile on her face. "Watch this." She sets Lula down on her own two feet, holding her by the tips of her fingers, and then slowly letting go, allowing the little girl to balance for herself.

"Is she—" I start as Lula takes one step forward, then two and three. I laugh and run a hand over my head. "She's walking."

"Yeah. She started yesterday with both of her grandmas there. It was almost perfect."

"Almost?" I say—that sounds pretty perfect.

"Yeah, don't tell Jude. He was gone, and I want to surprise him. Besides, it's completely okay with me if he thinks she took her first steps toward him."

I shake my head and laugh. "He'll be fine knowing she took them toward one of your mothers too."

Coco gathers her little girl up before she can reach the row of standing easels. "I know. But give him this. He's been working hard, and he misses the girls when he's gone."

"I'm not going to say anything, but does Alice know?"

Coco's look tells me that she does indeed know about Lula's steps. Yeah—Coco isn't going to get away with anything. She realizes it too, now. "So, are you missing your wife yet?"

I swallow. No need to lie. "Yeah. I am. I've gotten used to her being around every day."

"I mean, you could work in California while she's there and she could work here when she can."

I give a curt nod. It's a good plan—for an actual married couple. But this relationship is pretty new for Delaney and me. I'm not sure she'd appreciate me following her around like a lost puppy. Not to mention—my dreams are happening over here too. I'm not sure I'm ready to leave the studio yet. Or my students.

"Well," she says, a hand on my shoulder. "I actually came because we've never set a date for your reception, and I was hoping to nail one down."

I clear my throat. "I'm not sure about a reception," I say, praying Coco will drop the whole topic. "I mean, Delaney is super busy and—it's not like we need anything."

"It's not about the gifts, Miles. It's about celebrating. You took your wedding away from our mother; don't take this too."

"Ouch," I say, running a hand over the back of my neck. "Low blow."

"Exactly on-target blow, actually. That's what happened and you know it." Coco has got bluntness down. "When will Delaney get back?"

"Honestly." I swallow. She didn't say, and I was too afraid to ask. "I'm not sure." Again—dating a rock star here people. I'm feeling a little self-conscious. It was easier to ignore the fame when I didn't have actual feelings for her. When I was sure she could never feel anything real for me.

"You don't know when your wife will be home?"

"No."

"She is coming home, right?" She huffs, frustrated with me.

I get it. I'm a little frustrated myself.

"I don't know," I say. "This isn't her home." It's more impatient than I've ever spoken in my life—and to my sister, of all people. I wipe a hand down my face. "I'm sorry."

She rolls her head back. "Miles, what is up with you? You don't want a reception, you don't know when Delaney will be back, and now you're denying she even has a home with you. What's wrong?"

I stand from my stool, run both hands through my hair, and *blow* all the air from my lungs. I might be the guy who doesn't talk much, but right now I have a whole lot to say. "I like her, okay? This was a whole lot easier when I didn't have any feelings, and now I have feelings *galore*. I might even love her." I pace in front of my easel. "And that's certifiably insane, Coco!"

Coco's brows lower. She wraps Princess's leash around a closet door handle and sets Lula on the floor before walking over and standing right in front of me, arms crossed. "All right, little brother, spill."

Secrets are easier kept when they don't mean anything. But now, Delaney means *everything*. If I thought it was difficult keeping this from my family before, it's impossible in this second.

So I talk. I tell my sister everything.

And when I finish, Coco's mouth is on the ground. Her hands and arms splay out on the table we sit at and she stares at me. The woman hasn't blinked in a minute and a half. "So, you aren't really married."

"Oh no, it's legit." I hold up my left hand. "This is real. Our certificate, real."

"But you don't actually love her."

I stir in my seat. "Actually, I'm pretty sure I do."

Coco sighs and sits a little straighter. "But she doesn't love you back?"

"Um, *love*." I shrug, "I don't know. But she likes me. She told me she has feelings—*strong*, real feelings."

"Miles, I'm so confused. Is your marriage fake or not?"

I peer at her, all my words gone because I'm not really sure anymore.

44

DELANEY

"Are you planning on telling Mom you're in town?"

"Do pigs plan on becoming delicious crispy, fried bacon? *No.*" I dig into my plate of enchiladas.

"Not even Grandma?"

I sigh, my fork hovering. "Eryn, you know how tricky this gets—if I visit Grandma, Mom will find out. That's the trouble of living in your ex-daughter-in-law's mother-in-law suite. Who does that?"

"We both know why Grandma never sold the house, why she rents it to Mom, and why she stays there," Eryn says. Her dark blonde waves wisp down her head, resting just above her shoulders. She gives me a pointed stare, waiting for me to admit the truth.

"Yeah!" I belt out like she's made a point for my side. "Mom doesn't even own the house. Grandma could kick her out!" But Eryn isn't wrong. We know why Grandma never kicked Mom out. Grandma paid for the house and let Mom live there with us for the past fifteen years with the stipulation that she got to keep her mother-in-law suite. It was her way of staying close to us so she could see us daily.

And thank goodness she did. I would have run away from home a dozen times had it not been for my grandmother.

Eryn's glare does not waver.

I groan. *Fine.* "I know," I say. She isn't wrong. I need to see my grandmother. One lousy phone call does not make up for the year I've been absent.

"She's getting old, Delaney." Eryn may be nineteen, but she is no stranger to manipulation. Thank goodness she doesn't have our mother's ruthless spirit, or she'd be one scary Cruella.

I purse my lips and glare.

"Well, she is." She shoves a bite of Cariño's spicy burrito into her mouth.

I clench my jaw. "How's school?" Yep—changing the subject on purpose.

My sister is studying molecular biology—she got all the brains in the family. And mother loves shoving it in my face. She wouldn't be so ruthless, except that my mother's dream for Eryn happened to match Eryn's while my dream for myself did not match up to Mom's.

I never had an interest in pageants. She may have demanded singing lessons for the talent portion of a pageant but I went along with it because I wanted to. It didn't matter what she did, she could not get me to perform in a pageant, not even at the age of five. But my heart wanted to sing.

"Nope, we aren't talking about me right now," Eryn says, refusing to answer my question. "You've got yourself a sugar daddy, and I want to hear all about it."

"Sugar daddy? We have no children, and the man barely has a dime to his name." I give her a pathetic smile—one that says *you've got it all wrong.*

"Okay, but how do you find someone willing to marry you—even you, Delaney—when you've only just met?"

Okay—I admit it—I told my sister the truth. I couldn't help

it. She was finally right in front of me and it all came out. She's my sister!

But I'm paying for it. I have all sorts of guilt knowing I told Miles he wasn't allowed to tell his family. That's why he'll never find out about this.

I blame this in-person visit.

I swallow, strangely unwilling to admit to my little sister that I have been crushing on my husband since day two. "It's a business arrangement, Eryn. I help him. He helps me. It's all working out."

She scoffs. "It's a bunch of phony bologna."

"Shh," I hiss, though we are the only two people in this dive. Cariño's makes the best enchiladas in the city, but hardly anyone knows it. That, and Claire Jones would never set foot in the place.

"So, you have a prenup?"

"Of course we have a prenup." Ash made certain that we did. I didn't think of it. I should have, but I didn't. I stumbled on Miles and the whole idea too quickly to think about a prenup. "Though we don't need one. Miles would never take anything that wasn't his. He isn't like that. He's literally a saint."

Her brows cinch and her eyes narrow. "You like him."

"What?" I shake my head.

"You like your husband." She scoffs at me, shoving another bite into her mouth. "I can't believe you."

"So what if I do?"

"Delaney, you went on a dating show—no, a *marriage* show. You had guys pining for you twenty-four seven, and you turned them all down."

"Well," I say, "they weren't Miles." Standing, I dab at my lips with my napkin, toss it to the table, and walk back towards the not-so-fabulous one-stall bathroom that Cariño's has to offer.

I lock the door behind me and pull out my cell. I haven't heard from Miles since I got here two days ago. Does he not believe in checking in? Or is he too busy with his real life back in play that he can't take a minute to text?

I'm not sure why I'm suddenly amped up and annoyed with him. I've only sent one text and it said, "I made it!"

I cram my eyes closed and breathe—only breathing in Cariño's not-so-impressive bathroom isn't my best idea. *Ick.*

I am Lane *Freaking* Jonas, for heaven's sake—if I want to text a guy, I will.

No, even better—I am Delaney Jones, valiant enough to defy my mother, brave enough to leave The Judys, daring enough to propose to a perfect stranger. I can do this, no matter my name.

> **Me**: Hey, how is your week going?

I am anxious and I send all the positive mojo in the universe to force Miles to write me back—*immediately*—because my nerves cannot hang out waiting all day. They'll explode all over Cariño's bathroom, and we know that won't get cleaned up until Friday.

Thankfully my husband is a good man who doesn't make me wait long.

> **Miles**: Hey, stranger. I've taught three classes and the building is a hit not only with my special friends but my elementary students. Tony Taylor is thrilled he no longer has to climb steps just to paint.

I laugh and, despite my better judgment, lean against the bathroom wall.

> **Me**: Who is Tony Taylor?
> **Miles**: A seven-year-old who has possibly eaten ten too many Little Debbie cakes. He's one of

> my private lessons. He's also a sweet kid—but
> for context, the snacks and the stairs do not go
> well together for poor Tony.
>
> **Me**: How's Alice?
>
> **Miles**: She was not invited to Sarah Parker's
> birthday party. It's a thing.
>
> **Me**: I'll beat Sarah Parker up.
>
> **Miles**: I don't advise beating up eight-year-olds—
> it never goes over well.
>
> **Me**: Well, why wasn't she invited???

My blood races with giddiness, and I hold my phone as if it were a lifeline. And in a way, it is a lifeline to the real world, or at least the world I want to be real.

> **Miles**: You've met Alice, right? She can be blunt,
> and I'm told she let Sarah know that snow
> boots do not go well with tutus and that her
> own dog is much cuter than Sarah's.

I chuckle, the sound reverberating off the walls of this bathroom. *Poor Alice.*

> **Me**: Well, she's right.
>
> **Miles**: Being right doesn't always make friends.

"Delaney?" Eryn says, pounding on the bathroom door. "How long are you going to hide in there? Did you pass out? You know, Cariños only cleans on Fridays. It can't be pretty in there."

45

DELANEY

"Eryn, you little pill," I say into the void because Eryn isn't around to hear me.

I've made it three days in L.A. before my sister has convinced me that I need to see my mother—if only to see my grandmother.

"Hello, then goodbye. Hello, then goodbye. Thirty minutes and a gift should be enough." I'm waiting to visit Grandma after Mom—then I can take my time, cool my jets, and make an excuse to my mother that I've got another appointment. However, with Grandma's house right behind hers, she's sure to notice my car still in front of the house. "Hello, then goodbye," I say again just to pump myself up.

I hold a hand up to knock. "Hello, then goodbye."

Without even touching the dark wood of my mother's front door, it opens up. Claire Jones stands before me in a pink pantsuit, her hair curled neatly around her face, wearing cherry red lipstick on her lips—so red it makes me wonder whose blood she's been sucking.

"Hello, Mom."

"And *goodbye*, apparently. Already chanting your departure,

Delaney?" Her tattooed brows lift. Her gaze roves over me from combed-and-curled hair—hiding any of the blue she hates—to my knee-length skirt—*ick* —and my not-so-sensible four-inch heels.

I'm dressing for her. And I hate it.

"Just lyrics." I swallow hard with the lie. "Uh, this is for you." I hold out the pink gift bag with white polka dots.

Mom smiles as she takes the bag with two pinched fingers, though it looks more like a painful grimace. "Thank you. It's been a year—so I'm sure whatever sits inside this bag says, *"I'm sorry for ignoring you for the last three hundred and sixty-five days, Mother."*

I'm guessing the sand wax candle and silver picture frame I bought won't add up to the loss she's sure she's amounted. "I haven't ignored you. We've texted. I've just been busy."

"Right. *Busy.* Busy quitting your job, ruining a network television show, and busy getting married without your mother. You have been busy, Delaney. Very, *very* busy."

The foyer of my mother's four thousand square foot home is large, and yet it feels pretty darn cramped at this minute. Like the walls are closing in on me. Why am I in heels again? What I wear won't change her mind about me. And I can't make a run for it in heels.

A door down the hall opens up, and I feel an ounce of relief when my sister comes hustling out.

"I didn't hear the bell... or a knock... or—" She looks at our mother. "You were going to tell me when she got here."

"Well, she's here," Mom says, her tone sweet as honey, while her eyes stab through me like daggers.

"It's been a while," Eryn says, pretending she hasn't seen me yet. She wraps me in a hug. I'd love for Eryn to get out from under the clutches of the woman I'm not allowed to call names because she's my biological mother but I'm so thankful that in this moment she's here and I'm not alone.

Mom's red lips are tight, and while the edges lift in a smile, it's anything but happy. Those lips speak without words, and they tell me what a disappointment I am.

A beautiful disappointment.

Man, I wish Miles were here.

I take it back. Why would I do this to him? I like him *way* too much to do this to him. And I'd like him to continue liking me.

"Well, come in. Let's go sit." Eryn loops her arm through mine, and we walk into the sitting room Mom only uses for guests. There's a family room in the basement with a projector for movies and a comfy sectional—but I haven't seen the likes of that place in years.

I invested in my own place and therapy the minute I joined The Judys.

"Nice outfit," Eryn says through a gritted grin. She knows perfectly well I'm wearing this for Claire; this is not a Delaney skirt.

"Yes. Too bad it isn't blue," Mom says in that sugary tone, "to better match your *hair.*"

I give Eryn a side eye, asking how much longer I have to do this. She pretends she doesn't see it.

"We've missed you so much, Delaney," Eryn says, hugging the arm she's looped hers through.

"As if I didn't know you've already seen each other," Mom mutters behind us. Claire Jones is scarily informed. There is no way that my mother has been to Cariño's, and yet somehow she knows that Eryn and I have already met up.

Eryn and I ignore her gripe and sit on the cream Diane Rove sofa she bought two years ago. It isn't comfortable, but it's pretty. Like everything in Mom's life.

Mom sits across from us in one of the floral armchairs she made Dad buy her after the divorce.

"Open your gift," Eryn says, smiling at our mother. How can

she do that so easily? But then, Mom doesn't nitpick everything Eryn does.

"Now?"

"Yes, now," Eryn says. "Delaney brought it for you. I'm sure she wants to see you open it."

I stay silent. I don't care if she *ever* opens it, let alone if I see her open it. It was meant as some sort of peace offering, and that peace isn't coming—that's clear.

Mom's nose wrinkles as she removes the pink tissue paper from the bag—as if I'd wrapped her gift with toilet paper. She peeks inside, then pulls out the sand wax candle—also pink, because I know it's her favorite.

"What is it?"

"It's a candle." There is a label right on the front of the pretty jar of sand. It's not rocket science.

"Hmm." Can the woman say nothing without wrinkling that nose of hers?

She reaches in for the last item—the silver picture frame. I know how my mother likes her silver and gold. At least this she will appreciate.

She peers at the empty frame as if she's confused.

"It's silver," I tell her.

"Ooo," my sister adds for good measure. "Pretty."

"There's nothing inside." Mom flips the eight-by-ten around to show me as if I didn't know. As if I've left something out by accident.

"Yeah. Well, I thought you'd know what you want to fill it with."

"You mean this isn't for you and your new… *husband*? You don't have a photo for me?"

Even if I did, where would she put it? Mom doesn't display photos of her children. There are framed flowers, dead ancestors, and photos of a young Claire Jones on these walls. That's it.

"I do not."

Mom crosses her arms and her legs at the exact same time. "Why is that, Delaney Sage? Do we get to meet this so-called spouse of yours? Or is he just a figment of your imagination?" Her brows lift as if to test me. She knows I have issues backing down from a fight.

"He's real." I pull out my phone and open to the photo Coco took of us the day we had a family gathering at the studio. She sent it to me, and I saved it, feeding that crush of mine.

That not-so-little crush I've got on my husband.

Is it still called a crush if he likes me back?

Never mind.

"Here he is," I say, holding my phone out for her to see.

"Wait—I want to see." Eryn snatches my arm and pulls my phone from my fingers. "*Delaney,*" she says, her tone overly eager—at least, too eager for speaking in front of our mother. "He's hot."

The fold of Mom's arms tightens, and she rolls her eyes away from us, away from my phone. "Eryn May, please do not use such horrendous terms."

"Okay," Eryn says, unfazed by the mini-lecture. "Your husband is a sexy stud, Dee."

With a groan, our mother stands and pulls the phone away from my sister. She turns it around and stares down at the screen, not nearly as impressed as Eryn.

"He looks just like he did when I called. Does he never brush his hair or change his clothes?"

That's right, she called me, and Miles answered. "You've already met him!" I yelp. "What do you mean, will you be allowed to meet him? You've met already." *So—ha!*

Mom holds the phone out toward me. "That measly two-minute phone call does not count. Has your father met him?"

I sigh, my chest heavy with the reality that is my family. "No. He hasn't." While Dad doesn't judge and project the way Mom does, he's not exactly begging to be involved in my life. He's not exactly dependable. Unless he's just been to Vegas and owes a few debts, then I can always depend on him to call up his "favorite" daughter. Sure, it's not ideal, but when I do see him, he gives me a hug and asks me what I've been doing with genuine interest. I just don't see him that often. While it's been a year since I've seen Mom, it's been two since I've seen Dad.

The cards must be treating him well.

Eryn is better than me—she makes more of an effort, so she does see and talk to him more.

"Does he even know?" she says, scoffing at something I've surely done wrong.

And I guess I should have told him. If he hasn't paid attention to the gossip news, then he probably doesn't know.

"Of course he knows," says a voice at the back of the room.

Grandma.

46

DELANEY

"*J*udy?" Mom says, her lip curled.

"Claire." Grandma smiles as if Mom didn't just sneer at her.

"What are you doing here?" Mom taps the toe of her high heel absentmindedly while staring at Grandma.

"I know I live in the guest house, but last I checked, I still own this property."

"Grandma," I say, ignoring their bickering. She looks older. And yet she looks the same. Has it really been a year?

I walk around Mom and pull my precious grandmother into a hug. She's the same height as me ever since the seventh grade: five foot six. Her hair is long and white and flows in one beautiful wave down her back. Her bright green eyes take me in with love and acceptance—always acceptance. And instantly I feel loved.

What was I so afraid of all this time? How have I deprived myself of her love for so long? Miles was right—my beautiful, seventy-five-year-old grandmother will always look at me with kindness and approval.

She's the only reason I can leave Eryn here.

She's the only reason I'd agree to come back.

Her embrace is tight and affectionate, and when we pull apart, she takes ten seconds to look me over and cup my cheek before turning back to my mother.

"You may not talk to Robert anymore," Grandma says, concerning whether Dad knows about my marriage, "but I do."

I'm punched with guilt. Sure, she's talking to my mother, but I haven't called Dad in months. I certainly didn't tell him about Miles.

"He's happy for your daughter and hopes we can all get together soon."

"He is?" I say, with eyes only for Grandma.

"Very much so." The skin around her mouth wrinkles with her reassuring grin, the most beautiful grin in all the world.

I swallow past a lump forming in my throat. Oh, how I've missed her.

"Of course he is." Mom's words drip with disdain. "She got her wisdom from him, so why wouldn't he be happy about our daughter marrying an absolute nobody?"

"Hey—" I start, but Grandma interrupts.

"I seem to remember you being a nobody when Robert married you." Grandma sets a comforting arm around my back.

"Mom, let's just—"

But Mom doesn't let Eryn finish her suggestion. "You're just like him," she says to me. "You have no idea how to use the skills you'd been gifted. What a waste. Such a beautiful disappointment. Thank goodness Eryn knows what's what."

"*Mother.*" Eryn moans.

"How is becoming a professional singer not using my skills? I'm confused, Mother." I scoff. "Oh, that's right. I never became a beauty queen. You're right, what a waste."

"Well, it's true. Eryn has a magnificent mind and she used it accordingly. You're beautiful, Delaney. You could have gone far. But you took those singing lessons and completely went wild.

I'd never intended for you to parade around like a hippy, disappointing your family."

I blink—nothing new, nothing shocking, and yet the words still sting. "I'm going. I need to call Miles." I hold my breath, walking past the woman who raised me. "I won't be back," I tell her.

"Delaney!" Eryn's feet shuffle after me. "Don't let her go. Make this right, Mom."

47

MILES

I stand outside the studio and stare up at the large plexiglass sign. Delaney must have ordered and paid to have it put up. "Hey, I was just going to text you," I say, phone to my ear.

"You were?" she says, and there's something in her voice that's off.

"Yeah." I squint in the sunshine, reading the sign one more time. "The studio has a new addition."

She gasps. "The sign came?"

"Yeah. It's up and it *isn't* the name I chose."

She's quiet on the other end as I reread for the millionth time—*Miles Bailey Creations Studio.*

"Buuuut," she draws out. "Does it look amazing and you realize I was right all along?"

"I've never seen my name that big before."

"And it looks good, doesn't it?" Her voice squeaks at the end of that sentence.

"I'm sending you a picture," I say. Five seconds later, I hit send.

"Crack bananas! It's even better than I imagined. Miles!"

There's a squeal on the other end of the line. "Tell me you love it. Do you love it? I love it!"

"Well—"

"Has Lucy seen it? What about Coco? Coco is going to love it." She's giddy over a sign with my name on it. She almost sounds normal; maybe she was just tired before.

I could kiss her. I would kiss her if she weren't twelve hundred miles away.

"I just barely saw it. So no, no one else has seen it yet. I heard the pounding, came outside, promptly got out of the way, and ta-da—sign."

"And then you called me?" she says, and her tone tells me it was exactly the right thing to do. I wasn't strategizing, though; it was instinct.

"And then I called you," I say.

"And you love it?"

"And—" I peer up at the sign. Seeing my name so huge might take some getting used to, but I don't hate it. "I might love it."

Delaney shrieks on the other end of the phone, a deep sigh falling from her lips. "Thanks, Miles."

"Thanks? Ah—Laney, I'm supposed to be thanking you."

"Oh, sure. Go for it."

My chest rumbles with a laugh. "Thank you," I say, meaning it. "How's L.A.?"

"Oh. Umm. *Fine.*" With that one word, her tone has changed. I hadn't imagined it before. "We've got one song recorded, and we should have the other two by the end of the week. It's just a demo to send to the actual recording studio."

I sit on a bench outside the studio and crane my neck to peer over my building, top to bottom. "Does that mean you'll be coming back or—"

"I mean, I can. Or—"

"Or if you have other things to do, that's understandable." I stand and push through my entrance door, returning to the privacy of my studio to pace. I don't want to be an obligation. She's done a lot for me. I don't want her thinking she has to do more. Or that she has to be somewhere she doesn't want to be. I know she has her own place in L.A.

"I always have stuff to do. And you could use a break—"

"A break?" Man, this is confusing. I'm guessing most guys don't have to wonder if their wives will ever come home. We started this relationship backwards, and sometimes I don't know which direction is forward.

"Sure. You don't always have to entertain me." She's stumbling over her words just as much as I am.

I pull in a breath. The world may not understand our arrangement, but Delaney and I do. We can be honest with each other. Right?

"Laney," I say, swallowing down the trepidation trying to keep my mouth shut. "I don't need a break from you. Anytime you're ready to come back, you'll be welcome."

"Yeah?"

"Yeah," I say into the phone. "I also understand that your job and lifestyle may need some attention there. That's okay too."

"But," she says, pausing, I'm certain, for dramatic effect, "you miss me."

I clear my throat. She's good. "Yes, Delaney, I miss you."

"Good. I miss you too, Miles."

48

DELANEY

I stand on the artificial grass that separates Grandma's house from Mom's. My mother doesn't come back here—not unless she's summoned. It feels like a safe place, even yards away from my mother's back entrance.

I hang up with Miles, already feeling more at peace.

He did that. He turned my chaos into peace.

My husband might be an adorable miracle worker, and I might be a chump falling way too fast and way too hard, but I don't care anymore. I'm just grateful to have talked to him.

In fact, I'm adding an event to my countdown calendar—three days from now I'll head back to Idaho, back to Miles. I'm almost finished when my phone rings.

My grandmother walks out the back door, not surprised to see me. I ended up on her front step constantly in high school.

"I'll wait for you inside," she says. "Take your call."

I nod to Grandma and hit speaker on my phone. "Ash?"

"Lane, what are the chances we get your husband here for a photo shoot?"

"A photo shoot?" I cinch my brow, confused. "Ah, not great."

"As far as I can see, he's getting the sweet end of this deal. You bought him that building and fixed it up, right?"

"Ah." I cram my eyes closed. I didn't tell her about the fixing up part. She must have her own sources—or just some investigating skills. It wouldn't be hard to figure out that Miles couldn't afford to do it on his own. "So?"

"So? It's his turn to hold up his end of the bargain. Remember, we're molding your image, girl. Not only are you switching to folk, but you're switching from single to married, alone to together, available to taken, undesirable to wanted."

Ouch.

"We need this to work and quick."

"Um—I don't know. I'll talk to him." But I don't want to. There's nothing I want less than Miles posing and being someone he isn't.

"Do," Ash says. "Remember your *why*, Lane. See you in the studio tomorrow."

"Your why?" Mom stands on her back porch, facing Grandma's place.

I jolt with her words, with her very presence—she never comes out here.

"What does that mean, Delaney?"

I shove my phone back into my pocket. "How long have you been there?"

"Just this second," she says. "And that—"

"*That* was about work and none of your business." I head inside of Grandma Judy's, leaving the toxicity of her company.

"You should listen to her."

I pause at the door. "You heard one thing. You don't even know the context of that question. Not to mention, you have always disliked my job. So why do you care?"

"Oh." She holds up her hands, innocent. "I don't."

The imaginary knife she's jabbed into my gut twists. *Yep, thanks, Mom. Love you too.*

I leave her, walking into Grandma's house.

Just before I fall face down onto Grandma's floral couch, I see the framed watercolor on her wall, the bright moon sitting on a lake, the sky a pinkish-blue. I'd know that work anywhere. *Miles.*

Tears fill my eyes, and I wail into one of Grandma's throw pillows.

"Is it time for me to move?"

I peer up from my screaming pillow. "What?"

"Should I move, Delaney? We both know your mother is the reason you haven't been to see me in a year. So, maybe I need to move out. Move on. I wouldn't mind *not* seeing Claire every single day of my life. I don't have much life left, you know. And I have to look at her on a daily basis."

I snort. "What about Eryn?"

"Well, your mother is a little less *Beelzebub* with Eryn."

I push up to my knees, my shoulders slumped. "Yes, but I'd still feel better knowing she had you, just in case."

"And that's exactly why I'm still here. That, and when I offered this home to your parents, it was with the stipulation that I stayed in the guest house until the day I die." She huffs. "You think it would be sooner than later. I'm sure Vaughn misses me—"

"Gram, you're seventy-five, in good health, with a great diet and exercise program. I am planning on you outliving me. Don't even talk about—"

"Fine. Fine. I just hate the fact that while you've avoided her, I've also missed out."

"Not on purpose. It's just, I—" I swallow and blow out a low breath. My heart pounds, but I have to say the words to her. "I quit The Judys and—"

"Was it right for you?"

"It was," I say, meeting her eyes. I'm sure of it.

"We've already talked about this, Delaney. I'm not upset. I

have no right to be. Besides, the only thing I want is for you to be happy."

"But you're the reason I helped create The Judys."

"And I expect a new song to be written in honor of me with this new journey." She grins and scoops her long white hair off her shoulder. I see myself in her at this moment.

And I feel so grateful that I do.

49

MILES

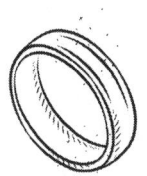

I hold the phone close to my ear and look out over the backs of my middle school students. My class size has more than doubled with the building, with the space that I have, and with my big fat name on the front.

The kids are working, I've given the majority of my instructions, and I couldn't stop myself when my phone came up with a Los Angeles area code. I had to answer.

"Hello?" I wait for Delaney's voice—but it doesn't come.

"Miles Bailey?" The woman on the other end says my name as if there is acid in her throat, as if my name burns her lips and tongue.

"Ah, yeah?"

"You did make a deal with my daughter, correct?"

Claire Jones. It has to be.

"A deal?" I don't know what this woman knows. Sure, I've spilled my truth to Coco. But Delaney was so sure we shouldn't tell anyone. And I can't imagine her telling this woman.

"Yes. Yes. I know all about your arrangement with Delaney." She sighs so loudly, as if making sure I hear it on my end. "I can't say I approve. But it has a purpose, does it not?"

Okay—maybe she did tell her.

I clear my throat. "Ah, yes. It does. But Mrs. Jones, you need to know I have real feelings for your daughter. I—"

"Of course you do." Her tone is condescending. She has a voice for every negative emotion in Pandora's box. "And it's *Ms.* Jones. Besides, if your feelings are as real as you say, why not come to L.A. and do exactly as she needs?"

"Ahh—" I have no idea what she's talking about. "She hasn't asked me to come."

"Right. That's because while Delaney is beautiful and talented, she's also as slow as her father when it comes to any common sense. She has no desire to take you away from your —*work*." She sighs once more. "However, you did make a deal. And I feel as though you should keep your end of that bargain. Don't you?"

"She needs me there?"

Why wouldn't she tell me? I've every intention to help how I can. That was our deal. My feelings about her don't change that I promised to help. If anything, they make me want to help more.

"*Ew*," Claire says. "I'd rather not be as dramatic as that, but yes, *she needs you*. If it helps, I'll add the word *desperately*."

∽

The only reason I am able to buy a plane ticket to California is because I've sold every painting I have on hand in the last three weeks. Who knows how many to my wife?

Still, I bought the ticket, with Claire Jones' address burning a hole in my pocket.

I'm anxious the entire flight. How can I not be? I spoke to Claire, not Delaney.

We land and I pull along my carry-on filled with clothes that

I hope will work for L.A, and whatever it is Delaney needs me for. I can't imagine what—

But at this point, I'm invested, and I'll do it.

Claire said she'd know when my plane would land and she would be the one to let Delaney know that I've arrived, but not before. She's certain Delaney would tell me to stay in Coeur d'Alene. And she might. But if she needs me—then I want to be here.

While I haven't known Delaney long, I do know that she and her mother have... *issues*. So, I wait until I'm in California, but I don't wait for Claire to call Delaney.

I exit the airport and order an Uber. And then, I call my wife.

It goes to voicemail, though. She's probably working. So, I leave her a message, sounding like the bumbling idiot I am. "Hey babe—*whoa*. Sorry, I don't know where that came from. Um, I don't even know if you'd be okay being called babe." I clear my throat and wish I could somehow delete and start over. "Anyway, I—" But her mailbox cuts me off.

"Crap," I mutter, peering down at my cell. "This is dumb. I'll just text."

My ride pulls up—a white Chevy—and I hop into the back, thankful my driver confirms who I am and then leaves me be. His efforts are on the road, leaving me to focus.

Me: Hey, you there?

I bounce my knee, knocking it against the passenger seat of the Cruze. Why am I so nervous? I haven't seen Delaney in six days. But we've talked. What could change in six days?

It's the wrong thing to ask myself. Six days is pretty much a quarter of our marriage. It took less than six days for me to start falling for Delaney.

A lot can change in six days.

My nerves are shot, and with the thought, I dial her number once more.

Voicemail again.

Great.

"Delaney, hey. Sorry for that last message. I don't know why I called you babe. Forget I said it. Umm... so, I'm calling because we need to talk." And then I promptly hang up. "Need to talk," I say to myself. "That sounds like I'm breaking up with her."

"Man," my driver says, his accent thick. He peeks in the rearview mirror at me. "You having girl trouble?"

"No, no trouble," I say, hoping he'll just ignore me.

I call—again. Because why not at this point? I'm in a hole, digging, and the hole is only getting deeper. There's no way out. I might as well keep going down.

"Weird, we keep getting cut off," I lie into the phone. "If you can, call me. If not, no biggie." I hang up and press one hand to my forehead. "No biggie? Who says that?"

"Okay, what is happening back there?" my driver, Ahmed, asks.

"Just trying to tell my wife I'm in town."

"She doesn't know?"

"Ah, nope." I swallow and peer down at my phone—I'm pretty sure it's the devil at this point.

Ahmed whistles. "Are you catching her in the act? Why so sneaky?"

"I'm not being sneaky. No act. She hasn't done anything wrong. Neither have I, to be clear. She just needs help and won't ask. So her mom told me to come." I swallow, but my throat has gone dry.

"How long you been married, man?"

"Four weeks."

At this, Ahmed laughs. But I don't see what's funny. How is four weeks funny? It's just a fact.

"Okay. Okay. Okay," he gets out through more laughter. He

makes a right turn and his GPS tells us we've only got ten minutes until I arrive at Claire's. Ahmed glances back again. He lifts one finger and says, "Short, sweet, and to the point. None of this chatty chatty. Okay?"

"Right. Okay." I nod, heart thumping as if I'm in the ring about to fight Mike Tyson rather than leave a simple voicemail for my girl. I hit call and wait for Delaney's automated message to play. "Laney," I say. "I'm in town. Headed to your mother's house. See you there." I pull the phone from my ear, but just before I hit end, I call out, "Here to help! Just here to help, babe!"

Ahmed blows out a tired breath. "We almost made it."

50

DELANEY

I strum and sing and listen to the rhythm through my headphones. The song fades to nothing and I feel in my bones that it's good. So, so good.

"Nice, Lane." I hear Ash's voice through the speaker in my ears. "Come on back," she tells me.

I leave the live room and slip into the control station. I lift my brows, waiting for Ash and the audio engineer's reactions.

Ash beams. "That was—"

"Fire," Hank says, giving me a nod.

"Thanks," I tell him, but I'm still waiting on Ash.

She gives a little head shake. "Why weren't we doing this all along?"

I laugh. "I wasn't there yet. I needed The Judys."

"And now you need a label."

"I do. And I like the indie house. They're good, and I don't mind starting small." In truth, I love the idea. They'll listen to me—more than a huge label would. I'll have input. The kind I never had with The Judys.

She narrows her eyes, giving me that smile like when she told me we'd hit the top ten. "Even if Sony's interested?"

"Wha—" I cough out a breath. "Did you say *Sony?*" Okay, that's bigger than big. That's *IT*.

"They saw your viral video and called me."

I sputter. Spittle flies outward. It's a good thing Ash stands two feet away from me. No words come into my brain. I am completely flabbergasted. They called her. She didn't solicit them. They came to us.

"Think about it—but don't take too long. You don't keep *Sony* waiting." She chuckles at my wordless response, then tosses my crossover bag to me. "Come on, I'll walk you out."

The walk isn't far, still I pull out my phone to see three calls and a text from Miles. "Shoot." I peer down at the device, my head spinning. Three calls in ten minutes? Something must be wrong.

"What is it?" Ash says, her dark eyes dragging down to my phone.

"Miles. He's called multiple times."

"Did he leave a message?"

"Yeah. Let me check." My hand trembles a little.

"You know, you don't have to stay married to him, right? Things have picked up faster and more explosive than we anticipated. You don't have to keep up with the charade. We don't need it."

I listen to Miles, sliding a glance and barely registering what she says. *No charade?* That should make me feel better—shouldn't it?

It doesn't. In fact, I'm pretty sure there are a million wasps attacking my gut. But then, Miles told me himself that he didn't *not* want to be married to me. We both like this charade.

I listen to voicemail number one, and when it cuts him off, I am thoroughly confused. "Babe? Did he just call me babe?"

Number two—he apologizes for calling me babe... and then, "*We need to talk.*"

Talk? Okay... maybe Miles doesn't want to be married to me

anymore. Maybe I am alone in my love of this charade. What happened? My pulse quickens and I click on message number three.

"My mother's?" I bellow, making Ash jump beside me.

"Whoa." Ash holds up both hands, her long red nails popping next to her dark skin. "What's happening?"

"Miles—he's here and he's headed to my mother's!" I can't stop the way the words shriek from my lips.

"Breathe," Ash tells me, one hand on my back.

"Holy snowballs, he sent that message half an hour ago."

Ash shakes her head, not following. "Which means?"

"Which means he's already at my mother's house!" A shaky breath falls from my chest. "What are the chances she hasn't already eaten him alive?"

51

MILES

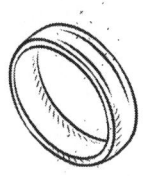

Why do I feel like I'm being buttered up—buttered up and about to be a snack?

Claire Jones sits across from me on the fanciest couch I have ever laid eyes on. Like—my butt shouldn't be touching this thing. After I leave, someone will have to come in and dry-clean the furniture.

I offered to take my shoes off before I walked on that off-white carpet. But she told me she had no desire to see my socks.

I'm not sure what that means. I'm clean. I shower and I wash my clothes and I'm not overly smelly—no more than any other man. And yet, I am one hundred percent sure a dry cleaner will be cleaning up after me.

Still, Claire is smiling and asking me question after question after question, and the way she acts after I give a short answer—well, it's a little too excited.

"I'd love to see photos of your wedding day. Delaney's the most beautiful girl. I'm certain she made a beautiful bride. It's a difficult thing for a mother to miss, you know?"

I clear my throat. I have zero pictures of that day, and Delaney was in jeans and a T-shirt—if I'm remembering correctly. "I don't have anything on me." I press my lips together. "Sorry."

"That's perfectly fine. I'll get my hands on them. I'll need one for the house."

I peer around this museum—I mean, sitting room. I don't see anything resembling family photos. Not like Mom's dedicated wall and mantel. There are a few photographs in this room, all in black and white and ancient-looking. Besides, if Delaney told her our marriage wasn't real, then why would she need a picture?

I'm anxious—but mostly I'm confused.

"You said Delaney needed my help."

"And she does. We don't want your little"—she wrinkles her nose, and strangely the action reminds me of Delaney—"*secret* getting out."

There's a buzzing in my pocket, and I feel as though I have literally been saved by the bell.

I swallow and peer at Claire, who clearly thinks I'm being rude. "It's Delaney," I tell her, hoping that will help my case.

"You can talk to her later," she says, and the perma-grin on her face falters. Which tells me she never told Delaney that I arrived or that she invited me like she said she would.

"I better answer," I say, standing and walking to the corner of the room, though Claire has no intention of giving me privacy.

"Delaney?"

"Miles!" she spouts as if we are stars in the next *Chainsaw Massacre* movie. One glance back at Claire, and I'm not so sure we aren't. "Tell me that was a joke and you are *not* at my mother's house!" She bellows each word—it will be a miraculous event, going in all the good books, if Claire hasn't heard her.

Still, I keep cool—just in case we are witnessing a phenomenon. "I'm here now."

"Nooooo! After she kills you, I will be bringing you back from the dead just so I can slug you."

"Sounds great, honey." I offer a grin to Claire. "So, I'll see you soon?" *Please tell me I'll see you soon, Delaney.*

"You're scared, huh?"

"You bet," I say, still smiling—though Claire isn't trying anymore. She's as good as grimacing.

"I'm almost there. Don't eat anything! And don't tell her anything about yourself!"

"I've already done both," I say through that frozen grin on my face.

Eat anything? Is she saying her mother would poison me? That's crazy. Right? She's strange, but she isn't homicidal. I slide my eyes back to Claire, who stares daggers through my head. Yep, she looks exactly like the kind of woman who'd poison a man for marrying her daughter without permission.

Delaney curses under her breath. "I am almost there."

Is this like a 911 call—am I supposed to stay on the line until help arrives?

I keep the phone to my ear, listening to Delaney's mutterings, giving a grunt and an "uh-huh" every now and then. I cup my hand over the phone. "She's on her way," I say to Claire as if this were a perfectly normal situation.

I'm not sure if I hear it over the phone or outside the house, but Delaney's car door slams, and I end our call, heading toward the front door. I don't care that this isn't my house. Or that Claire most likely finds my actions boorish.

Apparently, Delaney doesn't care whose house it is either because she opens the front door without bothering to knock.

We spot one another and all the questions and doubts seem to dissipate—or at least, most of them do. I am washed over with peace, love, and assurance, just taking her in.

"Miles," she says, breathless.

It's only been a week and we've only been together for four —so why does this absence feel like a long journey, like a battle? We've fought to be reunited, and here we are.

"Laney," I say, unable to hold back my smile.

My feet are nailed to the ground, so she walks to me. Her hand cups my cheek and I peer down, taking in every bit of her. Lifting up on her toes she snakes her arms around my neck and presses a kiss to my lips. My arms wind around her back, holding her close and forgetting altogether where we are until—

"*Please.* Spare me the show."

I loosen my grip on Delaney and her heels hit the floor. We both turn our heads, facing her mother, who has lost every ounce of sweetness she conjured when I first arrived.

"You expect me to believe that you actually married this hillbilly? This *painter*? By choice?" Claire snarls at her daughter, talking to her as if I weren't a real human, just an extra annoying figment of her imagination.

"Hillbilly?" I say. I've been called a few things in my life… but *hillbilly*?

"Believe it or not, I don't care." Delaney holds up her left hand, showing off her simple gold band. The ring we didn't even purchase.

I make a mental note to actually buy her a ring. Something that I pick out, something that reminds me of her. Or—maybe it's too soon for that.

I'm pondering things so much sweeter, things I want to think about when the word "hick" flies at me next.

"Hey," I say, though I don't know what else Claire has said.

"Come on," Delaney says, grabbing me by the hand. But she doesn't lead me out the front; we walk past her seething mother, through a large kitchen to a back door.

"I heard you, Delaney Sage. I know the truth. None of this is real, and I'm not afraid to leak it."

Delaney stops and turns back to look at her mother. She swallows. "I don't know what you heard. Or what you believe. But you're a smart woman, Mother. So, know this: my feelings for Miles are very, *very* real. And I know you see that."

I squeeze her fingers.

A month ago, I was sitting in my tiny studio, painting a piece that a handful would see and trying to figure out how to get Lars to rent me the building across the street. Today, I own that building, my name is on the front, and I've sold every painting I've created, with orders for more, *and* I'm holding Delaney's hand.

Funny how only one of those things feels important anymore.

52

DELANEY

I walk Miles back to Grandma's place. While it isn't far from Mom, she won't come back here. At least, she won't venture inside Grandma's house. I don't knock on my grandmother's door, I just open it up. Like always.

"Gram?" I call, with Miles' hand tucked in my own.

Grandma's steps echo from the short hall of her small suite. Her pink top goes from neck to wrist. Leave it to Grandma Judy to wear a turtleneck in June. Her long hair sweeps over her shoulders. Her cheeks and eyes wrinkle with a smile when she sees Miles.

"Hello," he says, holding out a hand to her. "You must be Judy."

Her grin turns to a beam. She shoves past his outstretched hand and wraps her arms around him, leaving him with a grandmotherly hug.

"I love this," she says upon releasing him. She points to her painting hung on the wall. "It's insightful and lovely."

"Oh." Miles' eyes light when he sees his painting there. "I didn't realize..." He looks at me. "You sent her something."

I nod.

"And I love it." She tilts her head, examining Miles. "You even look like Miles Howard a little."

I knew she hadn't forgotten her crush from that old soap opera.

"I didn't realize you were coming, Miles."

"He wasn't," I say before Miles has a chance.

Her brow wrinkles. "What brought you, then?"

"*Mom*," I say.

"Oh goodness." Grandma's lips purse. "Come sit, you're going to need some tea."

"Okay," Miles says.

Grandma takes him by the hand and leads him to her small kitchen. He passes by the green doily hanging on her wall—the one that Eryn and I like to fight over—and a light goes off in his eyes. He remembers. I see it.

It's strange how that warms my heart.

"Delaney, did you want to explain what's happening?" Grandma says, showing Miles to a seat at her small, round table.

"Well, I don't know. I was too busy yelling at Mom to ask her how she got him to come."

"She said you needed help, that you'd told her about our situation. She said you wouldn't ask, but you needed me to uphold my part of the bargain."

I plop into a seat next to Miles. *Holy crap balls. She does know.*

"What bargain?" Grandma says.

"But Laney, do you need help? You know I want to do my part—"

"Excuse me, young people. Old woman here in need of answers. What bargain?" Grandma says, refusing to be ignored.

"You told your mom but not your grandma?" Miles furrows his brows. He doesn't understand how or why I'd do that.

"I didn't tell her!" I bark. And then I cringe. "But I might have told Eryn."

Miles' eyes turn to slits. "I may have slipped to Coco."

"May have?" I say, and it's so unfair for me to be mad at him; I can't be. I told Eryn. And somehow my mother, apparently.

"Okay." His head rolls with the word. "I told her."

"Wonderful," Grandma says, setting her glass pitcher of tea onto the middle of the table. "Now someone can tell me."

Miles and I go quiet.

"Go for it," he tells me.

"The press took a photo of Miles bending down in front of me and construed it to sound like he was proposing."

Her brows raise. "He wasn't?"

I swallow—it's difficult; my mouth is as dry as the desert. How many things does a girl have to confess to her beloved grandmother in one month? "No," I say. "We didn't really know each other at that point in time."

Grandma's green eyes widen. "I see. Go on."

"I was never right for that TV show, Gram. But this—this was sort of perfect. Miles and I needed each other. We could help each other. So, we made a business deal."

"Oh, goodness." Grandma looks at Miles, then presses fingers to each of her temples. "Your building—" she says, putting two and two together. "But what for you, Laney?"

I shut my eyes. "My image. I needed to be seen as wanted, as progressing, and Ash thought marriage fit that bill. That's the entire reason I did *Celebrity Wife*. I never wanted that."

"Oh dear." Grandma's hands fall to her sides. She's going to need vitamin C and Coke—the only two things that help when one of her headaches comes on.

"She gave me one stipulation," Miles says, his soft hazel eyes drinking me in. "I wasn't allowed to fall for her."

"Yeah." I screw my lips up. "We both messed that up."

Grandma pulls in a breath through her nose. "You've been married to my granddaughter for four weeks, correct?"

"Correct," Miles says, turning his focus to Grandma.

"And you've known her for—"

"Four weeks," Miles says. Why does he always have to be so darn honest?

"Heaven help this nana's heart."

"Grandma, it's fine. It's no different than any other couple meeting and starting something up."

"Except that you're *married*," she says.

"Except that we're married," Miles agrees.

"That makes it quite different, my dear."

53

MILES

I sit in the passenger seat of Delaney's Audi, waiting for her to say goodbye to her grandmother. She likes me but thinks our whole situation is *bonkers*. I'm pretty sure she's right.

Delaney climbs inside the car and exhales all the air from her lungs.

"You okay?" I say.

She starts up the car and shoots off like she's afraid we might be followed. "Yeah."

"Are you worried about your mom telling the press?"

I peer over at her, the window just past her tinted dark. No one is getting a glimpse inside this vehicle. We pass by unsuspecting people who haven't a clue who sits inside this car.

We've got time to talk; Delaney's apartment is in Malibu, an hour away from her mother's house in L.A.

"I'm not." But she looks a little worried. "Bad press for me is bad press for her, in her eyes. And if there's one thing Claire Jones hates, it's looking bad."

"I'm sorry I misunderstood so massively. She said you told her about us. She said you needed help."

"And you came running." She peeks over at me. "My knight in shining armor—"

"Sure, only I'm armed with a paintbrush and I'm a pacifist."

A ping on my phone tells me my family text thread is still blowing up. Delaney glances my way before focusing again on the road.

"Just the family. I didn't have time to tell them I was leaving."

"Miles!" She barks. "Don't stress Lucy out on my account. Text them back right now."

I pull out my phone to see the number eighteen next to my texting app. *Geez, Baileys.* I start from the top.

> **Annie**: We need to talk dates for this reception thingy because Owen and I are booking a trip.
> **Coco**: Ooo—where to?
> **Coco**: Wait, check with Miles. He and Delaney may not want a reception. Now, where are you going??

My gung-ho sister now knows the truth and she's cooling her jets on this reception idea. It's fine by me.

> **Mom**: Wait, no reception?

Okay, maybe it's not fine by me.

> **Annie**: Aruba!
> **Coco**: Feel free to jump in, Miles. He knows more than me.
> **Levi**: Where are you, Miles? Meredith and I came by the studio and it was all locked up.
> **Owen**: He's got classes today. It should be open.
> **Levi**: There was no class happening.
> **Cooper**: Guys—does any of this apply to me? I've

> got one last final to study for, and I need to know if I can silence these or not.
> **Owen**: Silence away, bruh. We're talking about Miles.
> **Annie**: Who is conveniently ignoring us.

I chuckle.
"What's up?" Delaney asks.
I start from the top and read aloud my family's messages.
"Ugh. *Reception*. I want the out. I also don't want to disappoint your mother. I hope one day I'm just like her. So kind, loving, and unselfish that people give in to me all to keep me from getting hurt." She grunts.
I smirk. "Very unselfish thought, Laney."
"It was an oxymoron thought."
A tired laugh falls from my chest.
"What else do the Baileys say?"
I pick up where I left off.

> **Mom**: Oh Miles? Where are you today?
> **Coco**: MILES! (In case you couldn't tell, that's me yelling at you.)

There's an hour-long pause, and then:

> **Levi**: I went by his place and the studio again. Nothing.
> **Owen**: I called. No answer.
> **Coco**: I'll text Delaney.
> **Mom**: I'll call Nina.

"Crap—Miles, call your mother!"
"I'm just going to text. Those last two weren't that long ago.

Me: Hey! Sorry I worried everyone. I left town.

I hit send before I write out more. Just letting everyone know I'm alive. I can't have Nina searching all of Coeur d'Alene for me—not after the number of times I've asked her to clear the photographers away in the last month. I owe her a hundred favors at this point.

Before I can finish typing my next message, there's a string of texts.

> **Coco**: Dummy. We've been worried sick.
> **Mom**: Thank goodness. Is everything all right?
> **Levi**: Where'd you go?
> **Owen**: Levi, you owe Annie five bucks.
> **Annie**: YESSS! Glad you're alive and well, Miles.
> **Annie**: And with you out of town, I am five dollars richer.
> **Me**: I made the last-minute decision to go see Delaney in L.A. Sorry I didn't tell anyone. I'm here and safe, and I'll let you know when I head back home.

"Your family is…"

"Crazy?" I finish for her.

She laughs. "Involved."

"They are."

"I love that. I love them," she says, and it feels like a very intimate thing for her to admit. She presses her lips together. "Well, since you're here, you get to meet my sister tomorrow."

"Who knows the truth?" I say.

"Who knows the truth."

∼

*D*elaney's apartment building is tall—probably taller than any building in all of Idaho. She parks in the parking garage and I'm grateful to see there's not only a security guard who knows her but a keypad with a code that must be submitted before entering.

She parks, kills the engine of her Audi, and peers over at me.

"Your mom is kinda scary," I say.

"That's an understatement." Her eyes go wide. "Be thankful for Lucy."

"I'm always thankful for Lucy," I say.

She peeks over at me. "Yeah, it's no wonder you're so great."

"Well," I say, tilting my head to the side. "You haven't met my dad."

She laughs. "As scary as my mom?"

"Nah. That's a pretty high standard. But he is a bit of a train wreck."

"Hmm. Well, it's good to know you're not completely perfect."

I blink, rein in my grin, and peer down at my lap. "Not even close." I slide my eyes back up to hers. "But you—you're even more amazing than I thought. Did you raise yourself?"

"Nah. Thankfully, I had Grandma Judy." She lifts one shoulder. "Wait until you meet Eryn. She's so much better than me."

"Somehow that's hard to believe."

Her cheeks flood with pink, and I lean a little closer.

"I missed you, Laney. Is that crazy?"

Her body mimics mine, meeting me halfway. "Maybe. Maybe I've gone crazy too." Her warm hand cups my cheek as she pulls me closer... closer... closer. Until she closes the distance between us, pressing her mouth to mine. Her lips are soft and commanding. She tips her head, teasing my mouth open and making me crave her all the more.

Her fingers slip down my neck and snag onto the collar of

my shirt. There's a console between us, but she tugs me closer anyway.

We break apart, but just for a breath, her lips still brushing mine.

"I'm glad I'm not alone in my insanity," I whisper against her, pecking her lips once more.

She hums, eyes closed. "Come on. Let's go up. I'll show you around; it may be a slightly longer tour than your place."

"Well, that's not difficult."

54

DELANEY

My bed is too big.

In fact, my entire apartment is a ridiculously stupid size. I felt like an idiot today as I showed Miles around my place and took him into my *third* bedroom. I am the only person who lives here. Why three rooms? What's the purpose of that? My mother, sister, and grandmother live less than an hour away, and my father never visits. Who in the world do I need extra rooms for?

And bathrooms? Why three of those? Do I have the smallest bladder on the planet that I need one in every section of the apartment?

And now—my bed is *gargantuan*. Like HUGE.

I am one person—not even that large of a person—and yet somehow I convinced myself I *needed* a king-sized bed.

I kick my feet, feeling as though I may suffocate in these sheets, comforters, and down pillows at any moment. "Stupid, colossal bed that doesn't even do anything! Five grand, and it can't even dub as a couch," I say to no one—just the dark room and night air.

Miles sleeps three doors down. There aren't even three doors in his entire apartment.

He's in L.A., he's staying at my place, and yet he's so far away.

I had no problem falling asleep in this bed last night or the night before. I had no desire to curse it.

But those nights Miles wasn't three doors down. He was twelve hundred miles away. And while we haven't known each other long—our feelings haven't had all that long to marinate—he *is* my husband. And my feelings are very real.

Plus, I've gotten used to him breathing at night. And the way his massive shoulders take up more than half his couch bed and the way his body heat turns the entire mattress into a sauna.

I reach out an arm—it reaches the middle of this bed. Was this bed always so big? Did someone sneak into my house and add a foot onto the sides and end?

I peek at the digital clock on my nightstand. "Two?" *Ugh.* It's two in the morning. I'm recording tomorrow and I'm still awake.

This won't do.

For the sake of work…

For the sake of my music…

For the sake of sleep, I throw off my comforter that isn't nearly as warm as sleeping six inches away from Miles Bailey. The man is like a heater.

And while I may not need a *heater* in L.A. in June–I've gotten used to sleeping warm. I like it.

My feet hit the hardwood of my bedroom floor and I peer down, making sure I'm wearing bottoms to match my navy, polka-dotted night top. I am.

Which means—I'm decent enough.

Time to ditch this stupid bed. We're breaking up. The bed and I, to be clear. And there will be no *"it's not you, it's me"* discussion. Because it's *totally* the bed.

I quietly pad down the hall, careful and precise with my movements. I turn the knob to Miles' door as if I were diffusing a bomb.

The guest room door opens without even the slightest creak. There's a bed against the far wall, a standing mirror in the left corner, and a small bathroom attached to the right. There's no clutter or junk to trip over. I can just make out Miles' backpack at the foot of the bed. The moon outlines the form of it, sitting there, out of my way. It also lights up the lump in that queen-sized bed that is Miles. He's on his side, taking up only half the bed—*his half.* What a good husband. He's left my spot open for me. He sleeps, his chest rising and falling with even breaths.

On tiptoes, I make my way over to the left side of the bed. I swallow before pulling back the blankets and climbing inside. I rest my head on a pillow I've never used before in a bed I've never lain in before. I cover my bare legs and stare at Miles in the dark.

Comfort sinks in, settling over each of my limbs and head. It washes over me like plunging into a jacuzzi tub.

Complete comfort is rare in my line of work–and life. And yet I'm always comfortable with Miles.

My eyes adjust to the dark and space around me. His nose, lips, and closed eyes are all clear to me now. I can already feel his built-in heater warming me up in this air-conditioned room. I let out a breath, peace washing over me. I shut my eyes and—

"You're lucky I don't have pepper spray on me," the quiet man beside me says.

My eyes pop open. I let out the smallest of yelps. I was so sure he was sleeping.

"You're the one sneaking in on me, and yet I scared you?" he mumbles, his voice raspy.

"I am not afraid," I say. "You only startled me."

Miles hasn't bothered to open his eyes yet. He still looks like the dead. "Sorry," he says. There's a curl of russet-brown hair falling over one of his closed eyes. I reach out and scoop it back, away from his face. I run my palm from his hairline to his jaw.

And then, as if being pulled by some invisible magnetic force, I scoot my body next to his.

I roll over, pressing my back flush to Miles' chest. He wraps an arm around my waist and hugs me closer like we've been doing this for years.

"I missed you," he says, pressing a kiss to my temple.

He said the same thing earlier tonight. I don't mind him repeating himself. I could hear it again and again.

I rest my palm on top of his hand, lacing my fingers through his and hugging his hand to my chest. We are a bread-and-butter sandwich, stuck together in the best possible way.

I'm ready to sleep. It won't be long now. Why weren't we sleeping like this all along?

55

MILES

"Why are we coming back here?" I say, looking up at Delaney's mother's large L.A. home.

She pulls in a breath—it's possible she wants to be here less than I do. "Eryn said Mom was ready to apologize."

"You think she is?" I'm more than ready to go back home. L.A. isn't exactly for me. But Delaney is. If she goes on tour, I'll probably end up following her around just to make certain I spend every night for the rest of my life holding her like I did last night.

"Nope." She swallows. Her hair is up on her head in a stringy bun, leaving her long, pale throat exposed.

I'm not sure I've kissed every inch of that throat yet—and it's on my to-do list.

"But *what if—*" she says, her words trialing off. She breathes out a quiet sigh. "If the Baileys have taught me anything, it's that family is important. It's worth fighting for." She blinks, her gaze falling from the house to me. "If I could have some semblance of a relationship with my mother, isn't it worth the risk?"

I'm hesitant after the way Claire spoke to Delaney last night. There was no concern or love in her words. Not like a mother should have. While Delaney *deserves* to have a loving mother, I'm not sure that coming back here for repeated heartbreak is worth the slim possibility.

Maybe I'll mention that another day, as we're already here and Claire Jones is peering out the window at us.

I look at the house, at Claire watching us from the window. "Hey, babe—"

"Babe again, huh?" She flutters her lashes in question.

I turn back to her and shrug. "It keeps coming out. I don't know."

She sighs like I'm really putting her out. "Work on it, will you?" she says, but her mouth parts in a grin.

"I've been wondering," I say, my brows cinching. "Why did you tell me not to eat anything your mother offered?"

"*Blech*," she says, screwing up her face in disgust. "She puts brussels sprouts in everything. I was trying to spare you."

My face smooths over and I sigh. "I thought her brownies tasted a little off—but then you told me not to eat anything and... I thought the woman might be poisoning me."

Delaney snorts. "She is—with greens."

Eryn meets us at the door. Her smile is large, her glasses round, and while her shoulder-length hair is a much darker blonde than her sister's, there is no doubt that this is Delaney's sibling.

I watch as Delaney and Eryn embrace, their arms tangled around one another. Behind them, Claire's lips turn up—though she isn't smiling. It's more of a grimace. I've never seen anyone smile and pull off disgust all at once.

Judy sits on the couch in Claire's sitting room, and I've learned that while she is the mother of Delaney's father—Claire's ex—she owns the place. She's lived in the guest house for years and didn't want to leave when Claire and Robert split up. Delaney said she wanted to be there for the girls. So, she rents the place to Claire for cheap, and in turn, she keeps her home out back. This is the home she raised Robert and his brother in. I'm curious as to how similar the space is now compared to then.

But that's a conversation for another day. Today, I am keeping a low profile. I am hoping to chat with Eryn, hear a lovely apology from Claire to Delaney, and then fly home, Delaney by my side.

Claire brings us all a cup of tea. Now that I know her secret, I can't get the scent of Brussels sprouts to leave whenever I sip the hot liquid.

"Delaney Sage," Claire says when the chitchat between Eryn, Judy, and I simmers. "I'm sorry we argued." Her lips are tight. "I'm sorry that I'm such a bother, always wanting to be a part of your life."

Delaney glares at Eryn—it's an *I'll punch you later, little sister* kind of look. I know. Levi gives it all the time.

"Mom," Eryn says. "You called Miles here without warrant, without telling Delaney, and then you accused them of fraud." She clears her throat. "Remember? That's the apology you're making."

Claire's eyes search the floor—as if she's literally trying to remember.

Standing, Delaney huffs. "We have a plane to catch. So—"

"No." Claire breathes in and then out, the breast of her blue suit rising and falling with the action. "Fine. I am sorry I called Miles here."

"Thank you." Delaney nods.

"But I can't apologize for calling this what it is—a *sham*."

Delaney shakes her head—and while I never want to be in agreement with Claire Jones, and my feelings have changed dramatically since we first made the agreement, she isn't completely wrong. Delaney and I did make a business deal. One that somehow her mother knows about.

"Believe what you want," Delaney says. Her jaw is tight and her cheeks splotch with pink.

The thing is, everyone in the room knows the truth. Well, sort of—none of us knows exactly what or how Claire knows what she knows. None of us are willing to admit the whole truth to her. She'd construe it in the worst possible way.

"Here's what I believe—you're doing your best," Claire says as if she's offering Delaney an olive branch. "You needed some help, and you found some in this…" She peers at me, the right corner of her red lips curling. "*Painter*."

"He's an artist, Mother. An artist and a teacher. And he's ridiculously good, if you'd take a minute to look at any of his work."

"But Delaney. *I* can help you." And for the first time in the twenty-four hours I've known Claire Jones, she looks utterly sincere.

Delaney must see it too because she doesn't blow her off.

"Help how?" Eryn asks, and while Delaney looks hopeful, Eryn's brow furrows in skepticism.

"I've been in touch with Enrique—"

Delaney groans, all the light squelched from her eyes.

"Mom," Eryn gripes.

"Really, Claire." Judy stands, shakes out her arms, and paces once in front of Claire's picture window.

Claire holds up both hands. "Not to see if he'd take you back romantically. I've no hope of that after the scene you caused two summers ago."

"Who?" I say, looking to Delaney for help. I'm not exactly the jealous type, but even his name sounds like a man ready to swoon my girl away from me.

"He's willing to take you on as a model for his fall show."

Delaney scoffs and stands to face her mother eye to eye. "Model?" She shakes her head.

"You're trying to revamp your image. I spoke to Ash—"

"You called Ash? What the—"

"I simply asked her why the sham of a marriage, and she explained."

Delaney's fingers grip at her hips. "That manager of mine is so dead."

"I had my suspicions; she confirmed them. But the point is, Delaney, you don't have to do this. Marriage is fairly desperate, don't you think? There are other ways to alter your image. I'm all for the change, by the way. But not like this. You don't need him." She waves a hand in my direction as if I were an animate object without any feelings.

Judy wraps one arm around Delaney's shoulders, calming her erratic breathing.

"I don't want to be a model. I never have. I never will. So, how would working with Enrique help me?"

"Using your beauty is simply using your assets—"

"I don't *want* to model. I don't *want* to be Miss California. I don't want to!" Delaney's face and neck blotch with an angry pink. "Besides, Mother, I *like* being married to Miles. He is funny and kind. He's creative and loving. *And* he is the sexiest man I have ever met!"

Claire rolls her eyes with Delaney's last declaration. And maybe she said it purely to annoy her mother, but I'll take it.

"He thinks about *me—me*, Mother. And what *I* want."

"But you don't need him—"

"Maybe I don't!" she bellows with a humorless laugh. "But maybe I want him."

I slip my hand into hers. It's a silent assurance that I want her in return.

But the room has already grown stuffy and warm with their words and emotion. Claire must feel it too because her face is every bit as red as the lipstick she wears. "This is ridiculous. And you're going to end up right where you started—with your image in the gutter. Don't expect Enrique to take you then—"

Delaney runs a hand down her face.

"Mom, please—" Eryn hisses.

But Delaney is very good at taking care of herself. She doesn't need me or her sister to come to her defense. "I don't want Enrique's help or yours."

Judy paces behind us and tears glisten on Eryn's cheeks.

"You'll only drive her away again, Claire," Judy says.

Some of the blood drains from Delaney's face, and she peers back at her grandmother. "She won't. I won't let that happen again. I promise."

With a quick embrace to her sister and then grandmother, Delaney snatches my hand and starts for the door.

Claire yelps, stopping us in the entryway. "You'll never make it!"

"Excuse me?" Delaney peers back at her, stopping when we're so close to escaping.

I'd like to tug her out the door, but this isn't my fight. I don't get to make that choice.

"You and him," Claire says, bobbing her head toward each of us. "Your father and I knew each other for five years before we got married. And it still didn't work."

"Claire—" Judy says. "She isn't you."

"Well, that's certainly true. But experience… and life… and the odds all say they'll never make it. They've known each other for five minutes. He's small-time, and Delaney has always been meant for more—you and I both know that, Judy." She takes three steps closer, her eyes piercing her daughter. "You know how cruel life can be, Delaney. You know it." Her words are sharp and harsh, daggers that hit their mark. "Forget me, forget what I say. *Life* says you won't make it."

My fingers around Delaney's tighten. I lift my head and find my voice. "But love says we will."

56

DELANEY

I let myself cry for a solid ten minutes before pulling up my big girl pants and moving on. That's what Claire Jones taught me to do—put on a smile and *move on*. And when it comes to my mother, sadly, I think that's exactly what I have to do.

Miles' hand hasn't left mine since we drove away, and now here we sit side by side on a plane back to Coeur d'Alene. It feels like a good place to call home.

The plane hasn't moved yet—people are still boarding—when my phone in my pocket buzzes.

Ash.

I might murder her later for confirming to my mother about my unique relationship with Miles.

"Sony's heard the recordings," she says before I can even say hello. "They're all in, Lane. You just need to sign on the dotted line."

I pull in a small gasp. "*Sony.*"

"Yes. They want you in L.A. for the next six months. They've already got plans for an entire album and a tour. A *Lane Jonas* tour."

I swallow.

Sony.

A tour.

L.A.

Miles swaps from watching me to watching out the window, giving me privacy. But I know he's heard at least what I've said. *Sony*. It's the big league. Even bigger than The Judys ever saw.

"What about the indie label Afternoon Records?"

"You haven't signed with them yet," Ash says. "Of course, they're all in too. But what can they offer you compared to *freaking* Sony, girl?"

My brows knit together and my heart pounds in my chest. "That's a good question."

"What's a good question?"

"What is the indie label offering?" I ask.

She sighs in my ear. To Ash, this is an unneeded conversation.

People are taking their seats, and soon I'll be asked to hang up and put my device on airplane mode.

"They are offering a *fraction* of what Sony is. No guaranteed tour, no home base. You will get input on decisions. But, Lane, Sony never gets it wrong—*ever*. You'll have an album and creative leeway with the indie label. That's what they're offering. An album with a *fraction* of the pay, a *fraction* of the benefits, and a *fraction* of the listeners. This is a no-brainer, Lane."

I blink over at Miles, who looks out the window wistfully.

Love—when she'd given every practical reason we wouldn't make it, he gave the only one that matters.

Love.

"I like my indie label," I tell Ash.

"Lane, you're kidding. You aren't serious. This is—"

"Listen, I'm on a plane and we're about to take off. I can't talk anymore. I'll call you when we land." I hang up on my manager. I don't let her say anymore.

My mother dangled Enrique.

The Judys dangled steady success.

And now, Ash dangles Sony—with all of my folk dreams in reach.

But is any of that what I want now?

I pull in a breath and shut my eyes, leaning my head back against the headrest of this coach seat.

I want to sing what I want to sing, play what I want to play.

And Miles.

I want Miles. Sure, the world says the odds are against us, but for Miles—I'll take those odds.

"Hey," I say, as if I've just remembered something I need to tell him.

He turns, his bright hazel eyes peering down at me.

"I love you too," I say, though I know he didn't actually say it. It was implied, right?

His lips turn up in a grin, and his eyes drop to my mouth just before claiming my lips for his own. He kisses me far longer than he should in such a confined, public place. But I don't mind.

When the man behind us clears his throat, he breaks away, putting a centimeter of space between us. He pecks me once more, teasing me, leaving me wanting for more.

"I love you, Laney," he whispers against my lips.

"I thought you might."

"I have something else to tell you too," I say, making the decision as I speak.

He puts another inch of space between us, giving me room, and letting me talk.

"I'm sticking with my indie label."

"But Sony—"

Yeah, he knows what Sony means too. He's a smart man. "But Sony can't give me *everything* I want."

"And the indie label can?"

I smile, my eyes roving over his face. "I think it can." I tilt my head. "I've got my new stage name too."

"New? But why?"

"Yes, new. Lane Jonas was a Judy, a rocker. I can't go by that anymore."

"You aren't a rocker anymore?" His eyes narrow playfully on me.

"Of course I am. Always. But I'm also a bass-playing, banjo-destroying, folk-singing girl. And as such, I'm going by… Delaney Bailey." I swallow. This feels like telling him he's stuck with me forever and ever and ever and—*ever*.

His mouth falls open, surprise written all over his face. "Yeah?"

"If that's okay with you."

"Delaney Bailey. I'm pretty sure I can get used to that," he says, his sweet lips parting to a grin. He leans down, teasing me with another peck.

It's okay. I tease him the whole flight back.

EPILOGUE

MILES

TWO MONTHS LATER

There's a diamond burning a hole in my pocket. Which is pretty silly, considering the girl I want to give it to is already my wife.

Still, I've been stuffing it into my pants pocket for days now. A small, half-carat, princess-style diamond. Nothing crazy—but much nicer than the gold bands Ash purchased for us.

I'm not sure if it's the reception Coco and Mom have planned or the fact that Delaney and I have now been married three months, but I feel like if I don't give her this ring in the next hour, all hope will be lost.

Blood boils inside of my skin, and I feel like James Bond on a mission—it's now or never. Live or die—it must be done.

I storm over to the bathroom door, adrenaline pumping, and fling it open to a busy Delaney. Her hair is pulled back and up in a clip, flopping to the side in a whoosh on top of her head. She's barefoot with chipped pink polish on her toes. Her pajama shorts are short, with only one of her bare legs covered in shaving cream. And she's shirtless, only sporting a turquoise bra at the moment. With foam on her lips, she pauses the back-and-forth brushing of her teeth to look at me and my grand entrance.

"Hey babe," she says, past a mouth full of minty fresh Crest. "Do you need the bathroom?"

A splatter of white, minty bubbles falls onto her chin. She bites the purple toothbrush Coco bought her three months ago between her teeth and reaches for a washcloth to wipe off her chin.

Yep, that's my girl.

I have no doubt—and with that realization, no more fear.

I bend to one knee—this time with intention—knowing exactly what I'm doing, what I want, and what I'm getting myself into.

"Delaney Sage Jones—"

"It's Bailey," she says, toothbrush still between her teeth.

"Will you marry me?" I wrangle the ring from my pocket—dang, I should have gotten that out before I bent down—and hold it up to her.

Delaney stares down at the gold band and little diamond in my hand. Blowing, she spits her toothbrush into the sink and wipes her mouth clean with the back of her hand. All grins.

She falls onto my leg, setting herself there, and wraps her arms around my neck. Her lips press to mine, warm, sweet, and extra minty. She kisses me long and deep in answer.

"Is that a yes?" I say when she breaks our connection.

"Yes." She tilts her head. "I mean, you are conveniently already my husband. And I do love my new stage name. So, sure. Why not?" She leans in, pressing a kiss to my forehead.

"You missed," I tell her, cupping her cheek and pulling her lips back to mine.

Bonus Epilogue
Cooper

Wow. My sister can throw one heck of a party. Miles' new studio never looked so good.

Coco was smart when she talked Delaney into a wedding dress.

Whew. That new sister-in-law of mine looks pretty good in white. But... I don't think I'll tell Miles that.

Or maybe I will.

It's fun to watch my tamest brother get a little riled.

"Hey," Coco says, linking her arm with mine. "I need to grab more sandwich platters, wanna help?"

"Sure."

I stare out at the middle of the floor where Miles and Delaney dance. Next to them, Alice pirouettes in her pink flower girl dress, spreading rose petals all around her, while the crowd watches. Mom invited everyone she knows—plus Delaney's family and friends. Everyone but Delaney's mother showed up, and from my new sister-in-law's reaction, I think that's a good thing.

I am determined to get a Judys' phone number by the end of the night. I've always thought that drummer was pretty cute.

We walk by the three-tiered wedding cake, and while I don't normally care or notice things like this, I can't help but see the small stack of business cards sitting next to the confectionary masterpiece.

Leah Bradford is scrawled in fancy gold script over the card. Just her name and a number. And I am oh so tempted to snag one of those business cards.

I linger at the table, scanning the room for my nemesis.

"She isn't here," a high voice says from behind me.

"Who isn't here?" Coco says, peering around me.

I scan over my shoulder to Caitlyn, Leah's younger sister.

"Leah," Caitlyn says.

"Oh, the pastry chef. Do you know her?" Coco peers up at me.

"Oh, they know each other, all right." Caitlyn's green eyes—the same shade as Leah's—go wide. "But Leah is not a Cooper Bailey fan, unlike everyone else at Lake City High."

Coco stands beside me, now facing Caitlyn.

I puff my cheeks and blow out my breath. "No, she is not."

"I like him," Caitlyn says to Coco as if she's trying not to offend. "But Leah *so* does not." She giggles as if it's hilarious.

"Wait," Coco says, and for some reason, she's smiling. My sister finds this funny. "Someone doesn't like my little brother?"

"That's right." Caitlyn points at Coco, her smile growing wider. "I heard you got a long-lost sister. Mom told me. Wild."

"Super wild," Coco agrees, though the topic is a bored note on her lips. She's ready to skip back. "So, this Leah doesn't like Coop?"

"Don't be offended."

"Oh, I'm not offended, just in shock. Everyone loves Coop. He could charm a blind man out of his cane."

I cough. "You know, I don't think that's a compliment."

"It is," Coco insists, but she's still looking at Leah's sister. "*Mostly.* So, what did Coop do? How did he get on her bad side?"

She looks at me, but I'm not fessing up to anything, not in front of Coco.

"Well, for one—he ruined her prom."

"Nooo," Coco says, her eyes widening like this is juicy gossip. "Not Coop. He's charming and sweet. And a gentleman." Her brows lower, and she elbows me in the ribs, muttering, "Tell me you were a gentleman."

"He wasn't her date." Caitlyn sighs.

"Oh." Coco shakes her head, not following. I can already tell her mind is slipping back to that empty sandwich tray.

"Cate," Mrs. Bradford calls from several feet away. "We're heading out, honey."

"Coming," she says but pauses next to me. "You aren't *back* back, right Cooper Bailey?"

"Ah, no." I shove both my hands into my suit pants pocket. "I still have a couple more years of law school."

"*Whew.*" Caitlyn makes an exaggerated motion of her hand across her forehead. "Leah graduates with her business degree in December. Mom is hoping she'll move back home. No way that's happening if Cooper Bailey's back in town." She wrinkles her nose, then waggles all ten of her fingers at me. "Bye-bye," she sings.

Coco and I watch her go before heading off toward the back room, Miles' private studio, where Coco has coolers full of food.

Coco opens one of the coolers and hands me a tray of tiny square sandwiches. Man, I'm glad I wasn't here to be on the cooking crew. She could be feeding an army with what she's got left.

"Why would she say you ruined her sister's prom night?" Coco asks.

I think for only a minute about the pretty, green-eyed girl who'd always caught my eye in high school. "Probably because I did."

ACKNOWLEDGMENTS

Gosh, I love this book. Thank you for making it this far and reading all about Miles and Delaney. I love you, dear reader!

I love the Baileys. They feel like family to me! I'm so grateful for the inspiration and vision that has come with each of these books. I often pray before I write—because I know anything good I have to offer comes from Him. I am so thankful for a loving Father who has spurred on my desire to write and publish. All that I have and am, I owe to Him.

Thank you to my dear friend William—years ago you hired me as your teaching assistant. For two years I was able to help teach adults with disabilities life skills. Other than writing, it was my very favorite job. I loved those beautiful people and I loved teaching them, getting to know them, learning about them and their talents and gifts. It greatly impacted my life and inspired parts of this book.

Thank you to sweet Braleigh for all your bass guitar knowledge. I love that you researched and taught me! You're amazing!

Thank you to my beta readers and editors—Marisa, Pamela, and Caitlin. This book would not be what it is without you! Thank you for your love, time, and effort!

Thank you to my Lauren!! While you didn't proof this book—you are working your way through the ol' backlist. The group of stories that I love, but the ones that didn't get the love and attention from the kind of editors I have today. Gosh, I love you! You're beautiful and amazing and I can't wait to hug you! And your name needs to be in my acknowledgments!

Thank you to my awesome ARC team! I want to smother you all in a giant hug. For reals! Thank you for reading and sharing and sharing again! Thank you for your excitement for the Baileys. The success of this book would be nothing without you!

Thank you to the friends and family who constantly support my work and me! You are always rooting me on. Sam—you knew I'd make it long before I did! You're the Anne to my Leslie. Beck, Cash, Brynn, Lorna, Ruby, Jenalee, and so many others—thank you for reading and loving and sharing—every single time! I need your faith, friends! I'm so grateful for it and you!

Thanks and love to my sweet family, Jeff, Tim, Landon, Seth, and Sydney. I could dedicate every one of my stories to you. They are for you. I write for my heart and love. But I also write for you! Thank you for always believing in me and loving me. I love you to the moon!

xoxo,

Jen

ABOUT THE AUTHOR

Jen Atkinson has been dreaming up love stories and writing them down since she learned her ABCs in elementary school. While Jen has written a variety of genres, from romantic suspense to laugh out loud romcoms, all of her novels contain three things: a love story, a happily ever after, and all are closed door reads! If you want to feel all the feels, and get a little light head from swooning over cinnamon roll heroes, grab one of Jen's books.

When she isn't writing... or editing... or creating fun graphics about books to share online, Jen is dating her husband, hanging out with her children, and forcing her family into epic board game competitions—that she will surely be the winner of.

To learn more about Jen, follow her on Instagram at @authorjenatkinson or join her Facebook group.

Made in the USA
Middletown, DE
29 April 2024